KIRSTY MCKAY

UN

FED

Chicken
House

SCHOLASTIC INC.
NEW YORK

All rights reserved. Published by Chicken House, an imprint of
Scholastic Inc., *Publishers since 1920.* CHICKEN HOUSE, SCHOLASTIC, and
associated logos are trademarks and/or registered trademarks of
Scholastic Inc.
www.scholastic.com

First published in the United Kingdom in 2012 by Chicken House,
2 Palmer Street, Frome, Somerset BA11 1DS.

Library of Congress Cataloging-in-Publication Data
McKay, Kirsty.
Unfed / Kirsty McKay. — 1st American ed.
p. cm.
Summary: Fifteen-year-old Roberta wakes up in a hospital after
the incident which turned many of her classmates into zombies,
only to be told that her mother is dead and all of Scotland has been
quarantined — but something suspicious is going on and it is up to
Bobby to figure out what it is.
ISBN 978-0-545-53672-1 (alk. paper) 1. Zombies — Juvenile fiction.
2. Conspiracies — Juvenile fiction. 3. Scotland — Juvenile fiction.
4. Horror tales. [1. Zombies — Fiction. 2. Conspiracies — Fiction.
3. Scotland — Fiction. 4. Horror stories.] I. Title.

PZ7.M47865748Uo 2013
[Fic] — dc23
2012040707

10 9 8 7 6 5 4 3 2 1   13 14 15 16 17

Printed in the U.S.A.   23
First American edition, September 2013

The text type was set in Alisal.
The display type was set in Alisal Bold.

Book design by Phil Falco

To Ma and Pa,
for always making me believe that I could

PROLOGUE

When you're staring into the jaws of death at the age of fifteen, there's not a whole lot of life to flash before your eyes.

"Brace! Brace! Brace!" a voice cries.

Huh? This is a bus, not a plane, silly.

There's a huge skid, I've got a face full of seat, and all the kids around me are screaming. Before I can grab something, there's a *whack* and a *thud* and for a split second we've stopped. Then I'm flying, weightless and silent, up through the air. The bus flips. My world is spun round and round and I bounce helpless off edges of things, like a sad little kitten in a tumble dryer. Glass smashes and the cold thrusts into the bus. A tearing, wrenching sound — the bus peeling open. In spite of the dark outside I glimpse a tree through an open window. We're still falling. The whole bus jerks from side to side as it pinballs off immovable obstacles, and with each hit there are new and terrible howls from my fellow passengers. I try to hold on — to the overhead lockers, the seats, the bodies — but everything seems to come away in my grasp. I bash off the back of something. A booted foot lands *thonk* in my throat, choking me.

There's a *boom*, so loud that the sound punches me in the chest. I curl up tight. Did we explode?

I chance a peep. Bits of bus. Cushion stuffing bursting out, a back-pack with a lunch box in it, someone's leg. I'm curled in a ball between what might be the bottoms of two seats.

Father, Son, and Holy Goat. I'm upside down.

Hair hanging. Pressure of blood running to my face, banging in my head.

A slither.

My hands shoot out, but it's no good. I'm in free fall.

I hit the floor with my head, an arrow in the ground, and I flick-flack like the worst gymnast in the world. An ominous rattle — a shadow moves across my view. I shut my eyes and something tumbles on top of me, a heavy thing, pressing me into the floor and crushing the air from my chest. I should hurt, but I don't.

"Bobby!"

There's a voice in my ear, breath warm.

"Wake up, Bob!"

And again. Soft, but urgent.

Smitty.

I open my eyes. But I can't see him. Everything's blurred round the edges. He must be behind me, and I think I'm twisted kind of funny, and the crushing thing is stopping me from turning over.

"Are you OK?"

I try to speak, but nothing comes out. I must look like a fish gulping for air. *Mucho attractivo.*

"They're coming, Bob. You have to move. You have to get up."

I try, I really do. But my body doesn't listen.

"I can't shift this, Bobby. You've got to help me!"

He's shaking the thing on top of me; it's kind of annoying. Right now I really have to sleep. When I wake up, then I'll help him. I'm sure he'll understand.

"Bobby!" He sounds really upset. I mean, like, crying. *Wow.* That's so not Smitty. Maybe that gunk we injected in his leg had a weird effect on him.

The memories of what happened out on that frozen lake move in — Smitty bitten by one of *them*, the infected Undead, and the only known source of the cure in a syringe in my hand — but the darkness draws in faster, tempting me to slip away.

For a moment, I do.

Then I'm back with a rush of cold. And everything is real again. The thing that was on top of me is lifted, and a pair of sturdy black boots appears in front of me.

I peer up through the debris at my rescuer. Not Smitty. A man in black — balaclava, ski jacket, thick gloves.

My rescuer looks down on me, crouches low, and stares into my eyes. There's a tiny yellow insignia on the lapel of his jacket, an *X* with a swirl around it. I know that logo. Xanthro Industries. The big bad. An evil pharmaceutical company, and — oh, did we forget? — my mother's employer. Last on my list of desirable rescuers.

Pain rushes through me as my nerves finally catch up with reality.

And that's the last of it.

1

I wake up, rasping at the air like I've been held under freezing water.

On my own. Lying in a bed.

The only sounds are my gasps and my heart beating loudly in my ears. Am I paralyzed? I kick out with a foot and swear as I stub my toes on the end of the bed. No, apparently not paralyzed. *Goody.* Hands gripping the cold metal sides of the bed, I stare up at the bright white ceiling, steadying myself while the room stops spinning, hanging on, waiting for the calm. I slowly roll my head from side to side, trying to push the fog away.

Where the hell am I?

Uh-oh. The memories pop up violently, one by one, like a malevolent gang of jack-in-the-boxes.

A school trip from hell. Me — the class newbie — born in the UK, but transplanted to God Bless America for the last few years. Freshly back in Mother England, with zero friends and a weirdy accent. We were on a bus; there was a blizzard, a stop at a café called the Cheery Chomper, some poisoned Veggie Juice. My classmates turned feral with a capital *Z*. And then, hello! My mother is the creator of a stimulant called Osiris that turns normal folks into brain-hungry ghouls.

Just your average school trip.

And of course there's Smitty. The most maddening boy in the world. A fountain of insults, a kiss, and those terrible bites on his leg. And how I gave him the only syringe of antidote in existence so he could cure himself.

But we were rescued — yes! — by a bus of school kids not so very different from my former classmates, before they went Undead.

Oh — but then the bus crashed.

Smitty . . . ?

Mum . . . ?

The others?

I remember the moans, then something else. Rescuers? Who got me out? Why can't I remember that?

My heart clenches, breath tightening.

Don't freak.

I'm alive, that's huge. Someone rescued me. I'm in a bed in Whoknowswhere, but it doesn't matter because I'm *alive*.

There's a bedside cabinet to my right with a thick book on it. I reach out; it's heavy in my weak hand. *Ow.* There's a taped-over thing stuck in the back of my right hand by my wrist, a thin plastic tube leading up to a clear bag of liquid held high above the bed on a silver metal stand. *Urgh.* I want to pull the tube out, but I'm scared of what will happen if I do.

I rest the book on my chest, flicking open the bottle-green cover. A Bible, with a stamp on it saying PROPERTY OF ST. GERTRUDE'S.

So, where you at, Gerty? And are you coming back for your Bible anytime soon?

I thump it back onto the top of the cabinet.

At least I know where I am.

A Hospital.

This is it. This is what happens in the zombie apocalypse — the empty hospital. It's a classic. Survivor wakes up alone. Everyone else has disappeared. The hospital has been abandoned; the corridors are streaked with blood, littered with overturned gurneys. The phone is off the hook, with a dead tone coming out of the receiver. There is no one left alive.

But there are dead people.

And Undead ones.

I swallow. This is real. It's happening to me.

Focus. I blink. *Try to sit up.* I roll onto my left side and try pulling myself up to somewhere approaching sitting. On the left there's a window, blinds open. The light outside is dim, so I can't see what's out there, only a girl in a bed staring at herself.

Bollocks!

The figure is deathly white, with huge dark eyes and spindly little limbs. *Me.* Man, I'm skinny. Like, modelorexic thin. But that's not the half of it. I raise a shaking hand to my head.

My hair has been shaved off.

I lean closer to the window, trying to see my reflection better. On the side of the front of my skull is a huge scar. I run trembling fingers over a patchwork of nearly healed wounds, a network of stitches. What happened to me? Tears of self-pity prick my eyes. *Don't do this. Don't break down, you coward.*

Enough already — I need answers, now.

"Hello?"

My voice sounds like I've been gargling wasps. It would be funny if it wasn't so completely alarming.

I grip the sheets and push myself up to sitting. Bare feet touch a cold tiled floor. Can I stand up? Things hurt. But I have to get out. I have to escape. I have to survive, all over again.

Behind me, a door flies open.

I twist around, unsteady. A figure stands there, mouth pulled back in a grotesque smile. Arms outstretched, the thing rushes toward me, and before I can fall in a dead faint, it has grabbed me.

I hear it cry out as I collapse onto the bed, fighting with all I have, which is nothing. Scrabbling pathetically under the bedsheets, I screw my eyes up tight and wait for the bite, curling my legs up in a ball in a futile move.

"You shouldn't be out of bed!"

Whoa, nelly.

It's talking to me. They don't usually talk. And it is not trying to chow down on my brains. Maybe I was a little hasty with the judging. I peeka-boo over the covers.

"Sorry if I scared you."

Woman. Live one.

The smile comes again — that huge mouth with tombstone horse teeth. Not attractive, but not monstery. She has apple cheeks, glasses, curly sandy-gray hair. And she is huge. Humpty Dumpty on steroids. I'm not being cruel; she's actually the roundest person I've ever seen in the flesh. And what a lot of flesh.

I blink at her. Open my mouth to say something, but nothing comes.

"My name's Martha." Her voice is low, calming, her eyes intelligent.

I sit up in bed a little.

"Hi." I find my voice, although it's more of a croak.

"I work here at the hospital. You're safe with me." She waits, almost as if she's politely allowing me to invite her farther into my territory. Nice, but I'm always kind of suspicious of adults who treat me like I'm their equal. "I'm sorry if I shouted at you. It's quite a shock to see you awake — a good shock, of course!" She beams. "May I sit?"

"Sure."

She moves toward me as if she's on wheels, delicately, seemingly effortlessly picking up a chair on her way over to my side. She places it silently at the head of the bed.

I look at the slight plastic chair, and she reads my mind.

"They build these things to be robust, don't you worry."

I flush red.

Martha sits slowly, the chair creaks a little, but holds. She folds her hands across her huge bulk; they're weirdly slender, the nails perfectly manicured and painted pale pink. There's an iridescent opal ring on one slim finger.

"You must have a lot of questions. Let me give you the rundown first."

"OK."

"You were in a bus accident. You sustained some head and leg injuries, but you're doing very well indeed. There's nothing to worry about on that score. You were unconscious for quite a period of time. We have been monitoring you. Do you remember anything in the hospital before today?" She leans forward ever so slightly.

I shake my head. "How long was I out?"

She takes a breath, as if assessing whether I'm going to flip. I might flip, I really don't know.

"A little under six weeks." Her eyebrows shoot up, as if she's only just totted it up herself. "Forty days, to be exact."

I swallow. Coulda been a hell of a lot worse. It's not like I've been cryogenically frozen and I've woken up to find all my loved ones are dead and I have a fashion faux pas hairstyle. Oh, wait . . . I do have the hairstyle.

Martha suddenly reaches into my bedside cabinet and retrieves a large trash bag.

"Your personal items, recovered from the bus." She offers me the bag, and I take it gingerly. It is white, with HAZARDOUS MATERIALS written across it in red. "Sorry about the bag. Nothing dangerous in there, I promise. But it's all I had on hand."

I open it a little and peer in. There's my phone, my T-shirt, my fleece, socks, and boots, and my underwear.

"Your clothes have been laundered. I'm afraid they had to cut off your leggings in the ambulance." She rubs her hands as if washing them, and the opal ring flashes at me. "Hope they weren't a favorite pair. I'm sure we'll be able to furnish you with something to wear once you're up and about."

I silently drop the bag to the floor. I'm gonna wait until she's out the door and then I am straight on that phone.

"Roberta . . ." she starts again.

"It's Bobby."

"Of course it is." She nods. "Bobby, I don't know how much you know about what was going on, but it's been an interesting few weeks."

Interesting. Yuh-huh. You could say that.

"I don't want to shock you . . ."

"You won't."

"Quite . . ." She still looks unsure. "There was an outbreak." She pauses to see what I'll say. I decide to play dumb for now. "A dangerous disease spread around the area you were traveling through, and a relatively large section of the local population was affected. The infected became violent and attacked others." She narrows her eyes. "This isn't news to you, is it?"

"Not exactly."

She nods, like she was just confirming something she already knew. "Unfortunately the disease is highly contagious, and it was passed on to others. Many others — it spread very quickly."

OK, now she has my attention.

"It spread? Where to? How many?"

"Rober — sorry, *Bobby* — Scotland has been quarantined."

I rub my eyes. "Say again?"

"Scotland has been cut off from the rest of the UK — and the world, for that matter. For the time being, no one can get in, or out. The government is trying to contain the disease, but it took hold quickly and threatened to overwhelm the entire population. There are steps being taken to rectify the situation, make it safe again —"

"Hold the phone." I raise a hand. "Where are we?"

"We're in Scotland." She nods grimly. "Just outside Edinburgh. For now we're in lockdown. You don't have to worry, though. This is a military hospital. We have a perimeter fence and the toughest security measures. We're really in no danger at all . . ."

I sit bolt upright in bed.

"You're telling me they're out there?" I shout at her. "Right now they're at the 'perimeter fence'?" The blood rushes to my head, making me dizzy. "You mean this wasn't all cleared up? How did it get out of control? How could they let it? Oh god!" I clasp my face in my hands and slide my back down onto the bed. "How difficult could it be? We killed a bunch of them ourselves and we're only kids. You cut off the head, it kills them." I stare at her intently. "Or blow them up. That works, too."

The tears shock me, running down my cheeks freely and furiously. I can't stop myself shaking, like I'm coming off some major drug — which I suppose I probably am.

"I promise you we're safe here," she says as she places a delicate hand on my arm. "We're lucky. We have food, water, electricity. The government assures us it should be a couple of weeks more, at most."

I breathe, the sobs pass. I feel kind of embarrassed. But I guess I had license. OK, she says we're safe. Military hospital. In a way, it couldn't be better. Military. That means weapons. And big strong people to use them. I can do a couple of weeks here. And then life totally goes back to normal. I go home with Mum the Evil Superscientist, with my friend Smitty, the Only Known Source of the Cure. I close my eyes.

"What about everyone else on the bus?"

She sighs, almost imperceptibly. Here it comes.

"Bobby, I'm really sorry to say, there were fatalities."

"Who?" My fists are balled up and pressed against my eyes.

"Some were infected. Some perished in the crash."

"Who survived?" *Give it to me quick.*

"You were one of four."

I look at her, not bothering to cover up my gaping mouth. *Only four? Out of a whole busload? Kids, teachers, everyone?*

"I'm so sorry, Bobby. There's no easy way to say this."

"Say what?" I bite down on my lip, already knowing the answer.

She shakes her head sadly.

"Bobby, your mother is dead."

Her words float up into the air and hang there between us. I look up at them, not letting them in yet. I can't.

And then the sirens start.

Sirens; loud, screaming sirens. So sudden and deafening they make my chest hurt. Or maybe that's my heart breaking — I don't have time to tell.

"Stay here!"

Martha's face reads panic. She rises and crosses the room with surprising speed, opening the door a crack and peeping out. She's scared. She tries to hide it, but nobody peeps round a door like that unless they're pretty damn terrified.

"It's probably just a drill." Martha's face is stretched tight, telling me in no uncertain terms that it is Not. Just. A. Drill. My head is buzzing, but I'm not allowing myself to take in that last piece of news.

She leans over me, and I can smell stale deodorant on her, the sweet mixing with the sour.

"Bobby, you have to trust me. You are my number one priority."

Before I can answer her, my head starts to spin. Martha is pressing a plunger into the liquid that is going into the back of my hand.

"No! What are you doing?" I scream at her. I feel myself lurch forward, my head seemingly floating behind me while my body is being carried on a roller coaster climbing the steepest track.

"Don't worry," she tells me. "It's for the best."

The roller coaster peaks and starts the long descent into oblivion.

"No!" I try to yell more forcefully, but it sounds like a woof.

"You'll be safe," Martha shouts from somewhere near the door. "I'll come back for you!"

And with that, I sink.

2

"Wake up, Roberta."

Smitty leans in close, and I smell the raspberry shampoo he uses. He kisses me softly on the forehead, his hand warm against my cheek.

I can't see him. My eyes are blurred, and I rub at them, but that doesn't improve matters.

Oh, knickers. I know why I can't see. This is a dream.

"Get up. This is no time to be a-slumbering." I hear the smile in his voice. "We're all driving on the road to nowhere, and you're the only one who's got a map."

I crinkle my brow. "Seriously? We're doing cryptic dream messages now, Smitty?"

He laughs. "Best I can do, Bob. But don't lay blame for the lame. This is your subconscious, after all."

His hands have slinked underneath my bedsheets, and I can feel skin against my skin. There is soft, warm breath against the back of my neck. The flutter of eyelashes on my bare head.

Joy fills me. I reach out and touch him. The familiar leather jacket creaks a little as I pull him toward me, relishing the hug. I sense his face moving down to mine. I try to open my eyes to look into his, but they refuse to open. Lips touch; we kiss, deeply. I don't care about anything anymore, just this kiss. He rolls his body so that he's on top of me, and I let him, thrilled and a little scared by his weight. The kiss gets more fervent, more desperate, and I give in to it, a rush of heat pulsating through my body. I reach up to feel his hair, open my mouth, and his tongue pushes against mine. I feel rude. I feel wonderful. I feel happy.

And then his tongue pushes farther, filling my mouth, and before I know it I'm choking. I can't breathe, and I'm trying to push him off me, trying to scream, and he's heavy on me, and he's crushing my chest, and the hands that were soft and loving a minute ago are clawed and tearing at my flesh.

My eyes flick open. My hand wrenches a clutch of black hair from a bleached white skull with mad eyes. Gnashing teeth sink into my cheek, and my face explodes with pain.

He's Undead. And soon I will be, too.

The sirens are still screaming as I fall, panting, back into reality, eyes crusted and a dried trail of dribble down one side of my mouth.

Mum. Mum is dead and I'm having messed-up dirty dreams about Smitty.

I don't believe she's dead. I *won't* believe it. She always has a plan. Dying would not be part of it.

I scrub at my face to wash off the guilt and the beginnings of something that might turn into uncontrollable grief, push myself up, and rip the damn sleepytime tube out of the back of my hand. Rub it better, I'll mend. Teeth gritted, I swing my legs out from under the sheet, and press my weight down through my feet, gripping with my toes. And then I feel it: a quick sting between my legs.

Oh. My. God.

There's another tube. And this one is going up somewhere no tube should ever go. My good hand fumbles beneath the sheets, I claw at tape, and before I can even think about pain and consequence, I've yanked the tube out, flinging it away from me like it's on fire.

Think of Mum. Offset pain with pain.

Pale yellow liquid seeps from the tube. Horror of horrors. There's a hanging piss-bag on the side of the bed that is now emptying itself in a creeping puddle on the floor.

Ow, ow, ow.

This must be the crappiest wake-up ever. And believe me, there have been some crappy ones.

I rescue my bag of belongings before it can get wet, and dress as quickly as I can: underwear, T-shirt and fleece, socks and boots. No leg-wear; for now I'll have to have naked pins. I shove my phone into my boot, carefully step around Pee Lake, and tiptoe to the door. I turn the handle, but no dice. It's locked, of course. Pressing my ear up to the wood I try to hear something. Shouts? Screams? Relieved laughter? But all I can hear is the screech of the sirens.

And then they stop.

I spring away from the door.

Silence.

Now someone will come. Surely. It was all a big mistake, and they'll come and reassure me.

But they don't.

The silence is waaay worse.

As I stand there, I notice a clipboard on the locker by the door. ROBERTA BROOK is written on the top of a lined sheet, with times and dates and mystery numbers scribbled on each line. I reach for it and scan the notes. Random stuff I can't possibly hope to understand, not only because it's medicalese and shorthand, but because I can't read the handwriting.

That's not so surprising; Mum is a doctor and her handwriting looks like an indignant hen scratched something in the sand.

Mum. No, don't think it.

I make myself read on. Tests? Something-something *virus*? Cold shoots through me. They must think I have it — the Osiris zombie disease. Something about "carrier"? "Indicators" something-something "masked by other factors"? Huh?

"Carrier"? I shake my head slowly. One in a million people are, my mother told me. Folks who carry the virus but don't go zombie, they don't turn. My dad was one, a carrier. Kind of didn't make much diff in the end to him, because he got sick and died before she could save him.

Maybe it runs in the family? How much sense would it make if I was one, too? A whole lot. The thought sends chills through me.

I have to get out of here.

The window. It's lighter outside now; I wonder how long I was sleeping. I shuffle around the bed and lean over the sill to look.

A butterfly lands on the glass in front of me and flicks its wings prettily.

OK. So, not sure what I expected to see, but it wasn't this.

It's a tropical rain forest out there, the air filled with flutter-bys winging from leaf to leaf. I blink and refocus. Through the foliage and insects, I see walls and windows. It's a courtyard, set into the middle of the building. There are exotic flowers in bloom, little explosions of bright color among the green. Plants with huge, flat leaves. Vines up the walls, curling their way past the windows opposite me — darkened windows that I can't see into. And in the air, hundreds of butterflies of all sizes and shades. I cling onto the windowsill shakily as I take it all in. Some hospital. You could sell tickets for this.

Thunk.

The door. I jerk round so quickly, I crick my neck with an *Ow*. Someone's arrived.

A low groan. A scratching noise.

Either it's Martha back, or . . .

A moan. More scratching.

Not someone. Some*thing*.

Thunk.

Damn, they're here.

Some kind of doody military hospital this has turned out to be. I thought I'd have more time before they found me. A unique combination of chill and sickness moves over my body. I'd forgotten how they made me feel. And yet now that they're back, it's like no time has passed at all.

I back up a little.

Thunk. The door is moving slightly. Louder moans. There's more than one of them here now. Three or four, at a guess, because that door looked to be pretty thick. But I'm not taking bets on it holding forever.

Think. *Quickly.*

I reach for the bedside cabinet and shove it up against the door.

Now . . . the window? Take a chair to it? Smash the glass and make my escape? Not a great option. Escape to where? A courtyard with nowhere to go . . . *think!* I look around desperately.

There's a square up on the wall, not much bigger than a dog flap, covered by some kind of plastic grating. An air-conditioning vent or something? I seize the chair and pull it over to the wall, jumping up to get a better look. Meanwhile, the zoms back at the door are getting coordinated, their random *thunks* are in sync, and the door is complaining. Yay for teamwork. I won't have long.

I reach up to the vent and my hands grip the grating. A couple of rattles and it's off, revealing a welcoming hole, just big enough for this slinky gal to fit into.

But it's too frickin' high. Need something else to stand on.

I look desperately around the room.

Only one thing for it, the bed.

I jump down from the chair. OK, so this bed's on wheels, should be easy enough. With sweaty palms I try to drag it. Nuts, it has some kind of brake. I look for it. I can't see it.

There's a cracking noise from the door. They've managed to dislodge the lock — the fixing is coming away from the frame — I've got seconds.

Come on! I search for the brake, grabbing at various handles. The head of the bed shoots up, things *clunk* and sink and rise again, and the bed takes on all sorts of un-bedly shapes. But the sodding thing doesn't move.

The cabinet falls over and the door flies open. They're in. It's over for me.

I jump around the other side of the bed, so it's a zombie-Bobby sandwich with bed filling. I look at them. I can't not. I should be focusing on finding the damn brake and putting all my last good efforts into moving this thing, but I'm caught fast in the inevitability of my bloody death, ripped to pieces by these fiends.

Children.

Zombinos. Half a dozen of them, and then more, spilling into the room. Kids. Younger than me. Nine, ten years old? *God.* I feel my throat clench in sadness. Some are naked. The ones that aren't, their clothes are ripped and soiled, soaked through with patches of blood and spit and whatever else can seep out of a human orifice. Their young faces are caved in, hollowed, the color of bruises. Some of them have chunks of flesh missing. Fingers are bent back and broken, limbs are missing, and one boy is walking on a stump where his foot used to be, like a city pigeon.

Staggering, the leaders of the pack stop for a second and take me in. We stare at each other over the bed. The tallest is a girl, long and pale and bare, her flat chest and stomach engraved with a crude Y shape. They cut her open and sewed her up again. But this is not the most remarkable thing about her. She has crazy, curly red hair. I'll bet it used to be beautiful, her mother's pride and joy — but now it is tatted, almost like she back-combed it specially because she's gone zombie. And half of her head is missing, like it's a dippy egg with the top taken off. She stands there, swaying, naked and unashamed. I look into her cloudy eyes, trying to tell her *No, please don't hurt me, Red — I'm only a kid, a kid like you.*

The crowd does not move. Maybe they sense my helplessness?

I feel a sting of hope in my chest. Maybe they'll refuse to attack another kid, like we have some kind of unspoken understanding and they want me to live out the life they never had the chance to experience.

And then Red flings back her head and roars.

They move, as one, toward me. This is no young people's alliance. They want my brains.

Finding my strength, I crank the bed with all my might, lifting one end and forcibly dragging the thing on its wheels toward the wall and my only hope of escape. Red is reaching for me. I duck down, then leap onto the bed, making a grab for the plastic chair, planting it hopefully on the end of the bed, and jumping up onto it. The Undead kiddies pour toward me, hands out, and in my haste I slip and fall back down on the bed again. The bent and broken fingers find me, clawing, trying to rip flesh from bone — but I'm lucky because they only find my fleece, and before they can reach more I've rolled off the bed to the other side in a reckless tumble.

There's no time to languish on the floor. Tempting as it is to scuttle under the bed, I know that won't trick them for more than a couple of seconds. They're kids, too, and they know my moves; they probably hid under the bed from the monsters who bit them.

I try to spring up, but I'm wrapped in something — some kind of twine holding my arms to my body. I pull on it and there's a clatter. It's my IV line, still attached to a bag hanging off a metal pole. But now the bag has spilled out onto the floor, mixed with the Pee Lake, and soaked my legs. The pole lies next to me. I don't even need to think about it; I grab the weapon, scramble to my feet, and leap onto the bed.

Swinging the pole round my head, I let out a guttural yell as I clash a couple of kids. The first victim falls over, and my pole continues to a second. The head splits, an overripe pumpkin spraying foul-smelling gunk over its neighbors. I dodge the spatter and then I'm swinging again. The top part of the pole that held the bag has come off, and now the end is sharp and pointy. *Good. We like sharp and pointy.* I shove it at the boy with the pigeon stump; it's not a direct hit, but as balance is not his thing, he's pushed back and falls over.

So it's three down, four or five or six to go.

They pause for a second; maybe they're not used to this. They're kids, after all. It must be quite an effective turn playing cute little doe-eyed monsters. Their victims probably don't fight back until it's too damn late.

Red sidestepped the first attack; she's smart. People with orange hair always have great survival instincts. She launches herself at the bed, and she's quick, too — faster than any other zom I've seen. But not that fast. I bring my pole down flat on the back of her head, and she eats mattress. Reaching for the chair again, I turn and start to climb up onto it —

— but Red's not dead. She grabs my boot, and with surprising strength she wrestles it from the chair and before I know it I'm joining her down among the sheets again. She's on top of me, a writhing, skinny thing, more a bag of bones held together by sinew and fury, gnashing teeth mere inches away from my exposed fleshy bits. Her breath is rank and fishy. I want to scream but I don't dare open my mouth for fear the rancid stuff spilling out of hers will drip into me. The pole lies squashed between us, and I can't grab it — my hands are on her arms, holding her away from me.

But her wriggling helps me out, dislodging the pole so it falls to one side. I push her off me with one almighty heave, then seize the pole like a Crusader, and just as she falls on top of me again, I thrust it up through the soft skin under her chin. The metal pierces flesh easily, moves up through her face, and with another thrust, pops out of her eyehole, pushing the cloudy eyeball out onto her cheek.

It is, without doubt, the bang-up, A1, tip-toppity grossest thing I have ever witnessed in my entire life.

It hasn't finished her, but it's certainly rocked her world a little. She gulps and flaps, her attention briefly moving away from me and onto getting the pole out. And that's enough for me to *carpe* my *diem*. I push her off and clamber onto the chair.

The mob surges toward me, but it's too bad for them. Using the chair like a springboard, I jump and pull myself up into the vent, launching headlong into that hole. A hand brushes my ankle, but it's too late — I wiggle in and snap my legs up behind me, out of reach, safe.

It's only then I wonder if this goes anywhere. Could well be a dead end. *Ha. Ha. Ha.*

I realize my eyes have been shut. I open them. Darkness. Bloody hell. Coulda used a flashlight in this situation. There's only my phone for light, but I don't want to use up precious battery. This is the point in the movie where the hero normally reaches for a cigarette lighter to see the way, but smoking's not one of my bad habits, so that's not an option. Guess I'm going to feel my way.

The sound of their baby-groans follows me up the vent. I scrabble forward a little, then twist and try to look behind me. Who knows, one of those things maybe got clever with the bed-chair combo and is currently crawling up on my ass — but there's nothing back there except a square of light. I seem to remember they weren't too bright at climbing. Lucky for me.

I slither forward on elbows and knees, not quite enough height to fully crawl. It's slippery, and half the time I seem to propel myself backward. My damp palms make squeaky noises on the metal lining of the vent. Hope this is not a heating vent. If the heat comes on, I'll be roasted in this thing like the biggest turkey on the farm. Nom, nom, nom.

Ow! My hand shoots out and hits a solid thing. Dead end after all? My heart sinks. But wait . . . there's a draft on the top of my head. I look up. Can't see anything. I lift a hand. OK, so we're going up. I gather my legs beneath me and gingerly stand. I'm almost fully upright when my bald head touches the top. In front of me is another opening. *Sweet.* We just moved up a level. I pull myself up and wiggle into the new vent.

Now that I'm away from the room, the groans have gone. But there's a low hum, like a throbbing sound. I shiver as I imagine what may be waiting for me. Could one of these things be in the vent ahead? Sure, they can't climb for fudge, but what if they got in a different way, up ahead? It's totally possible. I stop crawling and lie there, listening to the sound.

Poop-a-loop, that could totally be moaning. I could be crawling to my death here.

But I realize there's a rhythm to it. It's got to be mechanical. I gather up my guts and go for it. Only one way, and that's forward. It's hot in here, I'm sweating in my fleece. Sure wish I had some kind of legwear on, though.

I hit another wall. Up again? No — the breeze is hitting my right cheek. The vent has doglegged — I've reached a corner. I wiggle onto my side and push myself round ninety degrees. The breeze gets stronger, the throbbing suddenly loud.

Hey, I can see something! A square of light, really dim, up ahead. I scrabble on.

There's a fan at the end of the vent, with light coming up from a grating in the floor. Or I can carry on to the right. *Decisions, decisions.* Either one could be my way out of the rat run.

I stare down through the grating into the room below.

A bed.

I shift myself slightly, trying to get a better view.

A head? Yes, it's a girl perched on the bed. I shift again to see more. Her legs are drawn in, defensive. I feel a rush of hope — we've got a live one, people!

I push gently at the grating — don't want to alarm her, but how do you not? *Shoot*, it's not budging. Should I call down? Better not, she'll freak. Plus, I want to be sure she's not infected or crazy or something. I put more pressure on the grating. Suddenly it gives way completely, falling down, down on top of the girl, hitting her square on her head.

She screams and rolls off the bed. *Shit!* Have I killed her?

There's crying. *Phew.* Maybe maimed for life, but not killed. I pull myself up and think about how I'm going to get down into the room. There's no space to squeeze my legs around, I'm going to have to go head-first. I hang on with my hands and birth myself through the hole: head, shoulders, then butt — upside down. Then I hook my knees so I dangle.

Maybe the girl will help me . . . ? I look around for her.

Before I can focus, there's a *screech* and I'm whacked in the face. I fall onto the bed — not nearly as soft as I'd hoped — and the girl is attacking me, hitting my head with something, hitting hard. I wrap my arms round my face.

"Quit it!" I cry out. "It's OK. I'm not one of them!"

The hitting stops. I peep out from behind my arms.

There, standing over me with a furious expression and a bottle-green Bible held aloft, is Alice.

3

"You!"

Alice spits at me, trembling. "Are you trying to scare the crap out of me?" She chucks the Bible at me.

"Hey!" I shout. "Cut it out!"

"What the hell are you doing here?"

"Lovely to see you, too, Alice."

"Is there anyone chasing you?" She's pushing me off the bed and trying to peer up into the vent.

"No." I pull myself up to my feet with difficulty, my arms throbbing from the Bible-bashing. "Are we safe in here?"

She shakes her blonde head. That hair looks glossier than ever, especially now that I'm bald.

"Probably not. Typical. That woman has been telling me I'd be fine in here; I should have known never to trust a fatty."

So she's met Martha. Cruel, and quintessential Alice, but also pretty accurate, it has to be admitted. I move to the door and place a tentative hand on the handle.

"They locked you in, too?"

"What do you think?" Abandoning the vent, she goes to the window and peeps out through the blinds. "I knew it was just a matter of time before stuff went *stupide* again. How many are there?"

"Don't know." I rub my hand. "Some of them broke into my room. Kids. Through the vent was the only way out."

"Do you think they'll break in here?" She frowns at me.

"They could." I start to pull the bed away from the wall. "Help me move this against the door, it's a good start."

She sighs and complains, just as I expected she would, but obliges all the same. Once again the damn brakes are locked, guaranteeing the whole exercise is superfun. We grunt and groan as we force the bed into position.

I clamber over and we both sit side by side at the foot of the bed on the floor. Alice squints at me.

"God, you're looking *très* fuglier than usual. What did you do to yourself?"

I run my hand over my head. "Not my choice."

"Army-licious." Alice curls her lip. "You smell of wee, too. And what about *that*?" She gestures at my lower half, bare legs sticking out of hospital robe. "What happened? Did they rip your jeans off, or are you going for the Combat Ho look?"

I eye her peach-colored sweats. "Whereas you're rocking that velour." *Right back at you, sista.*

"At least I'm not flashing my butt," she says with considerable distaste. "Did they do experiments on you, too?"

"No — what?" I get up and move to the window to check outside again. "I mean, for all I know, they could have done anything to me. I was out for weeks after the crash. Do you remember who brought us here?"

Alice shakes her head, and her hair moves prettily. *Gah*, I envy it. "I woke up in some plastic tent. Zombie quarantine. They told me I couldn't ring my parents, even. I've been going mental ever since."

No change there, then. I would have thought she could've killed a coupla weeks just looking in the mirror. I glance at her. "The others? Have you seen them? Pete? Smitty?"

She holds up her hands and shrugs. "They told me four survived."

"Didn't you even ask who else?" I give her a look.

"Of course I did!" she shouts back. "They told me nothing, just fed me airplane meals and stuck needles in me. All I know is that Scotland has gone all Och Aye the Ghoul." She stops and looks at me. "God, I hope Smitty didn't zombify," she says. "Because if he did, I bet you any money he'll come after me."

Personally, I think that if Smitty's a zombie he'll be far more discriminating than to chomp on Alice.

"He couldn't have turned. He had the entire syringe of antidote in his leg, remember?"

Alice blinks. "How could I forget? You chose to save your boyfriend before saving the entire human race!"

I do a complicated snort-cum-eye-roll combo that clearly screams *I did not!* and *He is so not my boyfriend!* But I find it interesting that I Don't Actually Say the Words. Partly because I don't need the drama of an Alice-a-thon argument, and partly because a teeny weeny bit of me thinks she might be right. On both counts.

"Maybe your mum could tell us." She nods behind her as if Mum is just waiting outside the door. "Help us get out of here. She was pretty good at that before."

"Yeah." I press my cheek against the glass and try to look into the windows across the courtyard. "Except they told me she was dead."

Alice gasps. "Are you serious?"

"Yep." I glance at her.

She has one hand clamped across her mouth, her eyes blinking rapidly. The hand falls away. "That's terrible!" There's a glint of a tear in her eye. "How on earth are we going to get out of here now?"

Nice one, Alice. Just think about how this is going to affect you, huh?

"I might have an idea." I lift my foot and pull my phone out of my boot.

"Oh my god!" Alice cries. "Have you tried to call for help?"

"Not yet." I switch it on, and make a silent prayer. It takes an age to spring into life. Alice gets bored and pushes in to look at the little screen. She groans and throws her head back.

"Don't tell me. No reception. Big fat surprise. There never is. Like, how do you spell YAWN."

I move to the window, but still nada. "So we go somewhere we can get reception."

"If that place actually exists!"

The pit of my stomach is warning me that Alice might be right. I check my text messages. Nothing new. Just a couple of old ones of Mum's. The sight of them chokes me up a little. I go to press the OFF button, but before I do, I see there's an icon in the corner of the screen that I don't recognize.

Was that there before?

It's a little book. I think it's telling me I have numbers stored, or something. Why is that bugging me?

"What is it?" Alice says.

"Nothing."

"Not nothing. Your crazy's showing. What's eating you?"

I shake my head, knowing how lame this is going to sound. "I'm Bobby-no-Buddies, remember? But the phone's telling me I've got numbers stored."

"Gimme that." Alice snatches at it and deftly navigates the menu. "Pleased to tell you you have friends now."

I take the phone back. There's a list on the screen:

Marigold

Mum

Poffit

Smitty

With trembling hands I scroll down the list, twice to make sure. Then I click on "Mum," and a number comes up.

A wave of relief crashes over me.

Now I know, beyond any shadow of a doubt, that Mum is alive.

And she's trying to tell me something.

Since the crash, somebody entered those names and numbers. Obvs, it wasn't me. I walk to the foot of the bed again, and sit on the cold floor.

"Mum put these numbers in."

Alice curls her lip in confusion. "I thought you said she was dead?"

"I think Martha lied to me."

I'm checking out that list. Mum, yeah, Smitty, fine. But the other two? Marigold is not known for her conversational skills. She's my grandmother's grumpy cat, who hates me so much that last time I stayed there she left a dirty protest in my bed.

As for Poffit . . . well, that's the one that seals the deal. And the most humiliating of the lot. Poffit is the name of the random bit o' blankie I used to toddle around with, Linus-stylee, until Mum made me go cold turkey from it when I started school. I'll admit I dug it out again at age nine, when we moved to the States. It was the only way I could sleep, early on.

So unless someone has managed to tap into my memories — and that's a pretty big stretch, even considering current developments — only Mum could have put all this embarrassing stuff in my contacts.

"Why would she give you fake friends?" Alice sits down beside me and squints at the phone.

I look at the phone again, willing it to give away its secrets.

"My mother does nothing without a plan. It must mean something." I open up the "Marigold" entry, and sure enough, there's a number: 3463764889.

"O-kaay," Alice says. "That doesn't even look like a proper phone number."

I hit SEND. I know there's no signal, but maybe this is like one of those urban legend distress numbers that work anyway.

Nothing doing. The call fails to connect.

I scroll down to the next entry, "Mum." Her number is 5555006005959.

"This one's even longer. Ridiculously long," I mutter.

I check out the entries for my kiddie comfort blanket and Smitty.

86337274343.

55461760328189.

"Weird," says Alice, leaning in. "Is it like code or something?"

I fling my head back and hit it on the bed. *Oh bloody hell, Mother.*

"That would be just her frickin' style."

I go back to the first number again. Jeez, are we talking 1 = A or something, here? I mean, that would be too damn obvious, but anything more sophisticated and I'm never going to work it out, especially with this cotton ball stuffing I currently have in my head. I can barely remember the alphabet.

All righty, so . . .

"Find a pen, some paper."

Alice rolls her eyes but gets something.

3463764889 would be . . . "Write the letters down as I say them." I concentrate hard. "C, D, F, C . . . nah, this is way wrong. No words start like that!" Besides, there are no ones or twos in this one, so that would mean she hasn't used anything beyond the ninth letter in the alphabet.

My head hurts.

"Come on, think!" I run my thumb over the keypad on the phone and beg it to give me the answer. And then it does. "It's a text message."

Alice crinkles her nose. "How?"

"My phone is old school. No QWERTY going on here, just a regular number pad, with the numbers corresponding to different letters, like on a landline phone." I feel a rush of blood to my head and search clunkily through the phone's screens until I can select the option to send a text. "If I'm right . . . we should type in the number as if it was a text message, and letters will appear."

Alice's eyebrows are causing major furrows on her pretty little face. "Do you have a fever?"

"No — I'm serious — watch this." I type the numbers in.

Cdfcgfdhhi

"Oh, yeah. Totally clear now," Alice snarks.

My hands are shaking. "We are not done yet . . ."

The phone beeps at me, and I nearly leap a foot into the air. LOW BATTERY flashes on the screen.

"No!" I cry. "Don't die now!"

"Get on with it, then!" Alice says.

"I am." I fumble with the phone, nearly dropping it, quickly scrolling until I find what I need. I choose PREDICTIVE TEXT from the menu and type in the number.

Finesmittw

My heart jumps into my throat. *Smitt*. That is no accident. I look at the phone keypad again.

"Fines-mitt-wuh?" Alice says.

W is on the same key as *Y*. *Smitty* . . . my thumb traces over the keys . . . of course, *E* is on the same key as *D*. I make the substitutions, and I geddit.

"Findsmitty," I shout, standing up and holding out the phone for Alice to see. "Find Smitty!"

She does not share my joy. "Couldn't your mum have just left an actual message? Like a normal person? Oh no — I forgot. She's related to you. You don't do normal."

"This *is* a message, Blondie! My mother's still alive, and she wants us to find Smitty."

"Are you sure?" Alice snorts. "Why would she care about him? Did she hit her head or something?"

"Look, it makes total sense." I stamp, impatient. "He's the only source of the Osiris antidote they were working on. Maybe he's the only hope for stopping the zombie apocalypse. And if he's gone missing, I'm guessing that just about every man and his dog are looking for him around about now."

"And us, too?" Alice groans. "Honestly, why does everything have to revolve around that stupid boy?" She shakes her head. "Like he's worth it." She looks at me. "Maybe you think he *is* worth it?"

I try to keep a straight face while I think of the snarkiest put-down. Unluckily, I fail.

Alice stands and walks over to me. "So where is he?"

I look at the phone again. "The other numbers — we decode them, they'll tell us!"

The LOW BATTERY screen flashes again, making a more insistent beep this time. Rats.

"The other numbers are going to have to wait. Not much we can do about finding Smitty until we find a way out of this room, anyway." I switch the phone off, and shove it down into my boot.

"That vent thing." Alice looks up. "There's a way out?"

I think about the right turn I didn't take. "There might be."

She sighs. "Vent it is, then."

I busy myself with trying to make a tower out of the cabinet and the chair, so that we can reach the vent, while Alice makes a big deal out of packing a small bag with heaven knows what.

"Hey," I call to her. "Pitch me that sheet, huh?"

"My covers?" She crinkles her nose as she picks up the bedsheet. "Why do you want them?"

"What, you're going to be sleeping here again?" I counter. "I need the sheet to make a rope."

"Great, Rapunzel." Alice clears her throat theatrically. "Are you expecting me to shimmy up it?"

"Rapunzel was hair, not rope. And she was climbing down, not up. So —"

"Bobby, like anyone cares!" She tosses her head and clambers up onto the cabinet with me. "Give me that!" She snatches at the sheet. "Like you're even going to be able to —"

"Hands off!" I snatch it back, and we tussle with it pathetically, wobbling together on top of the cabinet.

Clunk.

Our heads whip round to the direction of the door. It's the lock. It's unlocked itself.

"Thank god." Alice drops her end of the sheet rope and makes to jump off the cabinet.

"Wait!" I grab her arm.

She scowls at me. "What? The door's unlocked. Let's go for it while we can!"

She's probably right, but there's something stopping me. "It's just . . ." I can't take my eyes off the door. "It's been a long time since they locked the doors. Nobody's around, you've seen that. We don't know who could be out there."

Alice rolls her eyes at me. "You've been asleep too long. Come on! We didn't survive before by wasting time thinking about anything too much."

That's true enough . . .

"Go on, then," I tell her. "Go take a peek."

"What, me?" She sighs. "That was never my job. You're the She–*Man versus Wild* in all of this."

I take a breath and am about to tell her exactly how wrong what she just said is on Oh-So-Many levels, when —

Thud. Thud. Thud.

We look at the door.

Thud. Thud. Thud.

The handle jiggles. The bed is in the way, but the door moves slightly with each pounding.

Alice clings to me. "Oh my god, they're here," she whimpers.

"The bed should hold them," I say, and I'm convinced it will, right up to the point when it doesn't.

Thud.

The last one was the hardest, and the door opens, juddering against the bed, which skids forward on its wheels. *Frickin' brakes. They picked a great time to unlock.* The bed hits our cabinet, and we are thrown like Angry Birds, launched into the air. Out of the corner of my eye, I see Alice land back on the cabinet on all fours with the skill of a baby monkey, but I'm not in such great shape. I land heavily on the floor with a crunch of arm and ribs, the wind knocked clean out of me.

My view obstructed by cabinet and bed, I hear the things entering the room, footsteps scrambling. How many? Can we dodge, outrun? Must get on my feet, must pull myself up . . . But I'm stuck — arm dead, legs doing their own thing, but it's not helping any. This is no time to cut some slammin' break-dancing moves. And then Alice is there, above me — offering a hand, incredibly — and I reach up to take it and she pulls and I pull and I'm almost on my feet when her head turns toward the door and her face blanches with shock and she lets go of my hand —

I hit the floor again. But this time my body has remembered how to move, and I use the cabinet to tug myself up. Alice is stock-still and in shock beside me. Why isn't she moving?

I follow her gaze to the door. Two figures stand there. The first a boy, tall and broad, holding a fire extinguisher like a battering ram.

Beside him is another boy, with white-blond hair and the palest skin you ever saw. He steps forward and grins at us.

"Come with me if you want to live," says Pete.

4

Pete's been wanting to say that line, like, *forevah*. He's standing there like he's expecting us to applaud, and I check out his new look. The bleach-blond hair has been styled into a Mohawk, and he's wearing a tailcoat and some kind of *goggles*. The idea that Pete has gone all steampunk on our asses . . . well, that takes the biscuit.

And the fact that the hunk flanking him isn't currently cracking up at any of this may be even more disturbing than our predicament. The dude is tall and built like a tank, with buzz-cut fair hair, olive skin, and a pretty damn cute dimple. He smiles at Alice and me like he's sizing us up for smoochies at the prom. I wonder how Pete convinced him to join the ranks.

"What are you waiting for?" Pete shouts at us. "Move!"

Alice shoots me a look as if to say *What, we're taking orders from him now?* And I get her confusion, but this is no time to ask questions. I clamber down off the cabinet and reach up to help her, but the tall boy is way ahead of me. He smiles up at her and offers a hand. She may have doubts about Pete, but this guy's a different prospect altogether.

"Hi," he says to her. "I'm Russ." He turns to me. "Pleased to meet you."

"Hi," I croak at him, and wiggle my fingers lamely. *Nice to meet you. Is this your first zombie apocalypse? Do you possibly have a large weapon I could borrow?*

"No time for small talk, grab anything you need," barks Pete. "We're not coming back." And then he turns tailcoat and heads out of the door, followed by his new acolyte and Alice, toting her bag. I check that the phone is safe in my boot and follow them into the bright, long corridor. The sirens may have stopped, but there are amber and red lights flashing rapidly from the ceiling, like a deadly disco. The corridor is deserted. No one has come to dance with us . . . not yet.

Pete & Co have set off down the corridor toward a large desk, and they're not dawdling. Pete is on point; Russ, his wingman, carrying that fire extinguisher like it's nothing; Alice scuttling anxiously behind, checking out each doorway as we approach it.

"Where are we headed?" I shout-but-don't after Pete.

"Outside!" he stage-whispers dramatically.

"We're going out there?" Alice shrieks, stopping dead in her tracks. "With those things again?"

"That's right." Pete leads on determinedly.

"It's safer," Russ calls back to Alice. "Indoors is teeming with them. It's only a matter of time before they have us cornered." Alice dithers for a second, and I'm close behind. Pete has already scuttled down to the end of the corridor and is crouching by the big desk, beckoning us to join him. We scrabble after and squat in a line along the bottom of the desk, like bowling pins waiting to be scattered. The corridor stretches in front of us, heading away from the courtyard, deeper into the hospital, to territory unknown.

"Which way's out?" I whisper.

"Shh!" Pete holds up a finger and showers us with spittle. "Listen!"

We all strain our ears as the lights flicker above us. I'd love him to be wrong, to be over-egging it or giving way to Pete-adelic imaginings, but the sound hits me like a huge dollop of dread in my stomach. A keening noise. Barely there, but getting stronger.

"Kids!" I whisper. "Younger than us. I saw them; they came into my room."

"Were you bitten?" Pete snaps at me.

"Take a guess." I roll my eyes at him. Everyone eyes me suspiciously. "No, I wasn't bitten." Why, when you say these things, does it always sound like a lie? "You can check me if you like."

Bang on cue, the zombinos arrive, stumbling around the corner at the bottom of the corridor. "Martha's room?" Russ looks at Pete.

"It's lockable." Pete nods, and before I can question what we're doing, they're running down the corridor toward the mini-zoms.

The kids approve of this; they stretch out their little beaten-up arms and moan all the louder. Alice and I share a look. *Why are they running toward them?* But then I get it. Halfway down the corridor, the boys duck into a room on the right. *OK, time to follow.* By the time we get there, the zoms are approaching fast. We dive in, and door is slammed behind me by Russ, who slides a bolt and clicks some kind of lock.

"Thick." He pats it and shoots me a smile. "Safe as houses."

Yeah, I think. *You so don't know what you're dealing with. If you did, you'd lose the grin fast enough. Even though it is kind of pretty.*

"Nice one, people!" Pete shouts. "We made it."

"We did?" I look around. "Where's the exit?"

We're in a small room that is part office, part suburban living room.

At the far end of the room there are two armchairs with mismatched and faded flower patterns in muted hues, a trolley with teapot and sugar bowl, and a bookshelf, all illuminated by a standard lamp with a tasseled shade. Closer to us are filing cabinets and a large modern desk with a padded swivel chair. The main source of light is coming from a desk-top screen, which Pete is bent over like he's on the bridge of Starship St. Gertrude's. He clicks the mouse.

"There's an app with surveillance cameras on here — I saw it last time I had one of my little counseling sessions with Martha." He sits down in a chair with wheels on the bottom and makes a few clicks. The screen splits into six gray images of empty hospital rooms. "Got it! Now we can keep an eye on them on this floor, at least." He spins around to face me with a self-satisfied expression on his face.

"Let me see." I walk up to the desk. The screen changes and another six images appear, but these ones are moving. The Undead are walking the halls. "So we can use this to see which way to get out?"

"That's the idea." Russ looks over my shoulder. "We see where they are, plan a route."

"And hope they don't just surround the door and never let us out in the first place," I say. "Great."

"Any better ideas?" Pete snaps at me. "This will work. As soon as they gave me some freedom around the ward, I scoped out possible exits." He smiles, satisfied. "And if all else fails, we can wait it out here until the authorities regain control. I knew if something went down, this would be the place to head, and I was right." He leans back in the chair and cracks his knuckles, then smoothes the sides of his Mohawk.

"You hope so," Alice says from an armchair. "Next time you might want to *mullet* over."

Pete glares at her.

"So, care to share your thoughts on the exit, friend?" I lean forward onto Pete's chair, staring down into his pale green eyes. "Because if you get chomped, I want to know where I'm going."

He tries to suppress a gulp. "Well, there are several possibilities." He looks uneasy. "For example, in the direction where the zoms were coming from there's a door into the courtyard. There's bound to be a way out there."

"So why didn't we go that way to start off with?" Alice shouts at him.

"Er, the clue was in the bit where I said 'in the direction where the zoms were coming from,'" says Pete.

"Other options?" I say.

"Um. Well, a couple. But they involve the stairwell, which is down the other end of the ward."

"Where the zoms were coming from," I drone.

Pete nods, tight-lipped.

"We're trapped?" Alice yells, dragging herself from the comfy chair and stomping up toward us. She moves toward the door and points at it as if this is all its fault. "I'm sick of trapped! We've *done* trapped! Trapped was so six weeks ago!" She slaps both hands against the wall, as if trying to break her way out. Suddenly the dark-colored wall disappears and the monster children are standing there, inches away from us, dribbling and clawing at the air.

As one, we scream and leap backward into the room, Pete falling out of his chair on wheels and scrabbling under the control panel.

But the zombinos don't move toward us. It takes me a moment to see why they can't.

"Glass," I whisper.

The "wall" is now see-through. Russ moves slowly toward the little monsters and puts a careful hand out. His fingertips find something solid, and immediately the wall turns dark again. Once again we all jump and yell, but he keeps his cool. He reaches out and touches the wall again. The kids are back.

"Smart glass." Pete emerges from somewhere underneath the desk.

"A mirror on the outside?" Russ steps toward the monsters. "Look. They can see themselves, not us."

He lifts his hand up to where one small girl has her face squished against the glass in a terrible gurning of mushed-up cheek and dribbling blood.

I watch as a boy-zom reaches toward the girl's reflection in the mirror, then turns to her and repeats the gesture to her face. Then he runs a clawed hand up through his spiky thatch of hair, watching himself in the mirror. He grabs a clump, wrenches it from his skull, then looks at the tangle of hair and skin in his hand.

"Check it," I murmur. "He knows it's a reflection."

"So what?" Alice says. "Think he's pissed off he's forgotten his hair gel?"

"That's some clever thinking right there. The zoms of old wouldn't have stretched to that." I shake my head.

"Eh?" Alice says. "We're talking upgrades?"

"I'm sure of it," I say. "They're different from before, better movers, and they can think."

"Gosh." Pete stands up, his head on one side, studying the group before us. "I think Bobby's onto something. That doesn't bode well. Mindless, stumbling monsters are bad enough, but improve those motor skills and give them basic logic and we are talking a whole different level of hell."

"Turn it off," says Alice, and for once I agree.

Russ taps the wall at the girl's forehead, and they're gone.

"Fancy setup here," I remark. "Great views."

"We hang tight!" Pete says, plonking himself down on his chair again. "And we hang tough!"

Oh lordy. Can he get any worse?

"Where is the army?" Alice addresses me, like I would know. "They said this was an army hospital. Where're the soldiers?"

"Yes, well, we haven't seen too much of a military presence." Pete clears his throat. "The army have pretty much got their hands full with what's going on outside. I'd imagine that what we have here is just a skeleton crew."

"A skeleton crew versus zombies?" I give a low chuckle. "Horror-tastic." I look around me. "So, Martha's room. There's got to be something helpful here; we should search it."

"What for?" Alice sulks.

I shrug. "Clues to the way out. Weapons. The usual." I open a couple of drawers at the desk. "Pete? Have a look through those files, see if there's anything interesting on the computer."

He raises a bleached eyebrow at me. "What do you think I'm doing?"

There's a pinboard on the wall near me, and I scan it for a map, something about emergency drills, any information — but most of the things pinned there are meaningless. Memos about shift scheduling, a cafeteria menu, telephone extension numbers. In the bottom right-hand corner is a postcard with a lighthouse on it. I notice it because it's the only splash of color among all the gray scale. Something about it makes me pick it off the board and turn it over in my hands. The reverse is blank, except for the words ELVENMOUTH LIGHT printed in small letters at the bottom. I frown. Why does this bother me? I turn the postcard over again; the lighthouse is thin and white, with a band of yellow at the top and a black roof. I stick the pin in it and return it to the board. Something from Martha's vacay; no reason why it should be anything more.

"Hey, guys." I look at Russ and Alice. "Help out here. Look for food and water — or even information. Stuff about who runs this hospital, our medical files, who else they have here. The more we know, the better."

Russ leans against the door protectively. "Doesn't make sense to spend precious energy on a goose chase."

"Yeah," Alice agrees. "Someone will come and get us."

"You're right, Alice," I say. "Because that worked last time we were surrounded by the Undead." No one says anything. "So we just wait it out?" I raise my arms in a *Huh?* When no one replies, I slap them down by my sides, my palms striking my bare thighs with a smack that I instantly regret. "I guess that's a yes. Unless we want to try fighting our way out with a fire extinguisher and Alice's barbed comments."

Nobody chuckles at this. Nobody even gets it. *God, I miss Smitty.*

"Sure, look. And when the coast is clear, we will be out of here. But in the meantime, get comfortable." Russ opens the fridge door. "Blueberry yogurt, anyone?" he says. "No Veggie Juice, though."

"You heard about that," Alice says.

"A few times." Russ smiles into the fridge. "Can't help hoping I get to see the Carrot Man."

"No, you really don't." I slam one of the drawers of the filing cabinet. I'm too angry to focus properly on any of the things in them.

"These files are encrypted," Pete says from the swivel chair. "Same with e-mail. It's going to take a minor miracle."

"Pray to St. Gertrude." I open the only other door to reveal a small bathroom. Thank heavens for small blessings. At least we have somewhere to pee. I take a deep breath, close the door again, and turn back to face the group, who are now all searching the room, if a little halfheartedly. Looks like we have Catching Up time. "So what's the skinny?" I say, overly brightly. "What have you all been up to while I was doing the coma thing?"

Pete looks at me, his goggles glinting in the reflected light. "You've been out cold since the crash?"

"Apparently." I bat my eyes at him. "And can I just say, you've really let the place go since I was last conscious. I mean, I black out and there are just a handful of zoms stomping through the snow, and then I wake up and an entire country has been quarantined. Talk about sloppy."

Pete pushes his chair away from the desk and rolls into the middle of the room in a way he clearly thinks is impressive. "They had me in isolation for a week. Same with Russ."

I pull out a bunch of files from the top drawer of the cabinet, place them on the floor in front of me, and start skimming through them. Most of it is pretty boring. I look at Russ. "So you were on the bus, too?"

He nods. "We were on our way back home from Aviemore. School trip. In fact, I remember seeing your school there. I recognized you all when we picked you up on the road."

"And Pete has filled you in on our story so far."

He nods again. "The Cheery Chomper café. The apocalypse happened on your lunch break. Some evil corporation called Xanthro created a zombie virus. Intense. Sounds like you guys were pretty amazing, outwitting the students in the castle and escaping."

"Yep. We were." I wonder how Pete has pitched it to him. Probably heavy on the Pete-as-leader side of things. I smile when I think how I could correct that, if I was feeling nasty. Pete reads my mind and shoots me an anxious look.

"We had rooms on this ward, too." Pete takes over the story rapidly, before I get a chance to burst the bubble. "They let us socialize in a communal room during the day. We exchanged information, which was negligible. I think they may have been listening in on our chatter."

"And Martha 'counseled' you?" I replace all the files and move on to the second drawer.

"Basic post-traumatic stress therapy," Pete says. "Probably designed to find out how much we knew."

"So what's your story?" I look at Russ.

"Not much to tell." Russ shakes his head. "A little while before our bus picked you people up, we stopped at a garage and there was this bloke with free cartons of juice. The teacher took it, started to hand it out just before we ran into you. Then you know the rest. We crashed."

I'm still leafing through papers when suddenly something jumps out at me from a sheet in a file marked STRICTLY CONFIDENTIAL. My name. And Alice's.

I stare at the words, but nothing makes sense. I need to read this, and read it in private. I fold the paper, shove it surreptitiously into my fleece pocket, and jump right back into the conversation before anyone can realize what's happened.

"I'm sorry," I say to Russ. "Your buddies. Do you know what happened to any of them? Were their . . . bodies . . . brought here?"

He shrugs. "Martha wouldn't tell me any specifics. I'm guessing they died. But who knows." He shivers. "I just hope I don't bump into any of them out there."

"Yeah. That does suck," says Alice. "Especially when they try to bite you and you have to cut their heads off. Or run over them. Or burn them to a crisp."

"Thank you for reminding us, Miss Sensitive," Pete mutters. He scratches the side of his Mohawk with his stubby fingers. "Martha wasn't exactly forthcoming with very much information to either of us. She told me there were only four survivors, and that everybody had to be given time to recuperate quietly." He looks at me. "I guessed that you were one of them. I watched her face especially carefully when I said your name. It's all about the microexpressions, you see."

"That right?" I say.

"And Alice," Pete says. "I saw her file on the desk in here one time. I knew she'd made it. I guessed she was in isolation because her wounds were too extreme."

If I had hairs on the back of my neck, they would be standing up about now.

"Wounds?" Alice says. "I don't have any wounds!"

"What did the file say?" I ask Pete.

"What do you care?" Alice glares at me.

"I couldn't see anything," Pete says sadly.

"Ha!" Alice points at me.

"Could be they kept her locked up because they couldn't risk the social unrest," I mutter. I wave my hands in mock panic. "'Do not unleash the Alice!'"

"At least I'm fully dressed." She glares at me.

"And how!" I flash her a grim grin.

"Yeah, well — I'm not ill. You were in a coma. There's clearly something wrong with you."

The folded-up paper is burning a hole in my pocket . . .

"The only thing that is wrong with me is that I'm with you, *Malice*."

She jabs a finger at me. "Do not start calling me that again!"

"Hey, that reminds me. Smitty," Pete interjects, throwing me.

"What about him?" I snap.

"Is he here, have you seen him?" he says. "And" — his face brightens — "your mum. She must be able to help us. She did a pretty good job of that last time. Oh god." Realization dawns across Pete's pale face. "Four survivors from the crash. We are the four." He reaches to put a hand on my shoulder. "I'm so sorry, Bobby."

I spring up off the desk. "Forget it, Pete. If you want to make me feel better, get back on that computer and find us a way out of here, and fast!"

I stride off to the bathroom and slam the door behind me.

5

OK, so that was a little cheap of me, and Pete probably didn't deserve it, but I was getting majorly claustro in there. The truth is, I'm exhausted. I've never known tiredness like it, so much effort required to even keep upright. Like those six weeks of Sleeping Beauty didn't quite take the edge off.

And above all, I need to read that paper.

I get it out of my pocket quickly and scan the words that wobble in front of my wired eyes.

Persons of interest re O/vc retrieval . . . highest priority . . . individuals to be kept in strict isolation until further notice . . .

And then Alice. And then me.

A list of stuff — drugs? Tests they've given us? I have no clue what these words mean.

For a double doctors' daughter, I ought to know more than this.

I shove the paper back in my pocket and lean my forehead against the mirror. It feels blissfully cool. I'm running a fever, I'm sure of it. Maybe I *am* sick. In so many ways it would be easy if I just crumpled here, in this bathroom, into a bag of bones and skin with virus oozing from every aching pore.

"Get over it, Roberta . . ." Smitty whispers in my ear.

"And you can shut the hell up, too!" I yell at him. "Unless you say something helpful, don't say anything at all!"

I wait for him to reply, but he doesn't.

I look at my reflection. I'm really not coping well with the St. Gertrude's Experience. Am I going insane? Is this cold turkey or am I on the turn? I look at the dark spikes of hair beginning to poke out of my hairline. Maybe it will grow back curly, if I'm here long enough. I wonder what I'll look like then.

In the mirror's reflection, something behind me catches my eye. I turn around to get a better look.

Above the toilet, up on the wall, is a familiar-looking plastic grating. Thanks, Gertie. A way out? I take it all back.

OK, recess over. I gingerly put the toilet lid down and climb up on it, reaching up to remove the grating. Putting one foot on the cistern, I can just about pull myself up and look into the air vent. Leaning forward, I push my head and shoulders into the gap, my legs and still hanging out into the room below. There's a breeze on my face; I can't see much, but I can see enough. Ahead is one of those fans, set into the vent. No thruway. How totally annoying.

"Found something?"

I bang my head on the roof of the vent. Twisting round a little, I can see Russ standing in the doorway.

"No." I rub my head, and realize that from where he's standing he's got a front-row view of my butt in all its underweared glory. I hurriedly turn around on the cistern, and as I put a foot down on the toilet lid I slip, my hand grabbing at a towel rail to help break my fall. But all that happens is I break the towel rail; a length of shiny metal comes away in my hand, and I fall to the stinky linoleum floor at the base of the toilet bowl.

"You OK?" He reaches out to pull me up, but I decline to be pulled.

"I'm good, thanks." I push myself up to my feet, brushing off bits of plaster from where the towel rail came out of the wall.

"No way out up there?" He quietly shuts the door out to the control room.

"That's right." I pull at my fleece. *Gah.* Why couldn't my leggings have survived the bus crash, too?

"Least you found a weapon." He nods at the towel rail in my hand. I look down at it, too. He might be right. "And I know you know how to handle yourself."

"Fnarr, fnarr!" Smitty's voice pops into my head, and my cheeks flush red. *"Don't you just, Roberta!"*

"Don't believe everything Pete tells you," I mumble, sitting down by a cold radiator.

Russ looks at me intently and my face gets redder than red. "Actually, it's not that. I remember seeing you in action."

My eyebrows shoot up. "You do? How come?"

He drops to his knees and then sits beside me, back against the wall. "You ran me down." He looks at his feet ruefully, then glances at me again through thick eyelashes. "On the mountain at Aviemore. There I am, doing a decent job beating my friends on the last stretch of the trail" — he leans in, as if confidentially — "and some crazy ninja whooshes up behind me and wipes me out. As you can imagine, my friends thought that was pretty funny." He purses his lips in a mock pout. "Then it turns out she's a girl, and that makes things even better."

I think I do remember. There was this guy, totally out of control, making with the loco erratic turns in front of me . . . but ultimately, the collision was my fault for not reading him right. You can only control what *you* do, not other people, my dad used to say. So protect yourself, and don't let yourself get into a situation where your fate is in someone else's hands.

"I'm sorry."

"No worries." He smiles. His body is closer now; we're side by side, but somehow he's maneuvered himself so that we're almost touching. "The only thing you bashed was my pride. Oh, and my rep with my friends." A shadow moves over his face. "Then again, it's not like any of them are worrying about that now."

"I'm sorry about that, too," I say lamely. I scratch at my bald head, then remember how it must look, and stop.

"Don't worry about it," he says. "You had a friend on that bus, too . . . Smitty? And — oh god — your mother was on there as well?"

"Yeah." I shuffle, uncomfortable.

"Hey, I don't want to pry —"

"No." I turn to him. "I don't think things are . . ." I struggle to find the words. ". . . quite what they seem. There's a story I have to share."

"Yeah?" The brown eyes lock onto mine again. "I'm all ears."

"Well, with Pete, too," I say.

Russ frowns. "Sure you're happy with the others knowing?"

I stare at him. "Alice already knows. And Pete, well, I trust Pete."

Russ's eyebrows shoot up. "You do? That surprises me."

Now it's my turn to frown. "Why? He's an annoying little geek sometimes, but I'd trust him with my life. He's kind of, well . . . after what we went through last time, Pete and Alice, for all their faults, they're kind of family."

"Wow." Russ chuckles and shakes his head. "I had no idea. I mean, he's a great bloke and everything, but he is really interested in that virus, really wants to know all about the Xanthro people, what's happening outside, who's in charge."

"Yeah?" I say, surprised. "He's talked about that with you?"

"All the time. Kind of made me a little nervous." He smiles at me again and pats my arm with his large hand, then springs to his feet. "But that's great. Good to have friends in all this."

"Sure," I say, standing and moving to the mirror, just to have something to do. "Gimme a moment, and I'll come through and spill the beans."

Before Russ can question me any more, Alice bursts in.

"Get out! Get out!"

Russ leaps into action, grabbing the towel rail from my hands and brandishing it.

"Did they get in?"

"No!" Alice rolls her eyes and pushes past him. "I'm going to puke!" She just about makes it to the toilet in time and bends over with a series of little heaves, like she's regurgitating a particularly stubborn fur ball.

"Oh god, Alice." I put a hand out to rub her back, then think better of it. "Are you OK?"

"Blueberry yogurt," she splutters, then heaves again. "Go. Away."

I look at Russ, he hands me back my towel rail, and we thankfully follow Alice's order.

*   *   *

Back in Martha's room, Pete is still working at the computer. Russ is right, he has always been fascinated by all the Xanthro stuff, but that's no need to doubt him . . . is it? *Course not.* That's just the way he rolls. I plant my almost-bare butt on the desk beside him, and there's an attractive suction noise. I try to cover it with a kind of half cough.

Pete looks up at me with his big green eyes. "I'm sorry, Bobby."

At first I think he's talking about the weird thigh-fart I just made, but then I realize he's still stinging after I flounced off.

"'S fine." I cut him off and reach down into my boot. "So, I have stuff to share . . . I know Mum isn't dead, and I'm pretty sure that Smitty's alive and kicking, too." I say. "At least, they were when Mum wrote me a message." I hold out my phone.

"Whaat?" Pete gasps. "You got a text?"

I shake my head. "Someone — has to be my mother — inputted a load of contacts into my phone book. With these really weird, bogus numbers. It turns out the numbers are a kind of code. At least I think they are."

Pete practically wets himself. "Have you cracked it?" Oh, he really hopes I haven't. He's so desperate to do it.

"Yep." I enjoy the brief look of disappointment on his face. "Well, partly. In the first one, the numbers correspond to letters on the phone's keypad. When you type them in with predictive text, the words pop up." I try to shrug off the geekisms. "Kinda thing."

Alice slinks through the bathroom door, holding a wodge of tissue up to her lips.

"I'm still alive. Thanks for caring, everybody."

"Show us the message, Bobby!" Pete ignores her.

Alice sees the phone and rolls her eyes. "Oh, you'll love this."

"So what does it say?" Russ urges me.

"I've only worked out the first one." I switch on the phone and tap into the contacts.

"And?" Pete says.

"It says 'Find Smitty.'" I bite my lip.

They both stare at me.

"Give it to me!" Pete's Mohawk wobbles a bit as he stretches out an arm.

"Easy, tiger." I automatically close my hand tight around the phone.

"Show me."

OK, so I am quite excited to show him. Sharing this with Alice was about as gratifying as trying to explain long division to a panda. I show them the entries.

"Marigold and . . . Poffit?" Russ says. "You know some interesting-sounding people."

"Yeah." I falter a moment, but there ain't no getting round this one. "That's how I know it was Mum who put the names in here. No one would know about Marigold and, er, Poffit, apart from her."

"And they are?" It's Alice, of course. Calling from her corner. Because she knows it's going to be embarrassing.

"Marigold is my grandmother's cat." I wince. "And Poffit . . . Poffit was my, er, lovey." I flush red, try to laugh it off a little. "You know, the thing you carry around with you when you're a kid."

"Security blanket?" snorts Alice. This is way better than she had hoped.

"Got it in one, genius," I snark back.

"OK, so obviously no one would know about that apart from your mum," Russ steps in, to avoid things going catfight between the Malice and me. But somehow, that only makes it more mortifying.

"Look." I try to move things on by going into the "Marigold" entry. "Here's the 'Find Smitty' message. 3463764889. You type that number in like you're texting, it comes back as 'Find Smitty.'"

Pete grabs for the phone to try it, and I let him. He lets out a whistle as he gets the same result. "It works." His white-blond head nods slightly as he types in the numbers a second time. "She's telling the truth."

"Of course I am," I snap. "Now let's turn it off before the battery runs out." As if on cue, the phone beeps a warning. I hold my hand out for Pete to hand it to me.

"That's clever," says Russ. "She's smart, your mum."

"Smart enough to keep it simple so I'd understand it." I gimmegimme with my hand at Pete, but he ignores me.

"We copy out the numbers." He casts around for pen and paper. "We can easily work out the letters; then it's a simple anagram at worst." The phone beeps again.

"It's going to die!" I call out.

"It's fine," Pete counters. "They go on like this for ages before they actually conk out." He finds a pen at last and starts pressing buttons on the phone. "Oh."

"Pete!" I scream at him. "It died, didn't it? Great job." I collapse back down on the counter with another nekkid-butt squelching noise, but this time I don't care who hears it.

"Doesn't matter." He looks at the phone's bottom. "We'll get a charger. It takes the generic sort. And I know exactly where there is one."

"Where?" I refuse to get excited.

"The nurses' station."

"The wuh . . . ?"

"The big desk in the corridor that we crouched behind."

I blink at him. "The big desk in the corridor. The corridor that is currently swamped by zombinos."

"*Quelle marvellouse!*" Alice treats us to one of her best flounces. She looks at me. "Go fetch, then."

"What?" I hold my hands up. "As in, out there, with them? Slow your roll, girl."

"It'll be easy!" Alice shouts.

"So you go!" I shout back.

"Like that's going to happen!" she screams at me.

"I'd like to see the day!" I scream back.

"I'll go," Russ says quietly.

We all look at him. Then we look at the screen. Then at him again. He smiles.

"I will. I'll go. Simple," he says, and he walks over to some pegs in the alcove. "Look what Martha keeps handy for those special occasions." He holds up a dark-colored jacket and raps it with his knuckles. "Reinforced. Kevlar."

"Bite-proof . . ." I mutter.

He gives me a big smile. "Here's hoping." He slides an arm into the jacket and retrieves a helmet with gloves nesting inside it. "Nice."

"What, you're going to just run through them?" Alice says. "You'll completely die."

"Very foolhardy," Pete shakes his head. "Besides, these messages — as valuable as they might be — aren't our ticket out of here. We still have to find an exit."

"Yeah, Pete," Alice says. "About that . . ."

Russ taps the smart glass on the wall, revealing only a couple of zoms. "They've thinned out at the door now, I can get out, no problem." He pulls on the helmet and starts with the gloves. "Besides, it could be a practice run for our great escape. Maybe I can frighten enough of them off so they'll clear a way for us to get out of that door into the courtyard? The phone needs time to charge up before we can even start deciphering the code. So I go now, and that gives us time to hole up here before we make our exit."

"But the zoms!" Alice cries.

"They're only small. And I'm big." He gives her a winning smile, his caramel eyes twinkle, and I see her melt a little. He turns to Pete and claps him on the shoulder. "Where exactly is this charger?"

Pete gulps, then remembers he's Grand Leader. He straightens his goggles. "It was plugged in. There's a socket on the wall on the right-hand side of the counter." He shuts his eyes for a minute, as if picturing it. "But if it's not there now, search the drawers."

Not such a simple dash and grab, then. More of a search and rescue. Russ is going to need more time to get this done.

"Piece of cake," Russ says, not a trace of snark in his voice, and pulls down a reflective visor over his head. He looks like the love child of Buzz Lightyear and Iron Man. He unbolts the door and then grabs the handle. "Wish me luck."

"Wait!" I cry.

"It's OK, I won't let any in," he says.

"No, it's not that." I dart over toward the pegs. "I'm coming with you." I pick up a second jacket; Martha was well prepared. Hot diggity dang, it's heavy. I throw it on over my fleece; more padding. "You can't go out there by yourself, you'll get mobbed." The jacket is huge on me. What's good is that it covers my ass a little better than what I was wearing before. But I still have bare legs, and there's no second helmet or pair of gloves.

"You can't do this," Russ starts.

"Of course I can," I argue. "One of us provides a distraction, the other goes for the charger. I'm fast." *Well, I used to be . . .* I shake off the thought. "I'll keep 'em busy while you get to the desk." *What the hell am I doing?*

"If you're going, you should go now." Pete is fiddling with the computer. "Big ones, maybe heading this way."

"At least take these." Russ begins to pull off the helmet and gloves.

I shake my head. "Won't be able to see with that on my head anyway." I look at Alice. "I could use some legwear, though."

"What?" She's shaken. "So now you want my velour? Naff off. You wouldn't fit into them anyway."

"Come on, Alice. Gimme," I tell her. I have no other options; even my skinny behind would be hard-pushed to squeeze into Pete's tiny polyester slacks.

"Oh my god, this is too gross for words. DO NOT get zombie on them." She begins pulling them down. "Or your own sweat. You!" she shouts at Pete. "Turn around! I refuse to strip while you're perving and getting your jollies off."

Pete splutters and objects, red-faced, but turns around anyway. Curiously Alice is not bothered by the prospect of Russ seeing her in her skimpies. She chucks the peach fluffy legs at me, and I pull them on. Hmm. Wouldn't have been my choice, but I'm not sure that Alice has any biker leathers I could borrow.

"Let's do this." I'm all Captain America now. What I lack in actual armor, I make up for in spirit. I grab my towel rail, Russ picks up the fire extinguisher, and the door is opened and closed before I have time to think what a stupid idea this is.

6

The flashing amber-and-red lights have stopped. Maybe the Undead don't like to disco. The Lil' Zombinos have given up on crowding the door, but to our left they're clumping up beside the nurses' station, probably because it smells of warm human a little more than these scrubbed-down corridors.

"Let's draw them down this end!" I say and point to the right beyond the courtyard entrance, where the corridor takes a sharp turn. "Then I'll keep 'em occupied and you run up the wing for the try."

"Don't you mean for the touchdown?"

"Yeah, you're right. We're way too armored for rugby." I grasp my towel rail and set my jaw, and together we scoot down the end of the corridor. I've already spotted where I'm going; just before the corridor turns, a pair of double doors is open, with a gurney beside them. I'm becoming an expert at this — with a leap and a bound I reckon I can get up on top of one of the doors and balance there for the duration of Russ's charger retrieval. There are a couple of large pipes suspended from the ceiling; they'll give me something to hang on to.

I never used to think like this, I never used to look for the emergency exits, the free-running routes, the easy weapon, or the barricade. But I'll never be able to stop now. Not even when I get old and crusty and all this is just a bunch of bedtime stories I frighten my grandchildren with.

That's always assuming I get to grow up.

"Now what?" Russ shouts at me from under his RoboCop visor. We're at the doors. The corridor continues a little farther beyond here, then takes the ninety-degree left. I run to look down the dogleg and am glad to see it's clear. For now. Meanwhile, back at the nurses' station, the mob has turned around to see what all the commotion is, and is heading our way.

"They're coming, just wait." I clamber up onto the gurney. "They'll thin out as they start moving. As they get closer you can make your run."

"You've done this before, haven't you?"

"Pete told you the tales." I grit my teeth. "Once or twice." I shove the towel rail down my jacket, and use a dispenser for antibacterial hand cleaner as a foothold to hoist myself up and plant my butt on top of the door. I wobble there, not exactly limber in this fleece-jacket combo, but I cling on to the pipes on the ceiling for balance.

The mini-monsters are homing in on us now, smacking their little chops, excited as zoms can ever get, the fish-sick smell emanating from their foul breathy moans.

"There!" I point up to the nurses' station. It's practically deserted. Just what the doctor ordered. "Do it!"

Russ lets out a roar and pushes the gurney, using it as both a weapon and a shield, legs powering it from behind and straight through the little zoms. It's moving fast — he throws himself down onto it like it's a greased lightning sled and barrels along the corridor, knocking bodies left and right. I cheer him on, distracting some of the zombinos to my perch.

Russ's gurney hits the nurses' station with a *KerPlunk*, and he goes flying headfirst over the desk. Lucky he didn't give me that helmet after all. It's kind of funny, and it does more to endear him to me than all the brave stuff. You can't knock a piece of comedy gold. My laughter makes the door shake, and I grip tighter to the pipes above to keep from falling.

"I'm OK!" He stands up and shouts at me, his helmet wonky. This is even funnier, but I don't think it will do his morale much good to see me in hysterics, and I can't give him the big thumbs-up without falling, so I don't do anything. He's not looking, anyway — immediately he's searching for the charger, ducking down behind the desk, using every second like it's a matter of life or death. Which, of course, it is.

Below me, the mob is pressing at the door, reaching their little arms up to try and snatch a foot. I keep my legs out in front of me; it's quite an ab workout, and the edge of the door bites into my rear end. But they can't reach me, and they're not going to shake me loose. There are six or seven of them now, jostling for space, bumping each other against the wall, against the antibac holder thingy, against a big button that says OPEN/CLOSE on it . . . *Shit!*

My door starts to move from under me. The little rascals have had a lucky accident and hit the button. The door is closing. I can't go with it, so I have to jump or hang. Jumping down among the dead men is not an option, so I hang, my legs dangling, arms burning, grip slippy on the dusty pipes. Heat moves over me, a rush of adrenaline and danger-sweats. I feel my stomach muscles crying out as I try to raise my feet in front of me and hook them over the pipes, but the stupid towel rail shoved down my jacket keeps me from bending my body. Dammit! I hang, legs kicking, and the kiddies reaching up to bash at me like I'm the fattest piñata at the zombie birthday party.

"Russ!" It's hard to scream when you're dangling, but I manage it. "Have you got it?" He's still out of sight, somewhere behind the desk.

"Not yet!" A muffled cry comes back at me.

"Wanna speed it up for me?" My shoulders feel like they're dislocating. I shuffle a nervous hand forward, knees bent, feet only just out of reach. Can I monkey-bar hand over hand along these pipes? At least to get clear of the zoms below? Sweat dribbles down into my eyes. I have no choice, my grip can only hold out for so long. I've got to go for it. Right hand, left hand, right hand. My legs swing, giving me a rhythm. I'm doing it! Left hand, right hand, left hand . . . the towel rail slipping down my front every time I swing. A girl with lips bitten away in a permanent smile looks up at me and makes a lucky grab. I kick my foot free, but she's on me again.

"Russ!" I up the urgency a notch or three. "I can't hold out!"

"I've got it!" he shouts and pops his helmeted head above the parapet. "But it's tangled in some other cables —"

"Untangle quickly!" *I don't need an explanation, just get on with it!* But I know that no matter how fast he works, I've reached the end of my endurance. The mob is all around. No place to jump free or run clear. I try one last, desperate effort to somehow wedge my feet in the pipes and take some of the weight, but I know as I'm doing it that it's useless. The towel rail finally clatters to the ground, and I'm all set to follow it. My grip gives out on me, and I fall to the floor below with a yelp.

I land on one on them, and it kind of splats and crunches below me — I try to roll free of the crowd but hit a pair of legs. Instantly I curl into a ball, shrinking into my flak jacket like a turtle. Little claws scratch at my back, the bulletproof stuff in the jacket doing its thing and keeping me safe. But I have to move before they manage to find a fleshy bit or roll me over like a hedgehog. With a shriek I tumble over and over, with as much speed and force as possible, through the gaps in the legs around me until I bash up against the glass of the door leading to the courtyard, and I've found my answer. There's a bar halfway up the door saying PUSH TO OPEN, and I raise both hands to smack it and willingly obey. The door clunks and gives way. I roll out into the courtyard, twist round, and slam it shut behind me with both feet.

I lie there panting, my boots against the glass and my back on the concrete. I raise my head to look at my pursuers. They're there on the other side of the glass, pressing up against it and clearly quite flummoxed as to why they can't reach me. I laugh out loud.

"Gotcha!"

The door shudders as one zombie raises its hands and smacks the bar on the door. Others join in. Dammit! They're *copying* what I did. They're going to open it exactly the same way. I brace my legs against the bottom of the glass, unable to move.

Anywhere to run to? I screw round from my prone position, my head wrenching my neck in an effort to see behind me. *Gah, it's hot in here. Wait* . . . I spot a ladder, bolted to the wall in the far corner. I follow it up the wall with my eyes. Presumably there's some kind of hatch in the greenhouse roof, to the outside. It's hard to tell from here. But they wouldn't have a ladder leading to nowhere.

Thud.

The door wobbles again, and my knees are jarred. Where is Russ? He's not going to leave me here, is he? The thought is genuinely worrying. He seems like a straight-up kinda guy, and I think he sorta likes me, but you never can tell.

The faces at the window turn away from me, and then there's a spray of white goo that spatters across the glass and the zombie mob part. At first I think the white stuff is brains, that Russ has found a pump-action shotgun and is going crazy. But even pus-marinated zom brains are more of a pink-thru-red kinda color. This is something different. Russ is at the door — visor up, battle-drunk face — but his weapon is the fire extinguisher, and the white stuff, foam.

I let my knees relax and roll out of the way just as he bursts through the door.

"Come on!"

I leap to my feet, just as Russ uses the extinguisher's end to ram a blindly stumbling zom. They all have foam all over their faces, they can't see, and it's cramping their style.

"You got the charger?"

"Yep." He pats a pocket. "Quickly!" He beckons me, and I'm about to follow him, but the lure of that ladder and the mob's incapacitation is too good to ignore.

"The ladder." I point. "Might be our way out! Let's get the others and make a break for it while we can."

He shakes his head first, then I see his face change as he looks down the corridor. "The adults. They've found us. We'll try it."

We run back into the corridor, past the feeble, blinded children. Russ uses the gurney to clear our path, and I miraculously trip over the bloody towel rail and scoop it up for future use. As we reach the control room, the door is already open and Pete is standing there. They must have been watching the whole thing on the screen, but I'm still impressed he got past Alice's inevitable objections to open up and let us in.

` "We can get out into the courtyard," shouts Russ. "There's a ladder to the roof."

"I want my sweatpants." Alice is perched on the desk, her T-shirt poking below her hoodie and stretched out of all proportion to cover her modesty.

"Jeez, Alice, there's no time!" I shout.

"Not moving until you give them to me!" she cries and thumps the desk with both fists.

"Do it!" Pete shouts at me.

"Are you both frickin' crazy?" But I'm already struggling out of them, because I already know the answer to my question. The bottoms catch on my boots, and I am hopping around trying to pull the damn peach fluffies off. It's OK, though, because at this rate the zombies will probably kill themselves laughing at this performance. "Thanks for the loan, lady." Finally I win the battle and I fling them at Alice, who dons them in record time.

"Hitch a ride!" Russ is patting the gurney, and we load ourselves onto it — me on the front, then Pete and Alice, squealing. Russ is behind, pushing us off, running until we've built up enough speed. And then he leaps on, too, and we're flying, screeching, the wind whipping over my bald head, a little part of me enjoying it as the gurney flies down the corridor again. As we come level with the door to the courtyard, Russ jumps down and acts as a human brake, the front of the gurney swinging from left to right as we skid to a stop.

"Aargh!" Alice flies off the side and splays out onto the floor at the feet of a boy Undead, who makes a move on her. As tempted as I am to leave her, I raise a leg and boot the zom in the head. As I reach down to give her a hand, she screws up her face in distaste.

"Do me a favor? Cut out the high kicks until you've found some pants."

I pull her to her feet, unnecessarily roughly. "You'd like me to leave you to be eaten?"

There's a furious roar, but it's not Alice. Undead Seniors have arrived. We've been playing tag with the kids long enough. The big guys are here, and it's time to go.

We run to the door just as Russ opens it and bust out into the courtyard. The door is slammed shut and Russ wedges the fire extinguisher against it. I guess it's not the easiest weapon to tote around, especially when you're scaling buildings. The hotness hits me again as I scan around just to make sure no little monsters have slipped out while we were otherwise occupied — or whether there are any other survivors — but we're alone. For now.

"God! God! God!" screams Alice. "Get it off me!"

I turn expecting to see a zom clinging to her leg. She has a large spotted butterfly sitting on her outstretched hand, fluttering its wings prettily. Alice flaps her hand back at it, not quite daring to touch.

"Die!" Russ splats it with his fist. *Wow.* Alice gives a yell, and the poor butterfly gives a flutter and falls to the ground, broken. Russ's eyes blaze. I guess he really hates insects.

"The ladder!" Pete cries, pointing to the corner.

"It's so high," Alice gasps.

"It's leading to the roof, what did you expect?" I mutter.

Russ grabs her hand and squeezes it. "We can make it, Alice."

She doesn't look so sure, but I'm guessing the combo of imminent zoms and a leg up from Russ will be enough for her to give it a shot.

I reach the bottom of the ladder first, seizing the sides and pulling myself up before my foot has even found the first rung. The metal is so sharp it feels like it's cutting into my hands. I wish I'd taken those gloves now — but then again, as I ascend and realize the world has a great view of my ass, I really wish a whole lot more that I had fought Alice for the sweatpants.

I take the first few rungs as fast as I dare. It's slippery going, and I'm grappling with the towel rail. The ladder is attached so close to the wall there's barely room to find a decent foothold without feeling like you're falling backward. I glance down. Pete is on the ladder after me, with the best view in the world, and Russ remains on the ground with Alice, doing the persuading. I feel a wave of dizzy from looking down, and turn my attention back to where I'm headed. Gotta keep moving.

The roof looms up at me, and for the first time I wonder what will be waiting for us. I don't relish being met by a dribbling fiend.

There's a crash below, and a shattering of glass.

Crap. They're through the door. I chance another look. A flow of Undead, big and small, stream into the courtyard. It doesn't take them long to spot us.

"Frigging hurry up!" Alice screams, halfway up the ladder.

I pull myself over the low wall at the top and step out onto a crunchy surface, eyes darting to see what foes we'll have to face.

Hard to be sure, but I think we're alone up here. The courtyard is a hollow square below, at the center of the hospital. There are some air-conditioning vents rising out of the surface of the roof and some bricked blocks with small doors set into the side — probably electrical junction boxes or something like that. But beyond the odd adventurous butterfly, there's nothing moving.

And then there's this glass ceiling above us. I suppose I expected to reach the top of the ladder and find a hatch, open it, and emerge out of the tropical oasis into gloomy old freezing-cold Scotland again. But that's never going to happen. The glass ceiling covers the entire roof area. Weird. We're still inside. The ceiling is not far above me. Put it this way: If my current escape gang formed a human pyramid with a sulky Alice at the top, even she wouldn't have to strain to touch it. And what's more, the glass rises out of the outside edge of the building, like the whole hospital is a miniature model inside one of those terrarium things that you grow plants in. I look around again. Where's the exit?

There's something more than a little off. If I think about it, I kind of knew it as soon as I fell into the courtyard the first time round. The light is weird, and as I was lying there on my back holding back the zombies behind the door, I knew it just didn't look real somehow.

I look across the roof in search of a horizon in the distance, and my brain can't quite compute what I'm seeing.

I run to the far edge of the roof, the outside wall, and look beyond the glass.

There's nothing out there.

7

The sky really is the limit.

Behind the glass walls is blackness. Not as in outer space or anything like that. A cavity, then solid matter. Rock. I can see texture, cracks, roughness.

Why in the Name of Butt would you have a hospital surrounded by rock?

I rub at the glass. It's slightly frosted, and above us there are lights behind it, giving the impression of daylight. If I squint I can actually make out the individual bulbs.

Pete joins me, panting hard.

"Status update?" he gasps, pushing his goggles up onto his head.

"OMG, today I'm, like, *totally* inside a giant fishbowl," I suggest.

He looks at me impatiently. "What on earth are you talking about?"

I point up to the glass. "The outside has gone."

I watch his face as he follows the ceiling along to the far wall . . . and he sees what I see.

"I think we're surrounded by rock. Like we're in a cave or something."

"This is incredible! Why would they . . . ?" He runs — and it takes a lot to prompt Pete to run — to one of the walls, feeling the glass like the original Marcel Marceau. He shouts back at me, "We're completely encased!"

As if on cue Alice arrives, with much fanfare and overdramatization, seeming to fall at the last hurdle before Russ lends a helping hand and hoists her onto the roof from behind. Her cheeks are flushed, and I don't think it's just from the thrill of the chase. I never cease to wonder at that girl's ability to irritate. She glares at me.

"Couldn't you move your fat arse any faster?" she says. "Those things were practically snapping at my heels."

The retort is so tempting, but I ignore her and look over the side down into the courtyard again. It is fast filling with zoms, the bodies pooling around the bottom of the ladder. They're looking up. It's worrying; they've figured out where we've gone, and one of them is reaching up for the rungs, trying to climb.

Russ blocks my vision momentarily, smiling at me as he reaches the final rung and steps out onto the roof.

"So where to?" His eyes dart to Pete, who is still doing his wall-fondling over at the other side of the roof. "Hey . . . what's . . . ?" He looks up at the ceiling and I see him making the same connections. "Where's the exit?"

"Doesn't appear to be one," I say.

Russ shakes his head and runs over to where Pete is. We all follow.

"What are you all talking about?" Alice's worldview hasn't quite grasped the truth as yet. "Oh my god!" She slaps the glass wall.

"Got to be a door, something." Russ takes off, running. He's fast; you can't help but admire that. Team Cheery Chomper stand and watch while he runs a circuit around us like a collie dog, finally returning barely out of breath.

"There's no way out," he says.

"We're underground," Pete mutters. I look up at him sharply. Alice stares at him like he smells bad.

"Excuse me?" she says.

"You're excused." He sits down on the gravel and puts his head between his knees. "We're still underground, though."

"Explain," I say.

Still with head down, Pete shoots out an arm and gestures around him. "I should have guessed. Where would the safest place be for a military hospital? Underground. Hidden, protected, secret."

"Seriously?" Russ says. "Seems pretty incredible to me."

"Why?" Pete lifts his head and fixes him with his pale green eyes. "There are subterranean military hospitals in the Channel Islands left over from the Second World War; they are tourist attractions now. And there's an old nuclear bunker in Scotland that housed several hundred people during the Cold War. One hundred feet below. I visited it last summer."

"You would," says Alice.

"And those are just a couple of examples we know about," Pete says. "Just think of all the ones we don't."

"So if this place is so secret, so hidden and so protected, how come it's overrun with the Undead?" I say. "Did they come down the chimney while no one was looking? Hide in the laundry baskets and smuggle themselves inside?"

"Perhaps they were here already," Pete says. "It's a hospital, after all. Perhaps they were trying to treat them, or perhaps they were dead bodies who reanimated."

"Whatever," Alice says. "Chances are they just sniffed her out." She points at me. "Everywhere she goes, they follow. What matters is how we escape."

"Right," Russ says, then shoots me an apologetic look. "About the last bit, I mean."

"Very right," says Pete. "Quite often these places are booby-trapped. Or there's some kind of fail-safe. When a facility is compromised, it automatically floods to ensure no one gets out."

"Are you kidding me?" I yell at him.

"Well, the ones with the Nazi wounded were," he says.

"Nazi zombies now?" Alice groans.

"Keep your big-girl panties on, Alice, there are no Nazis here," I snap at her. "Isn't it enough for you that we find out we're several stories below Raccoon City?" The ref is lost on her, as I knew it would be. "What's important is there must be a way out, and chances are, we gotta get back in before we get out." I point to the air vents. "So I'm thinking that's our way."

"Oh god oh god oh god," groans Alice. "Why do you always insist on crawling through things?"

I jog up to one of them and tug at the screen on the front.

"Er, Bobby." Pete has a smarmy look on his face. "We could just walk through the door." He points over to the opposite roof. In the middle of the flat roof, there is what looks like a block of bricks. I think I must have written it off as another vent or a chimney or something, but it's obvious now that it must be a small room housing a stairwell down into the building. "Let's check it out."

Before we can respond, there's a cracking sound behind him, and we all look. It's something down in the courtyard. The noise comes again, and a third time.

"Hey!" Alice shouts. "They're shooting them."

We rush to the wall.

"Where?" I scan the courtyard. Another shot rings out and, instinctively and as one, we all duck behind the wall. I poke my head over it. As far as I can tell, the shots are coming from somewhere across from us.

"There." Pete gasps. "Top floor, third window from the right."

We look. There's a shot and a little flash, confirming he's nailed it. But then another shot from a different direction. There are zoms down. Whoever's firing is doing a pretty good job of picking them off.

"How many shooters?" Pete pushes up beside me, trying to get a better view while using me as a human shield, just in case. When I shrug, he looks exasperated.

"So sue me," I hiss at him. "This is my first sniper scenario."

"Who cares anyway?" Alice says. "They're on our side." And before we can anticipate her madness, she stands up and waves her arms. "Hello-ee! We're over here! Can you save us, please?"

There's a *ping*, brick dust flies, and Russ has tackled Alice to the ground. She lies there, her eyes wide. "They are shooting at *us*?"

"Must have been a mistake," Russ says. "Itchy trigger finger."

"Itchy trigger finger my arse," says Pete, and we know what he means, but it still sounds bad. "They're trained men. They don't make mistakes."

And he's right, I'm sure of it. They know the score; they know the zoms don't stand on roofs and wave and shout.

"Wait!" Something on the ground has caught my eye. "Survivors!" Three moving figures emerging from the remains of the glass door we had come through. There's a gray-haired man clad in green scrubs and a woman in a suit helping a younger guy who is injured. They stick to the sides of the courtyard, away from the mob who are still mainly underneath the ladder. They've seen the shooters, too, and they're waving at them and calling out for help.

Crack.

Crack.

Two shots. Two hits. The man in scrubs falls first, then the woman. For a second the younger guy looks up — and I can just make out the terror and confusion on his face.

Crack.

He's not confused anymore. He's still.

I drop behind the wall, a dread-ball of sick forming in my stomach.

"Oh my god oh my god oh my god!" Alice whispers. "They shot them in cold blood." Tears start to drip down her face. "They just wanted help, and they shot them." She looks at me, frantic. "What will they do to us?"

We flatten ourselves against the place where wall meets roof and try to disappear.

"They know we're here, we have to move," Russ says.

I turn to Pete. "Is this the fail-safe, then? Wipe everyone out, just to be sure?"

Pete shakes his head. "No. Fail-safe is a last resort. If we were at that stage, those shooters would be dead, too."

"That's something." Russ sends me a look, and I feel a little heartened. "Come on." He beetles along on all fours, heading to the end of our wall. "Let's get to the door."

I'm not sure about that. Isn't it the way the shooters will come, now that they know we're here? Then again, we're kids. They have more pressing targets, namely the zombie hordes. There's just a chance they'll leave us till last, as long as we don't get in their way.

"Ow, ow, ow, ow." Alice delicately picks up her two front paws as she crawls after Russ. "This is so uncomfortable on my hands!"

"Sorry, we'll pick the nice velvet-soft roof next time," I say, overtaking her.

Crack!

Crack! Crack!

The shooting is almost reassuring, because it means the snipers are still where they were. Once it goes silent then we know they've bagged every last courtyard monster and will be on the move. I keep as low as I can, fearing for one inch of body to rise above the wall and give them something to hit. We round a corner and keep on going. So long as there's wall to cling to, we're OK. The real test will be to break cover and run to that door. Better hope it's open when we get there.

And then the shooting stops. Russ must have stopped, too, because I barrel into Pete, and Alice smashes into my scantily clad behind. It's a total pileup.

Just an expanse of roof stands between us and the door.

Russ goes for it, keeping low. I guess it's hard to keep him back, and he's the trailblazing type, wanting to check out the door so that the rest of us will be safe. It's kind of sweet, but kind of irritating at the same time. I think if I'm honest, I'm just pissed he's not Smitty. Smitty would have gone for it, too, but he'd have cracked some lame-o joke and given me a wink and managed to insult Alice all in one go. And it would have been annoying as hell, but wonderful.

"*Roberta! Don't get all sentimental on me now!*" Smitty says in my ear. And he's right. That's the kind of nonsense that makes a girl soft. And gets a girl killed.

Russ is crouched by the door and turning the handle slowly. That's good. It would be oh-so-typical if the thing was locked. He opens it a little, then looks inside. This should probably be the part where something pulls him into the blackness. But luckily for all of us, it isn't. He gives us the thumbs-up, then beckons, and we go for it. I cast a glance behind as I reach the door; the courtyard is still silent, and no one is shooting at us. I follow Alice in through the door, and Russ gives me a smile, last in, and shuts the door behind us.

We are standing at the top of a stairwell, lit with a small bulb encased in a metal mesh above our heads.

"So down to go up, right?" I grab the metal rail.

"Wait!" He holds out a hand. "Remember those guys are trained, they have weapons, and they have a plan. Don't get too smart, don't think you can fight them. If it comes to close quarters, leave it to me to disable them."

"You can do that?" Alice looks like she's going to swoon.

"I know some things," Russ says. He winks at her. "But if I told you . . ."

"You'd have to kill me?" She flirts back. But somehow the whole thing gives me the shivers.

We run down the stairs. I count seven landings, and still the stairs go on. Journey to the center of the earth. My ears are popping. This is getting ridiculous. And panicky. I stop and turn to Pete.

"Ground floor is where, exactly? If we continue any farther we're going to find the molten core."

Pete makes a face at me, but I can see he's grateful just to stop for a second.

"All the way down, I'm guessing. There's got to be a lift to the surface from the lowest level," he gasps.

We reach the next landing. I skid to a stop.

"Look!"

There's a body. Someone in a white coat, lying down. Lying still. At first I think it's a woman, because this person has a long, brown ponytail, but as I get a little closer, I realize it's a man.

"Curious," Pete says. "The hair."

"God, I know," says Alice. "Dreckitudinous. He must have been living underground since 1977."

Russ chuckles. "What Pete means is that he's supposed to be military. Who heard of an army guy with long hair? They give them all buzz cuts."

"Yeah," Alice replies. "Like her."

"Maybe he does their website for them." I crack the joke, but something is wrong with this picture.

And then it gets even wronger. Ponytail wakes up.

He slowly rises, arms dragging up his body, head lolling until the last second, when it pops up to reveal it's half blown away. The remaining eye sees us, and, I SWEAR, he smiles. Arms out, he advances.

I grip the towel rail. I feel Russ stiffen beside me.

"He's only one. We can get past him."

Upstairs a door slams.

"The soldiers!" Pete squeaks.

"Stay calm, folks," Russ says. "Bobby, give me the towel rail."

I hold it up to give him, but at that moment the door behind Ponytail opens, and a surge of Undead spills through. In shock, I clatter the rail against the metal banister on the stairs. The vibration travels through my hands, up my arm bones, and into my shoulders, and in shock I drop the rail. It falls down the stairwell and lands somewhere below with an almost tuneful clanging. *For whom the bell tolls.* I lean over the banister, as if somehow I can take back the loud noise. And then comes the buggy feeling. I turn round quickly and look up though the stairwell, feeling eyes burning into the back of my skull.

A head, in a black balaclava, is hanging over the banister several floors up.

A second head appears, a little farther down.

Then a third, a mere two or three floors above.

"Run!" I screech, not trying to be quiet anymore, because I clearly failed the silence thing. Down is not an option, so we run up a flight and through the doors and into another short corridor, round a bend, and keep on running. But as we near the end of the corridor, a mob appears in front of us, doctors and nurses freshly turned, hungry-looking, as yet unfed.

"Fall back!" Russ cries. We sprint back to the bend in the corridor, and I spy a door with a small sign by the wall. I can just make out the letters.

"There! The door doesn't have a handle." There's a keypad entrance system, but the door is already ajar. We can get in and shut it behind us. I point down the corridor. We race for it, Russ pulls the door open, and we bundle inside.

The room is very small, with lockers and shelves storing boots and clothing. And a doorway leading to something else beyond.

"We're trapped again!" Alice screams. "And they know where we are!"

Russ shakes his head. "We were too fast. The zoms didn't see where we went. As far as they're concerned we melted into the wall."

"Now all we've got to worry about are the soldiers," Pete says grimly.

"No doubt, but they won't look here," I say. "At least not for a while."

"What makes you so sure?" Alice says.

"They'll assume we won't hide here."

"Why?" Alice frowns at me. Then her pretty little nose curls up in distaste, and for once, it's not me that is provoking the reaction. "God, what's that smell?"

It hit me as soon as we came in here, but then again, I knew to expect it. It's strong, so overpowering that it's making my eyes water.

Pete knows. As we rushed inside, I saw him clock the word written in small letters on a subtle plaque on the door. He walks to the doorway to the other room, and peers around tentatively. Below his feet is a tray with some kind of liquid in it.

"Disinfectant," he says, lifting each foot up and watching the stuff drip off into the tray. "That's the top note, anyhow. With a base of rotting flesh. The main smell, however, is . . . formaldehyde."

"For . . . what?" Alice still doesn't get it. But Pete's face is whiter than ever, and Russ knows, too. I decide to put Alice out of her misery.

"This is the morgue."

8

"The what?"

Alice ruins the effect of my announcement. I look at her face; she genuinely doesn't know.

"The morgue," I say. "Don't tell me this is a new word for you. It's where they keep dead people. You must know that."

"What, like I'm some expert on deadness suddenly?" she says. "Of course I've heard the word before, but I thought the morgue was that place in Europe where all the bad people go to court."

Russ bites his lip. "That's the Hague."

"Oh." Alice flushes red. "Same diff. It's not like I'm some saddo who cares. Such crapocity." She shoots a look at me. "Hang on a minute." She points at me. "So she's led us into some room where all the dead people are stored?" She balls her fists, and I can see the blood boiling behind that peaches-and-cream complexion. "Are you out of your little shaved head?"

I ignore her and push past Pete into the next room. The smell gets worse, and the smell behind the smell. The thing that it's supposed to be hiding. The fish-sick smell, so familiar to me now.

Bright light contrasts with the gloom of the little room I've just come out of. This is a far bigger space. There are a dozen or more empty gurneys scattered across the floor, some turned over on their sides. A scattering of black vinyl body bags, with a few sheets draped upon and around them. A bank of huge lockers lines one side of the room. Square doors set into a wall, stacked three high. I quickly count ten across. Thirty body lockers? That's quite a lot; they really planned for the worst case scenario when they designed this place. And just as well they did.

To the right of the body lockers, there's an open door. I wind my way through the gurneys and peep through into a large, empty room with ceramic-tile floor, walls, and ceiling — and nothing else. There are smears of blood here and there. I stand at the doorway, not wanting to go in any farther.

"This is where they kept them."

It's what I had been counting on. Because yes, if we are underground in a military hospital, this place probably *is* quite secure. No one is getting down here without some serious effort, and some even more serious firepower. And zoms — even the new, souped-up ones — haven't really shown themselves to have guns, in my experience. So once I knew the hospital had been overrun, and given that, *DUH, it's a hospital*, it seemed oh-so-much more likely that the threat had come from within.

They were here, but now they're gone.

"Clever." Russ appears behind me, making me jump. "You figured that if the dead peeps were running the halls, they wouldn't be in here anymore. Nice call."

"Pretty much." I can't help but feel a flush of pride. Stupid, but it kind of matters to me that Russ likes me. Heaven knows, with Smitty gone, I need all the fans I can get.

I turn back into the main room and eye the big locker things on the wall. I hope they're empty, too.

"So what now?" says Alice. "This is not the exit." Obviously she can't be seen to be appreciating me on any level. And that's fine. I'm totally comfortable with that.

"We wait. Don't touch anything." I turn to my little group. "I mean, nothing that looks bodily-fluidy. I think we're safe enough for a while, as long as we're sensible. We can charge the phone and make a plan."

Pete's not happy. He's shaking his head and the goggles are threatening to come off. "But we're giving them time to secure the exit. They know we're here, they'll search high and low, but ultimately all they have to do is seal us in here."

"What's the alternative?" I feel a panic coming, because I kind of know he's right. They could lock us in down here for good and let the zoms do the rest. Or starve us. Or implement the fail-safe thingummy — drowning, gassing, whatever.

"We plan quickly," Russ says. He looks around him. "Look at the stuff here — there're things we can use as weapons, protective clothing." He opens a cupboard, then a drawer or two. "Everyone gather whatever you think could be useful, then we'll scoot."

"The phone charger." I look at him. He reaches into his pocket and tosses it at me. I quickly locate a socket and jam the plug in. Then I fish the phone out of my boot. *Please, please, make this the right one.*

Every so often, something goes right. And this is one of those times. It's a match; phone and charger are totally making whoopee. The pin fits snugly into the little hole on the bottom of my phone, and a tiny pyramid of bars begin to build in the corner of the screen.

"Yes!" I stamp my foot, then instantly feel a tad ridiculous. "We are getting juiced."

"Great," Russ grunts. "Five minutes, tops — then we're gone."

"One second, Russ," Pete intones. It's a unique mixture of irritating and hysterically funny when he tries to do bossy. He turns to me. "Let me take another look at those numbers on the phone."

"Can it still charge while you do that?" I ask.

"Of course." He looks at me as if I'm clueless.

"Then go crazy."

Pete dives into decoding. Russ is searching a cabinet. Alice is pulling open drawers.

All busy being useful, except me. I know the other reason I wanted to hit this room, and now that we're in here, I've got to find what I'm looking for, even if it gets me killed. There's a PC terminal on a desk, but I ignore it — no doubt there will be passwords and protected stuff — and I head for the good, old-fashioned filing cabinets. Having grown up with two medical people as parents, I know that docs can be alarmingly technophobic, and I'm hoping that the info I'm searching for will be found on paper.

I pull open a drawer, and look inside. Alphabetized files hang within. I pull one out at random.

"Hey," Pete calls out. "This second number doesn't work at all. It's a load of nonsense with a dot and zeros — you can't have a zero, a zero's just a space."

"Nice one, Mother dearest," Alice sneers.

"Just give me time . . ." Pete thumbs away at the phone again, and I return to the file in my hands.

Hard copies of medical records. I scan the one I happened to pull out — a female, ten years old, name: Alderson, Isabel.

I pull out a couple of sheets. There are photographs, and they are gross. A brain. A swollen purple chunk of meat that is probably a liver or something. It's all kind of OK, until I see one more pic — a photo of her face.

It's Red, the young girl who wrestled with me back in my room. Isabel Alderson. The curly-whirly corkscrew hair is unmistakable.

Gulp. Now I know why she had that hideous half a head. Someone had opened up her skull with a saw and photographed the brain like a toy from an Easter egg.

"Cracked it!"

Pete's voice shocks me and I jump out of my skin. I look over to him, and he's jigging up and down like he's got a ferret in his knickers.

"The third message, 'Poffit'?"

"Yeah?" I answer.

"'Underbridge.'" He beams happily. "That's what it says."

"So is that where Smitty is, then?" Russ asks me. "Under a bridge? Or a place called Underbridge?"

"Way to be specific, *Mom*," drawls Alice.

I can't help feeling excited. This is making sense. I mean, it makes no sense — but at least we're getting answers. Even if we don't know what they mean. "Keep at it, Pete!"

"Not half." He taps pen to paper, double speed.

I start to skim through the notes, but it's pretty much all gobbledygook to me. Except one thing jumps out.

Hot damn. There it is in writing.

"Osiris."

I hardly realize I've said it out loud.

"What?" Russ says.

"This is a medical record from one of the kids who attacked me in my room." I face the others. "It says it here in black and white, she was 'Infected, tested positive for Osiris.'"

"Yeah, so?" Alice says. "Newsflash: She was a zom."

"But don't you see what this means?" I look to Pete. "Osiris." I stab a finger at the documents.

"The hospital has to be Xanthro," Pete says, putting the phone down.

"My god." Russ walks up to me and looks over my shoulder at the file.

"How come?" Alice says.

"Because the only people who know that the virus has a name are Xanthro," I say. "My mum and her team named the possible cure Osiris 17, and the stimulant Osiris Red."

"Possibly," Russ says. "But for all we know, that's what everyone's been calling it in the last few weeks. We can't be sure."

"Look at the clues, they're right there," I say. "The men in black who came to the crash site, they had little yellow Xs on their lapels, I remember now. That's the Xanthro logo."

"You sure you saw that?" Russ said.

"I think . . ." I say. "I was pretty out of it, but would I dream that kind of thing?"

"Yeah," he says simply. "You might."

"What about that guy in the stairwell?" I say. "Long hair and military doesn't add up, we know — but if he's Xanthro, then he's free to rock the ponytail." I hike a thumb in the direction of the door. "Biggest clue of all. They're shooting at us. That's a clue right there, with your name on it. I refuse to believe that the army would fire on uninfected kids."

Pete nods. "I certainly hope not."

"Maybe this is an army hospital, but there must be a Xanthro presence here." I point to my phone, which Pete has put on the counter. "Mum monkeyed with my phone. She must have taken it away from me at the crash site, then smuggled it in here somehow. Or maybe given it to someone else to plant. Either way, she must have connections with this hospital."

"Either way, can we get going?" Alice says, not unreasonably.

"Two minutes. I need to check something."

"Make it quick," Pete says.

I nod, and get back on task. I place Red's file back in its place and look farther, in several drawers, until I find the place where they keep the *S* surnames. I'm looking for something specific.

Smitty, Robert.

I run my finger along the tops of the files. There are lots of *S*s. Lots of Smiths . . . then a Snaith . . . I check back again to be sure. No Rob Smitty.

"Time to wrap this up," Russ says. "We've been here long enough."

"Nearly there." My hand reaches out, and I look for Lindsay, Dr. Anna. Mum always used her maiden name for work.

There's nothing there.

I check the *B*s . . . *B* as in Brook, as in my surname — my dad's name — in case they have her listed there. But there's nothing.

In spite of all the evidence that she's alive, I had to check. I feel a rush of relief and a little side order of happy, but mainly, I'm pissed. Furious. The nasty bastards lied to me.

I slam the drawer shut. "We go. Now."

"Oh my god." Alice is holding something up at arm's length. It looks like a bundle of cloth, wrapped in plastic, red and blue visible within. It looks . . . strangely familiar. She takes a breath, and delicately opens the package with her fingertips, shaking the contents to the floor. We all stare at it.

Alice's pep squad skirt has come back to haunt us.

"How did *that* get here?" Her eyes bulge, tears starting to form.

"I guess you were wearing it when they picked us up, after the crash." I move to get a closer look. "Where did you find it?" It's hers, for sure. I mean, how many cheerleading skirts do you find in a morgue in an underground Scottish hospital?

"It was in that drawer." Alice glares at me, like I hid it there. "Do you think they were testing it? For traces of *zombie*?"

I shrug, deliberately casual. "Maybe one of the lab techs just likes to dress up."

"Yeah, well," Alice snorts. "Solves your little problem, doesn't it?" She kicks the skirt off the floor. It flies into the air and lands on my chest.

High holy sheep shit. She expects me to wear it.

It slides down my front, back onto the tiled floor.

I look at Russ. He nods encouragingly — perhaps too encouragingly. Pete has already lost interest and is back at work with my phone. Damn, it *is* clothing. I can't really refuse it.

I pick the skirt up, shake it out a little, and step into it, fuming. Alice is elated. She's frickin' loving this. I turn on my heel and walk away from her. *Oh, gah.* The skirt flounces as I move. I don't think I have ever felt so low.

"Drat it!" Pete cuts through my misery. He's staring at the phone, shaking his head. "The other two numbers, I can't work them out."

"You got 'em on paper?" I say, glad to move on. He nods. "Great, then we go."

I look around for a weapon, and find my companions have grabbed all the best stuff. It's very scary. Alice has chosen to be driller killer with some kind of cordless implement tucked under her arm.

Russ has scored a heavy-duty battery-powered Stryker saw — you know, one of those things they use to cut through people's skulls on the crime autopsy shows? *Yeah, nice.* And Pete has the biggest butcher's knife I've ever seen.

I would have loved me a power tool, especially as there should never be a situation where Alice has a better weapon than me. This time, I'm just going to have to manage with the dregs. I open a drawer under the counter and settle on a large chisel. Might not be sexy, but it'll be handy in a tight spot, and it's definitely an improvement on the arsingly crap towel rail that was. Plus I probably won't cut my own arm off, which is a definite risk for Alice.

I bang the drawer shut.

"Everyone good to go?" Russ says.

"You bet." I stand up and make for the door.

"Pete? Alice?" Russ calls.

A garbled noise fills the air, as if in reply.

Alice screams, "They're here!"

"No," I say. "That was inside this room."

"An intercom?" Pete looks up hopefully. But I don't think he's right.

We hear the noise again — a longer, muffled babble this time.

There's no escaping where it's coming from.

"It's in one of the dead lockers." Pete points to the far wall. As one, we all take a step backward.

"Is it . . . talking to us?" Alice whispers.

"Don't freak . . ." I start to say. I know how this goes. One runs, and all run. We can't afford to let that happen.

"They're locked," Russ says. "We're OK." He puts a hand on Alice's arm. "Anything in there can't get out."

The noise comes again, and we all jump.

"Which locker?" Russ makes to move.

"No!" Alice squeaks. The noise squeaks back.

I walk carefully toward the lockers. "There," I whisper, pointing to the central locker a third of the way along the wall. "That one, I think. Or maybe the one below."

"Don't get too close!" Alice begs.

But something's not right. They don't usually make that kind of noise. Groaning, moaning, even a roar — totally standard. There's a retching thing that seems to be quite popular. And then there's this odd watery rattle that I've heard a couple of the more festering ones do. But not this. This is definitely new in the zombie vocal repertoire.

The babble comes again.

"It's a walkie."

"You what?" Alice sneers at me.

I look at them all. "Come closer, you'll hear. It's a walkie-talkie." The warbling sounds off again, briefly. "There." I tap the locker lightly with a finger. "In that one. Can't you hear them?"

Russ steps up. The others need more convincing.

"More than one voice," I say to them. "I think it's tapped into the soldiers' conversations!"

Russ puts his face next to the locker I'm pointing to. The voices happen again, and he almost flinches but stays put. The boy has guts, I'll give him that.

"She's right," he announces to the others, a broad smile on his face. "We might have just lucked out." He sticks out a hand to grab the handle on the door.

"Wait!" Alice squeals. "What if it's a zombie with a radio?"

"Could be." Russ looks at me.

"Heck. Do it anyway," I reply.

He nods. We stand ready with our medical implements. Russ takes a breath, pulls the handle.

There's a *clunk*.

The door swings open in his hand.

A shelf. Empty.

The walkie-talkie goes off again.

"Confirm new position, Alpha Team. Over."

The words echo in the locker, and we shrink back at the loudness. But there's no body, no zom inside. Russ moves around and pulls the shelf right out. It slides easily, as if on ball bearings. The walkie-talkie is about halfway along, with a single smear of red by it, as if it was placed there by a bloodied hand.

"Hey!" Pete pulls something floppy from a small cardboard box and throws it at me. I catch. "Rubber gloves!"

"Nice." I put a pair on and give the box to Russ. I reach in for the walkie, and pick it up gingerly. Then the voice comes again, and I nearly drop it.

"Black Fox, we're currently on four, east wing, headed north. Over."

It *is* the soldiers.

"They're on four." Pete's face blanches. "That's us. We're on four."

We are all crowded around the walkie now.

"You said this was the last place they'd check." Alice looks stricken.

"Alpha Team, this is Delta Leader. We have hostiles on eight. Civilians and crazies. Backup requested ASAP. Over."

"Oh my god." Alice's eyebrows shoot up. "They're totally doing army speak. This is, like, so *war*."

"Better believe it." Pete savors the grimness.

"Affirmative, Delta. This is Alpha confirming imminent backup. Finishing our sweep. We'll come and save your sorry arses. Over."

"Trying to miss all the fun, Alpha? Over."

"Save some for me. We have the north corridor and the morgue to check for the juniors, then that's an all clear for four. We'll be up in a jiffy, over."

"The morgue!" Alice gasps.

"Juniors. No prizes for guessing that's us." I toss the walkie to Pete and rush toward the coatroom. I turn round desperately. Russ is there. "Is there anything we can use to barricade?"

"We should go. Now!" Alice has joined us, with Pete behind her.

"There's no time." I grab a metal chair and try to wedge it against the door. Pathetic. "They're right out there, in the corridor." I see a walking stick hanging on a hook, and try to use it to shore up the chair. Useless. "God, Pete. It's around about now that I really wish you carried a welding kit on you."

"I absolutely could weld that door." He has my attention. "If I *did* have my kit, I mean."

"Wait." Russ grabs the chair and starts pulling it away. "If they try to get in and can't, they'll know we're here."

"Oh, you're right," I say. "Let's just leave the door wide open like we found it, huh? That way they'll totally think we're not actually here."

"Snarky." He gives me a smile, which I don't deserve. "No, what I mean is, we should hide."

"Where?" Alice is all for that idea.

"Come on." Russ scatters the barricade, and before I can object, he runs back into the main room, and we follow him.

"Oh dear." Pete looks like he knows where this is going, but it takes me another beat to catch up.

"Where?" Alice is ever more frantic, and she hasn't realized. "Show me now!"

Russ strides up to the first dead locker, bends down, and pulls the door open. He smiles encouragingly at Alice.

"Ladies first."

9

"You. Are. Shitting. Me."

Alice's eyes practically ping out onto the tiled floor.

"There is no way on this freaking earth I am getting in there," she says.

"Alpha Team, have you finished your sweep?" The walkie in Pete's hand comes to life again. *"We have heavy resistance on eight, live and dead hostiles. Requesting backup a second time."*

"Negative, Delta," the second voice barks back. *"Just the morgue, then we'll be with you."*

"Sod it." Pete opens up the locker next door and leaps back as if he expects something to jump out at him. "Do you think it's clean enough?"

"Just don't go licking it and you'll be fine," Russ says.

Pete gingerly climbs in. "It's really cold in here!" His voice echoes. "And there's no lock on the inside. How do we get out?"

"I'll let you out," Russ says. Pete makes a slight whimpering sound. I don't blame him. "Now mind your feet, I'm shutting your door." Russ slams him in.

"I am not going in there," Alice says.

"Hurry!" I shout at her. "Pick one!"

"No way."

"Yes way!"

She pouts at me. "They're not going to shoot me, are they? I'm too pretty to die, and people do what I say."

"Alice!" I grab her shoulders. "If you don't, you *will* die. Get it? *Très, très* for certain. *Au revoir,* Alice with a bullet in her head, *comprendez-vous?*"

She nods, and a tear runs down her cheek.

"You'll be fine." I randomly pull her toward me and kiss her on the forehead. She gives me such a look of surprise that I take advantage of how weirded out we both are by the moment and push her down into a locker that Russ has opened.

"Promise me you'll let me out?" She looks up at me with big, pitiful, damp eyes.

"I swear it." I make it sound just ambiguous enough to put the fears on her. I can't help it. I've got to get my kicks somehow. "See you on the other side." I blow her another kiss and slam the door.

"Now you." Russ is beckoning me into another door.

"Wait!" I say. "What about you? How will you shut the door on your own locker?"

"I won't." He makes a face. "I'm going to have to hold it open a crack and hope they don't notice."

I nod hurriedly and climb into my locker, wriggling so that my bare legs go down the far end and my face is by the door. *Ow.* My skin stings where it touches the ice-cold slab: Alice's skirt offers little protection, other than to my modesty.

"Just hold on tight, because if you get locked in it's curtains for the rest of us."

He nods back, and just as he's about to shut me in, there's the noise of a door being flung open. They're here.

"Get in!" I reach up to grab him, and he dives into the locker with me, his head to my feet, our bodies squashed together, him half on top of me, so I can hardly breathe. As he draws his feet in, the door swings toward me, and I just catch it in time before it shuts, the lock just resting on the latch, edging to go in, weighted to close. I hold it back with my outstretched fingertips, closing it as far as I dare without letting it go all the way. *Please, please let them not notice one door is not exactly shut.*

I listen for the approaching steps. Nothing yet; maybe they've changed their minds?

It's dark in here, and my bare legs are threatening to stick fast to the freezing metal of the slab I'm lying on, but it's funny how the adrenaline will make you not care about stuff like that. Top to tail beside me, Russ shifts slightly, trying to squash me less. It's kind of awkward how we have to lie like this, his body warm against mine. It makes being in here a whole lot less scary, gotta admit it. I only hope I don't drop an air biscuit. That would probably be worse than the soldiers finding us.

Then I hear some clattering. The soldiers are there, presumably moving gurneys, looking under body bags and in cupboards. Suddenly it strikes me how totally stupid we were to think we could hide from them in here. They're soldiers, after all — not nervous kids. They're going to check the lockers, because they're ruthless and they're thorough and they have big guns to shoot. My fingers tremble as I keep them stretched to the max, stopping the door from shutting, closing it to the tiniest crack that I dare.

"This place gives me the creeps." A thin, nasally voice rings out. One of the soldiers; I guess he's only human after all. Although not with so much humanity that he minds the idea of shooting kids in cold blood.

"Soft arse. Clear the room." A second voice, deeper. The one from the walkie, I think.

More sounds of banging and crashing. I guess you don't need to care about the element of surprise if you have firepower.

"They're not going to be here, are they? This is where the crazies were."

"Just get on with it."

"Poor little bastards," the original voice sneers. "Just a question of who finds 'em first, us or the crazies. Not like they got anywhere to run."

"Got to clear this room or the boss will be down our necks . . ."

"He's no boss of mine, he doesn't know his arse from his elbow. The company's so screwed they're putting bloody grunts in charge of us these days. This room's full of crap anyway. Nothing much worth taking." There's a sound of the soldier rifling through something. "Where you hiding, pills 'n' thrills? Daddy wants some Oxy."

"It's a morgue, not a pharmacy, moron. Anyway, those tranqs we picked up on five not good enough for you?"

"Gotta save for me pension, don't I? This gig's going tits up, you'll see."

I slow my breathing. *The company?* It's got to be Xanthro. My fingers ache horribly, outstretched, the tips numb. And that's vomit I can taste in my mouth. Never mind passing gas, if this door is suddenly opened, I can't be responsible for losing all stomach and bowel control and going for complete evacuation. I hope Russ is ready for it.

"Hey! What are you doing here?"

A new voice. Rough, rasping. I strain to hear, wishing I could see.

"Clearing this floor, *sir*. Like we was ordered."

"You were ordered, and ordered to do it quickly. And remember, if you catch them, your orders are not to kill. Capture them alive."

Did I hear right? Hope leaps into my heart. The rasping voice continues.

"Screw that part up and I'll make sure you end up in the pen with the crazies at feeding time, you savvy? I'll watch the corridor. Get moving."

There is the sound of boots on tile.

"Wanker," the whining guy says. "If them kids look like they're changing I'll put a bullet in their heads, no question. He can complain to the powers that be all he wants." He makes a frustrated noise and peels off a string of swears. "Give a civvy a firearm and he thinks he's God."

That hope that was leaping into my heart? It kinda missed.

"Or better still," the other voice says, "we find 'em and sell 'em to the highest bidder. Whichever side wants them more. There's your pension, mate."

"Alpha Team, this is Delta. We are surrounded and nearly out of fire! Requesting immediate backup."

It's one of the soldiers' walkies. Shit. I really hope that Pete remembered to turn the volume down on his walkie. Otherwise they're gonna be hearing that in stereo, and it'll be curtains . . . But I think he did. And I may have to kiss him, too, if we survive this.

"Oh, Jesus. Wot are Delta like?" the first guy says. "Can't even execute a simple clearance? Not like them crazies are carrying warheads. Let's go."

Yes, go on, go. I hear the boots on the tile, then they stop.

"Oi! We never checked them."

"What?"

"The freezer things."

Oh god oh god oh god . . . I feel a hand squeeze my ankle, and I nearly shriek in fright. It's Russ. He can clearly hear the soldiers, too.

"Come off it? Bunch of kids going to crawl in there? You're off yer rocker, son!"

Boots back, regardless. There's a *clunk*, then a *slam*, somewhere up to my right. Then another *clunk*, another *slam*. And then another. The guy is working his way along the lockers, one by one. I'm consumed by the desire to cover my face with my hands, like a child who thinks she's hidden if she can't see. But I can't, of course, because my hands are what are keeping this door from shutting. Not that it will matter in a few second's time. *Clunk, slam. Clunk, slam.* Thirty lockers. And as luck would have it, the soldier started at the opposite end from us.

"Speed it up, dickhead!"

"Stop calling me that. And give us a hand."

No, don't. But then again, maybe it's better to get this inevitability over with sooner rather than later. Rip the Band-Aid off quickly. Will being shot hurt? They're professionals, they won't mess about. They'll go for the head, the quick kill. I'll probably never know what hit me.

Clunk, slam.

That's much closer. He's starting low, too. He'll find us in seconds. Any last thoughts? I feel a kind of dizzy haze move across me, and I realize I've been holding my breath.

I hope they do me first; it would be too much to watch the others go before me. The anticipation is far worse than the actual bullet. The knowing you are going to die. Then again, maybe I hope they find Alice before the rest of us. She is very pretty. Maybe she can talk them round. If she saves us now, I'll never, ever say a bad word to her again, I swear.

Clunk, slam.

Clunk, slam.

That was right next door. It's us next. I brace myself.

Clunk, slam. No, he's working his way top to bottom! *Gah!* Why am I celebrating? It's only a few more seconds, either way. My stomach cramps. I don't think I'm going to cry . . . this is way beyond crying.

Clunk, slam. The locker above. We're definitely next. As he grabs the handle, I retract my fingers and push myself back into the locker as far as I can, and Russ, instinctively knowing what I'm doing, draws his legs up as far as he can. Anything for a last few seconds of being out of reach, a last few seconds of life.

The door opens.

"Alpha! Black Fox! Code Indigo! Code Indigo!"

I can see black-trousered legs, black boots. A memory sparks: the bus crash. Maybe this is the last thing I'll ever see. But the soldier hasn't bent down to look in here yet. Hasn't seen us.

"Alpha! Man down! It's Johnson — bitten. Oh god, we've got a gusher . . ."

"Shit, Johnson's down?" The boots turn round.

"Let's go!"

The boots are running, running — away from our locker, out of here.

And I can't help myself: As they disappear I pull myself forward to watch the man who would have killed me run out of the room. I have to check, I have to know. If he were to stop and turn around, he'd see me — but he doesn't. I see his back disappearing out of the doorway. He's all in black, the only dot of color being a small yellow insignia at the back of the collar of his jacket.

Xanthro. This is all Xanthro. Like we needed confirmation.

"Have they . . . ?" Russ whispers.

I don't answer immediately. I hardly dare. This might just be all an elaborate act to get us to come out, mightn't it? But the doorway stays clear. Could they have forgotten something they might have to come back for? The thought chills me. No, just get out of the damn locker.

"I think so," I whisper back. But still I don't move, and Russ doesn't push it, either.

In the end, the cold decides for me. I realize my teeth are chattering. It might be from being half scared to death, but I think I'm gonna blame the refrigeration.

"Getting out." I can barely form the words, my teeth are going so much. I reach my arms out onto the floor and haul myself out on the tile awkwardly, like a baby learning to crawl. It's only when I'm on the floor and the tile actually feels warm against my bare legs that I realize how totally frigid the locker was. And it's my whole body that's shaking, not just my teeth.

Russ arrives on the floor beside me; he's not in much better shape.

"Quick . . ." he chatters. "Have . . . to get . . . others out."

No kidding. I get myself up onto my feet with some difficulty, and grasp the handle of Pete's locker. I pull it open, with enormous effort.

The locker is empty.

At first I think my eyes are deceiving me, but I blink and, no, the locker is still bare. I squat down and look down into it. Was there some escape door we missed at the other end of the locker? Maybe all this time Pete and Alice are in some secret room, toasty and sitting round drinking hot tea and having a laugh?

"This," Russ is saying, pointing to the locker next door. "This one." He pulls on the handle, and there's Pete staring up at me. In my cold confusion, I'd simply got muddled.

I stagger over to the next one and haul open Alice's door. As I do she starts to squeal, and I think she thinks we're the soldiers who have found her, but as I bend down to reassure her she sits up and hugs me, sobbing.

"H-h-horrible!" Her body heaves. "Don't . . . ever . . . make me do . . . that again!"

I persuade her to stand, but she clings to me still.

"We did it?" she says. "We fooled them?"

I just nod, not wanting to share how close it actually came. I assume neither of them could hear like we could, with their doors closed, and that's probably for the best.

"What's up with Pete?" Russ's expression is concerned. I turn around, with difficulty as Alice is still suctioned onto me and is showing no sign of letting go anytime soon.

Pete is still lying there. On the slab, and not moving. Eyes still staring, only now I realize they're not focused on anything.

"What?" Alice unclings for a minute to take in the situation. She sees Pete and screams, "No!" She flings herself down beside him, pulling him off the slab, so that his head falls *clonk* onto the tile, and she rubs his pale, pale face with her palms. When that doesn't work, she shakes his shoulders, and when that does nothing, she starts beating his chest with the base of each fist, as if drumming on a barrel.

"Stop!" Russ goes to hold her back. But Alice clearly knew what she was doing. Pete takes in a massive breath and sits bolt upright, as if someone has jabbed adrenaline straight into his heart. He then starts to wheeze heavily, out of his daze, his eyes flitting around in distress and confusion.

"Inhaler!" Alice yells, shoving her hands into his pockets, searching. Pete looks nearly as distressed at Alice giving him a full body search as he is at not being able to breathe. But Alice manages to fish out a small plastic tube and rams it into Pete's mouth, his eyes bulging. Alice rubs his back until he sucks on the inhaler and the chemicals begin to do their job. His shoulders gradually lower, and his breathing becomes regular. His eyes are still popping out on stalks, but I think that's more to do with Alice suddenly going paramedic.

"You're OK?" Russ bends down to him and claps him on the shoulder. Pete nods. "Then we should get going." Russ straightens up, grabs a bag from underneath a gurney, and quietly runs to the doorway. "They've gone up a few floors," he tells everyone but me. "The bad news is, they are definitely looking for us. The good news is, they have orders not to shoot to kill."

I look at him. He heard that part, then?

Pete frowns from the floor. "Why? What makes us so special? They're killing everyone else."

"I wouldn't celebrate too soon." I grab my chisel. "It sounded like not everyone got the memo. And out of those who did, some of them might shoot us anyway."

Russ nods. "We should move now, go down and try and find the exit again, while the coast is clear. Get the hell out of this rabbit warren." His eyes flick back to Pete. "Can you stand?"

Pete nods again, and scrambles to his feet, shaking off Alice. I turn to follow Russ, but someone grabs my arm from behind.

"Stop." It's Pete. His grip is surprisingly strong. "The phone!" he cries. "What happened?" He runs up to the counter, his pale hands moving over the surface frantically. He turns to me, desperate. "They took it?"

I shake my head. "I don't know . . . I couldn't really see anything. I heard them looking through stuff, searching for pills, I think." They must have it. Because if they didn't take it, who did?

"I wrote the numbers on some paper," Pete says suddenly. "Where is it?" He frantically pats himself down with a panicked look on his face.

"Pete . . ." I start.

"Give me a minute." He boils red and turns out his pockets.

"You've lost the numbers?" Russ's brow crinkles in irritation.

"Did I say that?" Pete snaps. But he's run out of pockets.

"Check the locker!" Russ flings the door of Pete's fridge open.

"Here," Pete shouts from the corner. He's holding the paper. "It was just on the floor. It's a little wet on one end; I think it got dropped in some . . . brain matter."

"Give it to me!" I snatch at it, a dollop of goo flying dangerously off the paper. I pocket it in my coat.

"Now" — Pete runs to the door, full-on leader again — "it's time to discharge ourselves from this bloody hospital."

10

Pop. Pop. Pop-pop.

As we head out into the stairwell again, we can hear muffled shots from upstairs somewhere. Sounds like popcorn. I hope they're bagging zoms, not live people. I wonder briefly how many live ones are running scared, like us. For a second I think about if we can help them. Then I remember they're probably Xanthro, which makes them the enemy. They're on their own.

We retrace our steps back to the corridor with the exit sign; my heart is thumping like it's going to burst, but it's only partly the running. It's the hope that hurts. The feeling that we're so close now, but the hardest part may be yet to come. *Please,* I yearn, *please let us make it. It would be so unfair if we didn't after all of this.*

"This way." Russ is first, and fastest.

We round a corner and turn left down a short section of corridor, and suddenly there's stuff underfoot. The momentum keeps us going for a few seconds, and it's like an obstacle course where you have to run through the tires, except we're picking up our feet and skidding and hopping over something much more grisly. As one, we come to a halt and look down at what we're stepping in.

Bodies. And bits of bodies. Adults, children. I see faces, some stretched in pain. Cloudy eyes, skin sucked of color. These people, they have been chopped up. Someone set to and liberated hands from arms, and heads from necks. There is blood everywhere, pooling on the floor, splashed on the walls, dripping from the ceiling. The sharp smell hits me in the back of my throat, and the bright assault of red is blinding to my eyes. It's unspeakable.

Alice starts to hyperventilate. Pete grabs her and tries to talk her down. I lift one foot, mesmerized by the thick, dark red molasses slopping off the sole of my boot. Bloody, bloody hell. It covers the floor, not one single inch of white floor remains. I have never seen so much blood; I didn't know we had that much in us.

"We. Need. To. Keep. Going," Russ gasps through clenched teeth, like you do when you're trying not to be sick. "Don't look," he says. But if we don't look at them, then where do we look? They are everywhere.

"It's OK," says Pete. "They were monsters."

"All of them?" I say, pointing at a glint in the red. A round opal ring is drowning in ooze.

"Martha!" Alice gasps, sinking to her knees.

There's nothing left of her except red, and the ring. I didn't like the fact that she lied to me about my mother being dead, but I wouldn't have wished this on her. I wouldn't wish it on anyone. I pick my way through to Alice, grab her shoulder, pull her with me. We have to go before we sink, before we drown in this sea of red, this nightmare that threatens to overwhelm us.

I can hear the others behind me, but I don't look back. Alice and I reach the end of the corridor, make another turn, and the bodies thin out. We start to run again, slick feet against white floor, no doubt leaving a trail of raspberry jam footprints behind us. We pelt flat out and skitter to a stop in a large room, which is completely empty apart from a circular desk at the far side.

"Where now?" wails Alice.

"There!"

Set into the wall to our right is a pair of huge, steel doors. I run to them, and before I can question the wisdom, smack the UP button on the wall.

"What do you think, Pete? This it?" I'm oh-so-conversational, like we're taking a casual stroll and I'm asking him the way to the park. The smell of blood will stay with me forever now, the iron tang, the bitter and sweet taste in my mouth.

Before he can answer me, the doors open with a *ping*. A bright silver elevator. Without pausing, we run inside — me dragging Alice, Pete and Russ bustling each other in — and I push the button marked SURFACE. Nothing happens.

"Why isn't this thing moving?" I hit the UP button over and over, like that will make a diff.

"Drat it!" Pete points to a circular hole beneath the button. "We need a key. The lift won't work unless we find one."

"What?" I scream, but already I'm running out into the room and heading for the desk. Where else would you keep an elevator key? If not here, then our only option could be to sort through the body parts in the corridor.

And the others know it, too. Pete is searching cubbyholes behind the desk; Russ looking on the floor, underneath potted plants and rugs. Only Alice remains by the elevator, sitting there, sobbing, holding the door open. And then she screams.

A single figure, dressed in black, is coming toward us.

Not Undead, very much alive.

But this is no soldier.

The figure steps into the room, and the light falls on wisps of golden hair that have sneaked out from beneath a black knit hat. The face is young, placid, beautiful — and it breaks into a full-on smile when she sees me.

"Bobby!" she calls. "Thank god I've found you."

My jaw drops.

"They're coming." She moves toward me hurriedly. "We need to get out, now."

I take a big step back, the desk between me and her.

Alice screams again.

Pete shakes his head. "No, no, no, no!"

"Who is this?" Russ straightens up.

I blink. I'm not imagining her.

"This is Grace."

Once I've said it out loud, it sinks in. I make my run for the elevator.

"Who's Grace?" Russ says, running after me.

"The enemy!" Pete gives a choked yell.

"It's OK," Grace calls out. "Bobby, you can't go anywhere, you need a key!"

I get ready to bash at the UP button again.

"Hurry, hurry!" Alice screams beside me.

"*Grace*," says Russ. "One of the students at the castle? The ones who helped Bobby's mum develop Osiris, and did the dirty on her with the bad guys. That's right, isn't it?" he asks Grace directly, slowly moving toward us, his saw held high in front of him. "I thought Pete told us you died."

"Missing," Pete corrects him. "Shaq was bitten, Michael went up in flames, but we never knew exactly what happened to Grace." He looks at her. "What are you doing here?"

"She sold out to Xanthro, we know that much already," I yell at Pete. "Get in here, Russ!"

"You need a key for the lift, Bobby." Grace takes a step toward us. "You know you do."

"Get away from us, you bitch!" Alice screams, brandishing her drill.

"It's OK, Alice," Grace says calmly. "I'm here to help." She reaches into her jacket pocket and dangles something at me. "And I have the key."

I leap toward her, but she snatches the key out of reach.

"Ah, ah, ah!" she says, shaking her head. "We're going together. I've risked everything coming back here to get you out, Bobby. Now you have to trust me."

"Coming *back* here?" Pete says. "This place is Xanthro, isn't it?"

She smiles at him. "You've always had brains, Peter."

"But you obviously haven't," he bursts out. "Last time we saw you, you wanted to put as much distance between you and Xanthro as possible. You said you knew too much about how they'd caused this outbreak. You said they'd kill you."

"They will." Grace's mouth twitches. "It wasn't my idea to come back. But somebody persuaded me it was in my best interest to be your escape squad."

"Who?" Pete snorts, but I have an awful feeling I already know.

Grace looks at me. "Your mother, Bobby."

"No way!" Pete cries.

"That makes no sense," Russ says. "Why would Bobby's mother trust you?"

"Because she had no option." Grace lifts her chin. "Because she'd tried other means and it hadn't worked, too much time had passed. I was her last hope. I knew the access codes to this place from when we spent time working here, I had a key, I knew my way around. I released the infected as a diversion to bust you out." She looks at me. "It worked."

"Diversion?" Alice screams at her. "You nearly killed us!"

"I'm sorry about that. This batch is different. Xanthro has been experimenting on them, tweaking things to get them to be more efficient killing machines. That way they're more valuable; not only can Xanthro sell the stimulant, now they can sell the ready-made weapon, in human form." Grace takes a step toward us. As one we form a line of weapons at the doorway of the elevator, blocking her way. She steps back again, her hands up in surrender.

"Look," she goes on, "Xanthro is in pieces. The beast is wounded and desperate, and what's happened has only made it more dangerous. They still don't have a cure. And there are factions within the company who will stop at nothing to get their hands on you, Bobby, because you're the ticket to securing your mother, who in all likelihood will produce the cure. I'm your ride out of here. You need to trust me. Besides, you're not getting out without me, look at it that way." She leans forward slightly, her cool eyes fixing me, her voice low. "Let me into that lift, and in a couple of hours you'll be out of the danger zone and with your mum again."

"You know where she is?" I ask her.

She nods. "I do."

"And we're picking Smitty up on the way?"

"Got it in one," she says.

"You don't know where he is." I lean back into the elevator. "My mother wouldn't trust you with that."

"She did." Grace's eyes sparkle. "Didn't you work out the little clues on your phone? He's not too far from here, and he's waiting for you to help him, Bobby. Are you going to leave him for these guys to stumble over? Or shall we go and rescue him now?"

It's my turn to hesitate. Every bone in my body is screaming at me not to trust her, but I believe she's telling the truth. Right now I don't have the luxury of mulling this over. Right now I have to act, and live with the consequences later.

"OK, then." I beckon her in to join us.

She sighs with relief, rolls her eyes in a self-mocking way. "Thought you'd never ask."

There's a *pop*, and a kind of *thud*, and Grace stares at us. I wonder why she isn't moving. A trail of bright red runs out of her hat onto her forehead and trickles down into her eye, then onto her cheek, then runs off her chin and down onto her coat. Then she crumples and falls forward into the elevator with us.

"No! No! No!" Alice cries.

I don't think. I snatch the key from Grace's warm hand, tossing it up to Pete, who catches it deftly. I haul Grace's legs into the elevator as Pete thrusts the key into its hole and thumps the up button. Just as the doors close, I catch a glimpse of the soldiers rounding the corner. A masked man holds a rifle.

"Stop!" His voice is gruff and raw. "Stop now!"

It's the same rough voice as the one in the morgue, the third guy who the other two hated.

As if we're going to comply with his wishes.

We lurch as the elevator kicks into action and zooms upward, our ears a-popping, stomachs falling to our feet.

"Grace was shot," Alice mutters. "They shot her. Is she definitely dead?"

"Definitely." Russ has lifted her hat. I don't want to look, but I can't tear my eyes away from the neat hole in her temple.

"Oh god, hurry, hurry, hurry!" Alice slaps the elevator walls.

A pool of blood forms behind Grace's head, growing. I press myself against the wall of the elevator. I don't want it to touch my feet. Russ looks up at me. "We should search her. She may have been carrying something useful." He unzips her jacket.

"I'll do it."

I don't know why, but it feels like less of a violation if it's me. Russ stands aside, and I carefully bend over her. In Grace's inside jacket pocket, my hands close around a single key attached to a fat fob.

"Here." I hold them up for the others to see. "We get outta here, we have transport."

"Think she just parked at the front door?" Pete grimaces.

I check her other pockets, head down, swallowing back tears. She was shot. In front of us. I don't care that she was the enemy; a few seconds ago she was alive, breathing the same air as us, with the same fear and hope in her heart.

"Are there any clues to where she was going to take us?" Russ says.

I shake my head. "Can't find anything." I wipe my hands down my jacket, as if cleaning them of Grace's deadness. "I'm hoping if we find the car, it comes with a dirty great map and instructions."

Alice is sobbing. "Are you ... going to take ... her leggings?" She points down to Grace's legs, her face desperate.

"No." I shake my head. "I can't do that." I'd rather look like a cheerleader than swipe Dead Grace's clothing.

The elevator slows to a stop.

"Be careful, everyone," Russ says. "We don't know what's out there."

We brace ourselves. The doors *ping* and open onto semidarkness and the smell of damp cow. We're in some kind of outhouse.

"What do we do with her?" Pete points at Grace.

I jump over the body, then carefully pull her half out, so that everything waist up is still in the elevator. If the doors can't close, the elevator can't move, and that should slow them down some.

"She wanted to help us escape. She got her wish."

11

There's a crack of light, and we all hurry to it as quickly as the dimness will let us. This is a barn, complete with bales and a tractor and the farmyard smells. There's a constant drumming noise that I can't place, but I can't see any movement. We run to the wooden doors, fling them open, and we're outside.

Fresh air.

The rain hits us like a roar. It is pelting down, and I'm instantly soaked and gulping for air. I do a 360. There's a farmhouse almost directly in front of us and a couple of outhouses behind. There's a chain-link fence surrounding all of the buildings, with a gate to our right, through which I can see a road winding down a hill. A thick white mist hangs heavy over trees that I can just make out in the distance. But beyond that, nothing. I don't know what I was expecting, but I think it was something more than this.

"Where to?" Russ yells over the sound of the downpour.

"The gate — the road," I shout back. We run, grit skidding beneath my boots, water splashing up my bare legs. This is it, I realize. I could be on the run through Scotland with cold-beaten, ruddied pins poking out of Alice's ridiculous skirt like two boiled hams. The rain hammers hair down slick to faces (at least I don't have that to contend with), clothes to skin.

"Stop!" Russ — who is in front, of course — skids to a halt and holds his arms out wide, steaming like a thoroughbred after the gallops. We hurtle into the back of him, puffing and blowing from the chase.

Beyond the second building there is gate over the road. It is shut. And a good thing, too, because beyond is a huge chicken run . . . for monsters.

The hordes.

I've never seen so many. Even back at the road from the Cheery Chomper. Even on the ice at the loch — all those dribbling fiends coming at us from the castle — that was just an intimate gathering compared to this. They stumble around the vast coop, lumbering and moaning, some with arms out, head on one side, dragging a leg. They are drenched, festering — the smell is unlike any I've experienced before, like someone turned the odor volume up to eleven. And so many! Where did they get them all? I almost find myself waiting for the music to start. This is a *Thriller* flash mob.

"They can't get out, can they?" Alice says.

I don't know, but I'm looking. Looking for that breach in the fence, that hole, that break in the chain-link. Because it will be there, it's bound to be there.

"No, but we have to go in." Russ points. "The only way out is down the road."

The road divides the coop into two halves, straight down the middle. I can see that it used to be enclosed by fences within the coop, but those fences have been breached on the left-hand side by an army tank, which has torn through and now rests wrong side up in the midst of the left half of the coop. The mob roams freely onto the road.

"What about if we climb the fence somewhere else and work our way back round to the road on the other side?"

Russ shakes his head. "There's a drop."

I run to my right and slam into the chain-link fence. The whole of the compound sits on a little hill with a steep bank dropping off below. A modern-day citadel. If we climb over the fence, we'll have nowhere to go but a fall the height of a four-story house to the muddy ground below.

"There's no other way." Russ is behind me. "We have to follow the road to the bottom."

I shake my head but run back to the gate anyway, where Alice and Pete are shivering, eyeing the monsters who are reaching their rotten arms through the fence at them.

"Let me guess." Pete pants. "We're scaling the fence and tightrope walking out of here."

He looks over to Russ and gets his answer. Russ has already climbed the fence on the side and is heading toward us. By the time he hits the chicken coop, he's too high for the hordes to reach him. He moves swiftly, body bent over the rail at the top, feet finding holds in the chain-link, moving along like he did this all his life. He takes a look around, hangs for a moment, dangling tantalizingly just out of reach of the zom claws, and then springs down beside us again.

"Easy," he says. "We do what I did, then we descend the hill by the road fence. They won't reach us."

He grabs Alice's hand and hauls her over to the fence by the drop. Pete and I look at each other and follow. By the time we get there, he is already straddling the top rail and reaching down to encourage Her Royal Blondness.

"Pete next," Russ shouts. "Bobby, you bring up the rear. That gives me time to double back and help you."

The boy sure knows how to stoke my fire. I ain't gonna need no help from GI Joe.

Just as I'm about to start my climb, I spot something out of the corner of my eye. A chainsaw, propped up against the fence a ways down from us. *Wow.* This is better than a towel rail or a dumb chisel. Worth making a detour for. I run to it and claim it as my own. Heavy as hell, but there's a handy strap that I fling over my shoulder. I run back and begin scaling the fence, my new weapon weighing me down. It does occur to me that I have no clue how to use a chainsaw. But there's no time to figure it out now, and I've always had a knack for picking stuff up on the fly. How hard can it be?

Alice has made it to the top of the fence with Russ as carrot and Pete as stick. The climb is not as bad as it looks. The gap in the chain-link is conveniently teen-feet-sized, and the fence is taut and stable. You just have to ignore the huge drop on the other side and the fact that the metal digs into your hands and is slippery and ice-cold from rain. We shimmy along sideways, until we hit the corner and the start of the chicken run.

"OK, no lazy dangling feet, people," Russ says unnecessarily.

The zoms swarm at us, hissing, reaching, the sheer swell of them pushing at the fence and making us wobble. I can't look down at them or I will lose it and puke, but I do anyway. I retch; they are rancid, putrefying. I can't tear my eyes away as I marvel at the way their clothes have bonded with rotting skin, long shreds of flesh hanging off limbs like slivers falling off a well-cooked piece of meat.

"Keep moving," Pete croaks back at me.

The hands reach up for us, snatching at air. As long as we don't slip, we're OK.

"There's a second gate!" Russ cries, pointing. "Once we get there, we're home and dry."

He's looking at a gate by a sentry box down the road a little. The gate looks good, and the fenced-in road behind it is clear of Undead. It's just the same distance that we've already covered again. We can totally do this.

"Go!" Russ points again. "Get to that gate, now!"

We pick up the pace. But then something weird happens. One by one, the zoms that have been underneath us peel off and start stumbling down the road away from us. This is a good thing. Until I realize where they're going.

"Incredible." Pete has stopped, hugging the top rail and looking at the trail of zoms. "They heard what Russ said. They're heading us off at the pass."

The monsters are at the gate, pressing on it with all their might, rhythmically pushing it, *one, two, three,* working as a team to get it down.

"Remember what Grace said," I splutter. "Xanthro's been slicing and dicing in the gene pool, rewiring zombie brain, shooting them full of something."

"Whatever," Russ shouts from down the fence. "Keep moving!"

It's a race to get there before they break through. Russ is like a winged monkey on steroids; he reaches the gate easily and quickly, reaching down at the monsters and whipping out his mini-saw to cut off the stretched-out hands. It's totally gross, but it doesn't stop them pushing the gate.

Alice, Pete, and I get there together.

"Once we're down, we leg it," Russ yells to us. "There's no climbing up again!"

The road is clear, but to each side of the coop there are hundreds of monsters lining the fence. We won't have a spot to get out of reach if the gate is down.

"What if they can run fast now?" Alice cries, clinging to the fence, refusing to move.

"No evidence of that," Pete says.

"We need to go!" Russ calls as the gate buckles dangerously.

"No!" Alice shouts back. "What if there are more down there?"

She could have a point — we can't see the full length of the road — but there's no turning back. Pete groans, then climbs around her and gingerly plops down on the safe side of the road. It's not clear if he nudged her or if she simply lost her grip, but she slips and starts to tumble into the coop. Somehow she saves herself with one hand and an awkward foot that has stuck in one of the chain links, but she hangs there perilously, back to the fence, a mere inch or two from the nearest of the grabbing hands.

"Help!" she screams. "Oh god, help me!" She kicks down with her unfettered foot and wildly snatches at air with her free hand.

I'm nearest, and I throw myself forward on the top rail, reaching out to grab the hand that is waving in the wind.

"Here's the rail," I tell her, showing her hand where it is, above and behind her. She clings to it, but she's in such an awkward position, practically crucified on the fence, unable to turn round or pull herself up. I haul at her arms, but she resists, not able to let go and trust me to hold her weight, which is probably wise, because I probably couldn't.

"Russ!" I yell. He seems to be moving in slo-mo — and Pete is on the ground and useless — so I make one final effort to pull Alice up, with a mighty grunt.

But I don't have the strength I've learned to rely on, all resources used up. Plus, my new friend Mr. Chainsaw is pulling me down, the strap near-strangling me from behind. My hands slip from Alice's arms, and the momentum makes me fly backward and off the fence, down into the swarm of Undead.

My fall is broken by a body or two, and then I splat on my back in the mud below.

As soon as I'm down there, a switch flicks off in my head. I know I'm going to die. This is it. No way out for me now. It's easier to give in to it, to accept that within seconds my limbs will be torn off, my eyes gouged out, my bowels eviscerated and feasted upon. *Just make it quick.*

"Fight them, you tosser!" Smitty rasps in my ear. *"Get on your feet!"*

But as usual, he doesn't know what he's talking about. My hand scrabbles for the chainsaw, but I'm lying on it. I twist to one side, grab the handle, and look down at the controls. *Shit!* How do I turn this thing on?

And then it's useless, they're on me in a second, and all I can do is burrow, choking, into the thick mud. Hands on my jacket, pushing from all angles, it's only a matter of time before they exhibit some of that new-found teamwork and dig me out together. Or I'll drown down here, which is definitely preferable.

But it doesn't happen. And through the mud and the groans, I'm aware of shouting.

"Get up! Get up!" At first I think it's Smitty again, but then a strong hand slips under my shoulder and hauls me upward, and through the slop running down my face I see Russ there beside me, my chainsaw in his hand, no doubt in his mind how it works. He's spinning and kicking, lunging and ripping through flesh in a way I've only seen in the movies. He's cleared the zoms away from the fence, and I go for it, scrabbling up to the rail and over in one move, and landing in the mud again at Pete's feet.

"Good god," Pete says. "He's a machine." He watches in awe as Russ swivels — a well-placed kick to the jaw here, a decapitation there, until the chainsaw sputters and runs out of juice. Russ tosses it aside and swiftly follows the trail I blazed to safety at the top of the rail.

"Help me!" A scream rings out.

"Shit," I splutter. "Alice."

12

Alice still hangs, crucified, but both feet have wedged through the fence behind her, her knees bent down, and she's worked one arm through to the elbow and is clinging for dear life, unable to see the drama and beauty of Russ rescuing me.

Russ notices her, shakes himself, and manages to scoop her up and toss her over the gate to where Pete kind of half catches their fall, and the three of them land on the road beside me, like we're all catching some rays at the shore.

But not for long.

We run.

The road is steep and slick with rain, and we don't know what's ahead, but we run as fast as our bruised and bent limbs will let us, until we reach the bottom, a final gate to the outside, beyond the horror of the monster coop. We're over it and alone, only a stretch of road and then a line of thick trees in front of us. We skid to a halt and catch our breath, looking around.

"Where did you park, Grace? Where?" I mutter.

"The keys!" Pete does a gimme. I don't, but I get them out of my pocket at least. "Press the unlock," he says.

I look down at the fob. He's onto something. I hold the fob up and press the button. We all spin on our feet, looking and listening in every direction. I press the unlock again.

"Heard something." Russ takes off down the road. We follow, our feet splashing through the water that flows down the slight hill, turning grass to mud and road to river.

"Again!" he shouts as we hit the tree line. I press. This time I think I hear it, too, but Russ is sure of it, running over rough ground into the woods.

"There!" Alice jumps. "That way!"

There's a *beep* and a flash off to the left. I press again, and we have it. We run, dodging trees and leaping over bracken, until we're at the Jeep. We pull off branches and shove the tarpaulin that partly covers the vehicle into the back.

Russ flings the driver's door open.

"Keys," Pete says to me. I throw them. Russ pauses only for a second before he gives way to Pete; no doubt Pete regaled him with tales of his expert bus handling.

So Pete's in the driver's seat, and Russ riding shotgun (oh, yeah, how I wish we had one of them), while Alice and I hug the backseat like stupid girls on some kind of weirdo group date.

Pete fires up the ignition and flicks on the windshield wipers. They move at top speed, crazy noisy. He shifts the Jeep into gear and edges forward through the eddying water that covers the ground. I look for a seat belt regardless and try to fasten it across me surreptitiously, because in spite of my quite reasonable concerns, no one really wants to be that person who buckles up first. Alice checks me, and it only takes a couple of seconds for her to follow suit, without comment. Safety first.

"Gas?" I shout against the hammering of the rain on the roof.

"Plenty." Pete nods vigorously. "Enough to get us very much out of here, wherever exactly that may be."

"Just don't go freaky-deak fast, OK?" Alice clings to her belt. "Well, not unless you see any monsters or sniper people, that is. Then you can floor it."

"Yes, ma'am." Pete does a dorky little imaginary cap doff.

"So," I say to Russ as casually as I can under the circumstances. "Those were some moves you showed back there."

"Hmm." He's busy searching the glove box.

"You didn't tell us you were a closet Karate Kid. Looked kind of handy with the chainsaw, too."

"Done some kickboxing in the past," he says curtly. "And felled a few trees."

"As you do," I say. "Well, thanks for saving me: I thought I was a goner."

"Yeah," says Alice, "me, too. And I nearly *was* a goner, because you all forgot I was bloody there!"

"Eureka!" Pete cries before Alice can spin out the drama. "Thank you very much, Grace, I love you." He hits a couple of buttons on the dashboard.

Alice flutters her eyelids like she's going to expire. "What is he on about?"

"Satellite Navigation!" Pete shrieks, and as I lean forward, I see a small, illuminated screen move out of the dashboard.

"We have a GPS?" I ask him. We whoop and scream, and even Alice makes snarky applause. "So where the hell are we?" I shout to Russ, who has taken over pressing the screen while Pete winds us slowly down the watery road into the fog. It hangs there in patches, specters loitering in the damp air.

"Not sure," Russ says. "Looks like there's a signal, but this road isn't even coming up on the map. Surprise, surprise." He shoots me a look. "It's not as if the army — or Xanthro or whoever — is going to be sign-posting the way to a secret underground hospital."

"Has Grace programmed anything in? Like where we should be headed?" I ask.

"Give me a few seconds." He turns round to it again and resumes pressing the screen. "No. There's nothing here, not even her last destination. She must have wiped it clean before she hid the car."

"Great." I keep one eye behind us, but no one seems to be following. "So we're on our own. Again."

The road is getting steeper now, and as we wind slowly down the hill, the moor, with its muted, sludgy greens and purples, is giving way to the sharp emerald of pine forest. Through the patchy fog the color is shocking in its brightness, and it's quite a cheery greenness, but then again, I don't like suddenly being hemmed in by trees on both sides. Trees hide so much.

"OK, so it looks like we *are* outside of Edinburgh." Russ keeps us informed with his GPS fiddling. "If we can get onto a road that's actually on the map, we're about fifteen miles away. But there's a lot of nothing between us and the road on the map."

"Regardless of if it's mapped, we're on a road, obviously," Pete says. "We can do nothing but follow it and hope we hit something recognizable soon. Soon as we do, then we can navigate."

"Unless Xanthro controls the satellites." Alice plays with her nails.

Pete, Russ, and I stay silent for a minute. Then Pete spoils it.

"It's entirely possible that Xanthro controls satellites. They could be watching us right now."

We say nothing. What can you say? Can't satellites read the time off a wristwatch? If they can do that, they can certainly see the grim look on my face as I squash it against the glass and look up into the gray sky beyond the trees. *Hello . . . is there anybody out there?*

The rain thuds on, seemingly even louder now, although that doesn't make sense — the trees should give us a little shelter, surely. And then I realize that the sound isn't the rain. I twist around in my seat again, looking to check we're not being followed. But the road behind is clear.

"What is that noise?" Russ says. "Sounds almost like a helicopter."

Pete swerves the car.

"You're kidding! Where?"

We're all at it now, searching the skies. Russ opens his window and the car instantly fills with wet. He kneels up on his seat like a stuntman preparing to climb outside the moving vehicle.

"I can't hear anything," yells Alice.

"Shh!" I tell her. But I can't hear anything, either. If it was a helicopter, it's gone now.

Russ comes back in and closes the window.

"Didn't see anything. It can't be after us, otherwise why wouldn't it look on the road? If it was a helicopter, maybe it was just doing a flyby?"

Pete screeches to a mud-splashing halt, flings open the door, and he's out. A second or two later, he's back, with a large, smooth, black rock in his right hand.

"Screw it!" He dashes the GPS with the rock, smashing the screen so that it cracks like ice across a gray pond. "Don't! Follow! Us!" He hits it again and again.

"What are you doing?" Alice says. "You've killed it."

"We can't take the chance they know where we're going," Pete cries, hurling the rock out of the door.

"We don't even know they were following us," Alice says.

"Keep driving," Russ mutters.

Pete doesn't need telling twice. He wrenches the Jeep into gear and it moves off with a roar. The road levels out a little, and we veer round to the right and see a clear stretch before us.

So this is it. This is our outside. Snow given way to torrential rain, ice to fog. Where could Smitty be hiding in all of this, for all of this time? Is he actually hiding? Or is he being held? For all we know, he's been ferreted away into St. Gertrude's 2.0, somewhere deep under the sodden ground.

And then I see it, a few seconds' drive away. A humpbacked stone bridge over a river that has burst its banks.

"There!" I shout. "Under bridge! It must be."

Nobody responds, except Pete, who slows the Jeep a little. That might just be because the water level is rising the closer we get to the river.

"Like in the message." I try again. "'Underbridge'? That's the bridge, isn't it?"

My mother didn't feel the need to be especially specific, but if Grace was telling the truth about Smitty being close by, then this must be it.

"Hey, it's not like I'm hiding out in Sydney Harbour or dangling from the Golden Gate, Roberta," Smitty whispers in my ear.

"We need to stop, we need to check it out." I unclick my seat belt.

"Uh, how?" Pete shrugs. "Got your Aqua-Lung with you?"

"What are you talking about?"

"Under the bridge. Look."

He pulls the Jeep to a stop on the left of the road, wipes some condensation off the windshield and taps the glass. "See the water level? It's almost up to the stone. We'll be going some to clear the bridge in the Jeep as it is. But you want to get under the bridge. You'll need a wet suit."

I squint. It's hard to see, but I have a sinking feeling he's right. The brown water flows deep and fast all around the bridge. I dig my fingernails into my palm and hope that Smitty's waiting in a speedboat just around the corner.

"Smitty!"

What a nutjob.

I am standing knee-deep in running water, looking under the bridge. A rope from the back of the Jeep is around my waist, the other end tied to a small tree. Russ found me some waders in the car, but it is freezing.

The others watch me from the Jeep.

Am I crazy to even attempt this? I could drown or die of cold. I cast a look up the road where we came from. We really can't dawdle. They could be out looking for us at this very minute, and if they are, they won't have to look very far. It's now or never.

It is very dark under the bridge, and the water roars, black, deep, and fast.

"Smitty!" I yell again.

So maybe he's not here after all.

But then there's a noise.

13

A definite noise. A half gurgle, some kind of yell? I lean farther and listen intently, but all I can hear is the noise of the rain and the rushing of water. Was that a voice?

"Are you there?" I take a step, unable to see what's under the water, easing my foot forward in the sludge.

Nothing answers me this time. I try to remember the sound I thought was a yell. Could it have been him, hidden somewhere under there? Or in trouble?

"Hey!"

Smitty? The voice behind me makes me twist round awkwardly, and my feet almost slip from under me. A hand catches me under the elbow.

"Gotcha!" Russ beams at me, blinking through the rain. "Sorry if I gave you a shock. I know you wanted us to stay in the car, but I thought you looked like you could do with some help." He really is drenched. I should feel warm and fuzzy and grateful, but I'm too damn preoccupied with thoughts of Smitty. "See anything under there?"

"No. I thought I heard something, but . . ." I grit my teeth. "There's some sort of ledge halfway up the wall. I think there's a path underneath — I can reach up to the ledge and see what's there."

Russ looks, then shakes his head. "There's nothing useful under there. We should go. This is too dangerous."

"I'm checking it out anyway."

"Bobby" — he shakes his head — "have you seen how deep the water is? You'll kill yourself." He holds my arm tightly.

"Back off!" I holler at him. He does just that, at least for a moment, shocked by my ferocity. But then he's placed his hands on my rope.

"At least let me." He looks at me intently. "I'm strong."

"Yeah, I know it." I pull it away from him. "Good for you, big guy." I stumble and stomp through the rising water down to where I think the path begins, only too aware of how ridiculous I must look and how completely stupid I'm being. This is suicide. And I have to admit — as much as I hate to — that if I wasn't pretty damn sure that Russ was behind me, I might have turned back by now.

I put a frozen, wet hand on the rough stone of the bridge and edge my way until I'm underneath it. The water threatens to overrun my waders, the current strong against my knees.

"Hello!" I call up to the ledge, over the noise of the water.

I squint and focus. I'm going to have to get closer. My hands feel numb like I've only just woken up. Pulling the rope along with me, I reach the bridge and edge one foot gingerly down, hugging the stone for support. The water squeezes cold around the waders, but my toe eventually finds solid ground — smooth, flat stone. I step down with the other foot, and I'm almost swept away, my fingers desperately clinging to the side of the bridge. I flatten myself against the crumbling stone. It feels welcome against my cheek. Suddenly there's a tightening around my waist. With difficulty, I turn my head and look back, and there's Russ, holding the slack.

"Go for it! I've got you!" he shouts against the roar.

I pull a face like I want to laugh. *As if it was that simple, sucker.* At least there's someone to witness my demise.

Giving myself a lovely limestone facial as I turn my head back again, I edge carefully along the wall, trying to use the force of the current to keep me squashed against the sides. The bottom of the path is smooth, which has pros and cons. One slip and I'm under. The water pushes up against my thighs, under my stupid skirt, splashing up my backside. It doesn't matter. It's so cold I'm numb from the waist down.

I can reach the ledge now; it's not far above me. My arms stretch up and the edge of the stone actually provides a good grip. One hand reaches and feels the surface of the ledge, looking for whatever might be hidden there. Then I inch farther along, and we go through the same process again. I get a rhythm going:

Grab, grab, step, feel.

Grab, grab, step, feel.

Slowly progressing along the path, looking for heaven knows what. *Couldn't you have been a little more specific, Ma? Where under the bridge? What's there?*

For the first time it strikes me that she could have been warning me against something. I mean, all she actually wrote was "Underbridge." She could have meant, "Stay away! Don't go near! There's danger 'under bridge.'" My mind races. Isn't there usually a troll under a bridge? You know, in nursery stories or whatever? And muggers on canal paths. I don't think there's ever anything good underneath a bridge. Maybe we should have avoided it. Too bloody late for that now.

Just as I'm savoring the thought, my hand strikes something.

I risk standing on tiptoes to reach, and my poor sore digits close around it. A padded strap. I pull. It's heavyish, and caught on something. I give it a tug, and then another, with gusto.

The thing falls over, off the ledge, and almost over my head and into the fast-flowing river behind me. At the last minute I snatch it back, wrenching my shoulder and neck in the process — but that doesn't matter, I save it, and quickly stick an arm through, reattaching myself to the wall like an clam, and preparing to edge back to (relatively) dry land.

"What is it?" Russ shouts down at me.

"Backpack."

The disappointment is like bile in my mouth. *Backpack-not-Smitty.* After all of this, Mum had better have packed something damn useful.

"What's inside?" he shouts again.

I raise my eyebrows and shoot him a look, the effect of which is no doubt totally lost in the gloom of the underbelly of the bridge. "Wanna give me a moment before I check?"

"Sorry."

I can see him grinning at me in the light. He's so head-messingly cheerful, it's not normal. I wonder for a split second if he's some kind of android. Or alien. Or maybe he's an adult stuck in a teenager's body. Nobody my age I know is that weirdly smiley.

"Want me to pull you?" he shouts.

"I'm good," I reply quickly. It occurs to me I'm not overanxious to share the contents of this bag in public. Hadn't thought that far ahead. It's not like I want to linger in the icy river, but I need a few secs more to figure out how I'm going to get to look at this stuff on my own.

Then Russ drops his end of the rope and disappears.

"Great," I mutter, groping along as fast as I can. I'm almost through the bridge and out when Russ comes into view again. But this time he's not alone. A zom is holding him in a deadly hug.

"Russ!" I scream.

At first I think the zom is a kid, because there's not much to it, but as Russ struggles to throw it off I realize that it's a full-grown adult, but only half a zom. Torso, arms, head. Below the waist is missing, with a raggedy edge, little tatters of wet flesh hanging loosely down, shaking like decorations in the wind as Russ tries to free himself from it. Goodness knows how this one caught him, goodness knows how it moves, but it's swollen and bloated and I'm guessing it has been splashing around in the water for a while.

Russ and his dance partner wrestle, and Russ wins. The Thing with No Legs splashes into the water beside me and bobs up like a cork. Quickly its arms rotate with a front crawl action the likes of which I've never seen before. It has strength and enthusiasm, and the cold doesn't worry it. As it powers toward me, aided by the current, it opens its mouth and gives a gurgling bellow. It's a man, with meaty shoulders and no hair and a face so swollen and so pale it's almost violet, every little spidering purple vein showing the strain of effort. I'm struck with the certain knowledge that with this one I am hopelessly out of my league. I really wish I had saved my game before I took the decision to venture under this bridge. Because he's spotted me, and at once Russ is forgotten; he's homing in on his new target, and I know I am done for.

Unable to free a punching arm or a kicking foot, I scream. Vulnerable and stuck like a mouse on glued paper. Nowhere to run, nowhere to hide, and nothing to do but wait for him to land. It's pathetic.

Russ sticks out a faraway arm, and with no other option, I jump for it. I miss, of course, but as I splash into the water my hand grasps something — a trailing root? — sticking out of the bank, and I pull myself along it, the freezing water deafening me. No-Legs swooshes past, his big sausage fingers batting the water in a tantrum, as if he's trying to pull himself after me. But it's too late for him; as good a swimmer as he is, he's no competition for the river. The current carries him off and he yells in protest, whirling round and looking back at me with sad and resentful eyes, because it's not fair, and I would have made such a tasty meal.

As I dare to feel relief, my root gives way, and I'm underwater again, spinning, arms flailing, trying to touch the bottom or grab on to something, scared as much of being saved by No-Legs as of drowning. My knee scrapes something — I've lost a wader — and I find the bottom and push myself up to the surface.

I'm standing. I'm back on the path. But on the other side of the river.

The backpack is still on my shoulder. That's OK, then; all I have to do is to not die of cold, climb to dry land, and the others will meet me on this side of the bridge.

The others? They've gone.

Russ is no longer standing beside the riverbank, and I can't see the Jeep. Through the sound of the rain comes a sudden, shocking, juddering noise. A shadow moves over the sodden ground, and there's a strange flattening of the flood water as if something is forcing it down from above.

A helicopter.

Slick black and hovering, like an evil beetle. It pauses for a second only, and then drops. It lands, and I nearly lose my balance as I'm battered by its downdraft.

Three men get out and run toward me at a crouch. Soldiers in black.

Shit! Shit!

They'll see me any minute. I have to move, but I suddenly realize that I still have the rope around my middle, and that rope is still tied to the tree trunk on the other bank. With stiff little fingers, I try to ease the knot free, but the water has made it stick fast.

The first two soldiers have reached the riverbank. They're looking for something — or someone.

Behind me the helicopter has stirred up the water, and I'm caught in a rolling wave. I smack into the river and sink, the shock of the cold flooding down my neck and over my face, my eardrums feeling like they're going to burst with the sound and the pressure. The backpack weighs me down from behind, and I roll upside down, struggling, trying to swim, pulling myself toward where I think up is. My lungs are beginning to burn, and the huge urge to take a breath is becoming the only thing that I can think about. I fumble and fumble, but the knot isn't easy. I kick out with my legs — more out of panic than anything — but as luck would have it, my feet find the bottom and I spring myself up to the surface, gasping and flailing and full of shock that I'm still alive.

Finally the knot gives, but all that exists is churning water — frantic, icy, fast water.

14

"You're going to burn."

He's right, I am. I'm boiling hot. I twist my head sleepily, feeling the sand under my face, and try to look up at him. But he's just out of sight. The sun hurts my eyes, and I blink.

"So put some lotion on me." It's such an effort to speak. I think I hear a seagull screeching somewhere. I'm going to need a drink soon.

"Bossy." But in spite of his protests, I hear the bottle give a little squelching noise as he flips the lid. "Lying here is not going to help, you know," Smitty says. "You might feel like you need a vacay, but you ain't earned it yet, sweetcakes."

"Yeah, yeah. Sunscreen me," I mumble into the sand.

"OK," he says, sitting on the backs of my legs and placing his oily hands on my back. "But you've got promises to keep. And miles to go before you sleep. And miles to go before you sleep."

"Shut up!" I laugh. "You don't talk like that."

He laughs, too, and rubs the cream on me. And as he does, my skin comes off. He keeps rubbing my back, and the muscle and fat and flesh and ligaments slough off, until there's nothing left apart from shoulder blades and spine.

"Now that" — he taps my backbone — "that is what we need to see."

*   *   *

I wake, screaming with imagined agony. I'm so cold I feel burning hot, shaking, curled in a ball like a shrimp. My arms and legs shoot out along the ground to make sure I still have solid ground below me.

I have.

And it has stopped raining. After the deafening noise of the relentless downpour, the helicopter, and the amped-up roar of the river under the bridge, the relative quiet shocks me. And then there's the sound I'm making myself, although at first I don't realize it's me. I'm shivering uncontrollably, literally making *va-va-va* noises through trembling lips. It's almost funny. I pull at my jacket around my neck; I'm so screwed up with the frigid water that my brain can't work out my temperature. Freezing — boiling — freezing. *Choose one and go with it!* But the fact that I'm still breathing and still in one piece fills me with a tremendous sense of invincibility, and I almost want to laugh out loud. If I had the strength and the breath to spare, I would.

I've lost one wader. And Alice's dumb skirt. Incredibly, that seems to be the sum of my injuries. I look up and find I'm on a kind of grassy knoll in the river.

How long have I been out? At least I'm still alive; for all I know the others have been captured, or shot, or chomped.

Damn . . . where did the helicopter go?

I rub my eyes and look around, my breathing slowly returning to almost normal.

Fog. Thick, white, choking fog. It feels clammy against my skin; I can almost taste it.

No motor blades whirring, no shouts or shots being fired. Just the white noise of the river, and the squelch as I tentatively get up, testing my limbs to see if they still work.

I weigh up my situation. As far as I can tell, I'm not stranded, as such — the water around my little island is just overflow from where the river has burst its banks. I can see maybe ten feet into my future, but no farther. Close by, there's another grassy knoll, and on it, a hulk of brown, like a big balloon with four thin sticks pointing into the sky. It's not until I spot the horns that I realize what it is. A fat, dead cow. Full of fermenting dead-cow gas and bursting at the seams.

"Hey, fella," I shiver at it. "This water thing sucks, huh?"

But that's all I can make out. I have no concept of where the road is, where the trees are, how far away I am from where I started. Lost, and colder than I thought possible. I wonder if I should take off my jacket and fleece. What does the guy on the survival show do? I'm pretty sure he strips naked. That's all well and good if you've got a flint stuck in your shoe and a handy supply of flammable moss or whatever you're supposed to use to start a fire with, but not so great if you're marooned on a grassy knoll, and you're me.

It's only when I start to take my jacket off that I remember I have a backpack slung around my shoulder, and I almost whoop for joy. I pull at the drawstring with icy fingers.

The first thing I see makes me want to cry. Two tightly bunched balls of synthetic materials. I quickly unravel the first one, but I already know what it is. Waterproofs. My dad always used to keep a set or two in the car for any impromptu tramping through the countryside. That distinctive smell that takes me back to Dad, wet vacations, miserable walks, and stiff-upper-lipness. It makes me weep, but it's not just sentimentality that's providing the waterworks. For the first time I will finally have something to cover my backside. Some long waterproof pants and an anorak.

And I'm certain now — if there was ever any doubt remaining — that Mum left these things for me, and that she has a plan. The fact that I'm following her bread crumbs successfully makes me happier than I'm willing to admit out loud. And if she has a plan, then maybe this whole thing will end well. Or at least, it will end.

I dress quickly, and already I'm warmer. Great thing about waterproofs is that you always sweat like a bastard when you wear them, and for that I'm now grateful. I wring out my fleece and jacket as best as I can, then put them on over the waterproofs.

"God bless man-made fibers!" I slap my chest like a loon. "Oh lordy, I'm talking to myself now. Must have gone full-on feral." I look around me. "Well, at least it's better than having an imaginary friend. Dream Smitty is about all I can handle right now."

A terrible moan erupts from the grassy knoll beside me. I twist round. No, make that a terrible *moo*. My bovine friend is struggling to get up.

"Holy cow," I groan. But this cow is most unholy. And most Undead. Her face is barely there: a white skull clotted in places with clumps of bloodied flesh that used to be a nose, a mouth, cheeks. Browned teeth grind as she moos and leans toward me, the skin on her body stretched tight and transparent across her enormous, swollen belly, the visible organs twitching inside. She lurches forward, so bloated she can barely walk, and flops down into the water. But the eyes are on me, and Daisy wants blood. I put the backpack on again; further investigations will have to wait.

The fog swirls, and I take a step into the cold water with the foot that still has a wader on. The cow struggles to her feet again and moos her deafening moo, trying to propel herself toward me on her stick legs. But it's hopeless; she's so inflated that she can't keep upright. She smacks down into the water again, and as she does her huge belly splits and dead-cow stomach explodes into the dank air.

"Jesus!" The smell is beyond unbearable. I retch into my hands and stagger away through the water before the ooze can catch up with me. *Great.* We have zombie animals now, too. Did the zoms run out of humans and start chomping on the local wildlife?

Heaven only knows where the road is. Meantime, I need to get to someplace hidden. Someplace I can see the lie of the land and find my companions, or what's left of them. The fog thins a little.

There's a cowshed on a little hill up ahead. I limp toward it, slow and slipping with my unbalanced footwear. This will never do. I fling my remaining wader off into the wetness.

By the time I make it to the cowshed my socks are caked, gouging out chunks of sloppy earth as I power upward. But at least the effort warms me. And there's something to do with moving, one slow step in front of the other, that makes the adrenaline kick in, that reminds me we escaped, and that in spite of zombies, snipers, and water, water, everywhere — I'm alive.

"Mmm, yummy."

The cowshed stinks almost as bad as the Undead cow did. Actually, come to think of it, the whole of the countryside stinks. Must be dead things marinating in the wet: a funky, musty smell with the slightest hint of sickly sweet.

The shed is empty, except for a pile of hay or straw — I've never known the difference — and a substantial cow pie of dark green poo. I make the mistake of standing on it, thinking it's hard, and the crust slides off, leaving a brighter, wet mess underneath. Dammit, it's not like these socks were salvageable anyway. I carefully peel them off and throw them in the corner, my feet fuchsia, raw, and exposed. But now that I'm in here, I kind of feel worse than I did before, because there's a wall without a door, and at any moment there could be zombie flora or fauna sneaking up on me and hiding behind that wall. So I decide to climb up onto the roof. It's simple enough; a horizontal beam provides a foothold, and I pull myself up onto the sloping, corrugated iron pretty easily. And I lie flat on it, making myself small against the outline of the shed so if anyone happens to glance my way, they won't immediately spot me.

The fog is definitely on the wane, and there is a better view from up here, for sure. I can see back to where the river winds out of the woods, and I can see the extent of the tree cover, spreading back for acres upriver. And I think I can see the spot where the road emerges a few fields away. There's no sign of any Jeep, though. I wonder if they made it.

"Maybe they did make it," Smitty murmurs in my ear. *"But maybe they kept driving away."*

"Wot, you my bad fairy now, Smitty?" I murmur back. He doesn't reply. He's selective like that.

The sun is blinking weakly through the heavy clouds, casting rays down onto the glittering, wet ground. This is weird of me, but it makes me smile. It's the first time I've seen sun for what seems like a lifetime. Behind me, there are fields, and then the horizon drops away. We must be on a kind of plateau up here; either that or the world has melted away. I quite like that idea — walking to the end of the earth and then dropping off the edge. I could always stick out a hand when I pass Australia and catch myself on a gum tree. I'm sure things are a lot safer Down Under.

I lie on my back for a moment, feeling the uncomfortable corrugated lines straightening out the kinks in my spine. My hand is on the bag.

"Stop putting it off. Look in the bag, Roberta."

All right, already.

Rolling over, I pull the bag toward me, open the top, and stick a hand in. There's a plastic bag, and I extract it slowly. Granola bars. About a dozen; I can see them through the plastic. I break into the bag anyway and find water-purifying tablets, antiseptic cream, and a roll of bandage. I rip open one of the bars and cram it into my mouth; there are chocolate chips that explode their sugar over my taste buds, and gritty oat pieces that scratch my throat as I swallow. I've been all Nil by Mouth for weeks now. It's quite something to be eating again, and my stomach roars hungrily for more. I eat another and stop there. Who knows how long these things are going to have to last me? Besides, there's other stuff in this bag that needs my attention.

I delve farther into the backpack and find a water bottle, then something hard and heavy, wrapped several times in plastic and sealed with black tape. I place it on the roof with a *clunk*. I have a feeling this may be the main event. I run my hand around the backpack, and just as I think there's nothing else, my fingers catch on the edge of something rigid and flat. I pull it out.

A postcard. With a lighthouse on it.

A tingle fizzes down my spine. Same lighthouse as in Martha's office, I'm sure of it. I turn the postcard over. Yes, there at the bottom it says ELVENMOUTH LIGHT. There's also a tiny scrawl:

wish U were here

Mum's writing.

Seriously, Mother? Couldn't you have used the space to say something a bit more helpful? Like, starting with where the hell this lighthouse is, perhaps? Is it where Smitty is, or where you are? Or should we beware the lighthouse? Or maybe it's symbolic, another code to be worked out? And why the hell did Martha have the same damn picture?

I groan. I get that my mother is being über-careful and all, I truly do — I mean, if this backpack had fallen into the wrong hands, heaven only knows what could have happened. The enemy would have water-proofs! They'd have clean drinking water! And a charming picture of a lighthouse! It would have been game over, Mother.

I shove the postcard back into the pack.

Just the heavy, wrapped-up thing to investigate. And you know what? Part of me already knows what it is, and that's why I've left it till last. Because if I'm right, I'll have a big ol' dilemma on my hands, the extent of which we haven't seen the likes of before now.

I unwrap the thing very carefully, tearing off the tape piece by piece until just the plastic remains. Mum did a great job of making it water-tight, and it's as well she did, because the thing inside would probably not react wonderfully to being underwater.

As I reach inside the plastic to retrieve the thing that I'm going to wish was never there, I suddenly doubt myself. But as my fingers close around the smooth, cool object and I draw it out slowly, my very worst suspicions are confirmed.

My mother has gifted me a gun.

15

We moved to America, and I thought that guns would be everywhere.

That's what the movies and stuff have you believe. There are serial killers. Cowboys. Gangs. Wacko teens who shoot the kids who laugh at them in the hallway or, even worse, don't know that they exist.

The reality is, living in a leafy, liberal college town like we did, it all seemed very tame, and nobody appeared to be carrying lethal weapons. What's more, folks smiled. People said "Have a Great Day," and some of them meant it.

And yet the guns were there, somewhere.

One day when I was about twelve, my mum announced something to me over breakfast. This was unusual on several levels. First, it was a weekend, and she was home. Second, she wasn't exactly speaking to me at the time. I'd developed a great line in sulking whenever it looked like she might be thinking about talking to me, and it had worked great. Most of our necessary communications were conducted either through Dad or by one of us writing stuff on the whiteboard in the kitchen. But that Saturday morning she had cornered me on a cereal run from my bedroom, where I'd been peacefully watching really old episodes of *Doctor Who* I'd found on the Internet.

"So I thought we'd have a little trip out, if you're game." She kind of trilled, and I knew right then that something was amiss. We weren't exactly always going off on Mother-Daughter Happy Days.

"Where."

If I could get away with it, I always chose to be monosyllabic. And I probably had a mouthful of Cap'n Crunch at the time. And, crucially, I couldn't respond with a question — a question would have sounded like I was curious, interested, enthusiastic even.

"Well, I thought it was about time we tested your eye." She was grinning at me. Most discombobulating.

I remember I rubbed my eye at this point. I guess I figured she was talking about taking me to the optician's or something.

"No! Not like that!" She laughed, way too much. "I thought I could take you to the shooting range."

Well, you coulda knocked me on my ass. Didn't see that coming.

"Like, guns."

Again, no question. I was totally intrigued by this point, but there was no way I was letting on.

"Exactly like guns. Like this gun." She pulled this tiny, shiny *piece* out from behind her back and, honestly, my first instinct was to hit the floor. I almost lost bladder control. I thought she'd probably reached menopause and was going to take us down in a fit of hormonal rage. But she was still smiling, so I tried to smile back. Which isn't that easy when there's a gun in the mix.

"I think you'd be a great shot," she said quickly, as if she sensed that I was in total shock. "It's not like we're going to be out hunting or anything, but it's a useful skill to have, and I think you'll be good at it. Who knows, if you have a flair as I suspect, you could shoot competitively. You know it's an Olympic sport?"

By this time I was convinced she had flipped. I was just hoping that thing wasn't loaded and I could throw the bowl of milky cereal in her face to buy myself enough time to run upstairs and call the cops.

However, as if on cue, Dad appeared. He'd been on night shift at the hospital and was wearing his scrubs. There might have even been a little blood on them, but then again, that might be my memory embellishing. Anyway, he took one look at my mother holding a gun to me (well, kinda) and turned as pale as a peeled potato.

"What's going on here?"

"Just what we talked about." My mother doesn't really do Flustered — except when she's trying to be normal — so she tried Spiky and Irritable instead.

"But we decided no," my dad answered. His expression was already one of tired defeat.

"You decided no. I maintained it would be a great outlet for her." My mother had her mouth on. She only gets that mouth on when things are nonnegotiable. Which is most of the time.

"So not karate or horse riding or chess club, but guns?" My dad was incredulous. "I didn't even think you were all serious."

"Chess club?" I looked at Dad. "Do you, like, *know* me?"

"Chess is about strategy," Dad said. "Keeping a cool head. *Consequences*. It would be great for you." He pulled a face. "And maybe for your mother, too."

My mother shook her head, because she's above all this teen banter, and looked at me. "I'll be in the car," she said as if Dad were the kid, and placed the gun on the counter, and left.

Dad sighed. I sighed. I shrugged. He looked me up and down for a second, then walked up to me and put his hands on my shoulders.

"Want to do it?"

"I guess." I really *did* want to do it. It's kind of shocking how much blowing the crap out of something appealed to me.

He nodded. "Fine. I'd say knock 'em dead, but really *don't* knock 'em dead." He leaned forward and kissed me on the forehead. "Take extreme care. And don't let your mother get her hands on an Uzi."

"What's an Uzi?" I mumbled, but he'd left already. Left me alone with the gun on the counter.

(Except I don't think he said the stuff about the Uzi. I think I just made that up for my own amusement. But you get the gist.)

So I picked up the gun and I looked at it like I'm looking at the one in my hand now. And as surreal goes, looking down at a gun in your hands while you're sitting on top of a cowshed in zombie-infested, waterlogged Scotland is really not that much more bizarre than staring at a gun held in your hand in your kitchen at home when you're twelve. My decision then was easy, though. Go with Mum. Shoot the targets. Feel a reluctant and kind of guilty swell of pride when she praises you, because she was right — you do have a good eye, and you're a pretty hot shot, baby. And she never normally praises you, so you've got to take it when it's offered.

We went to the range a bunch of times that summer. Then Mum got busy again, and we stopped. Dad took me once, and he was mega-impressed at how much of a killing machine his only daughter had become. But I could tell he hated it there, and to be honest, after the initial excitement wore off, so did I. I liked the satisfaction of hitting something dead center, I liked that *badly*, but guns scared me, and they still do.

So I'm leaving this gun right here. I can't take it with me.

You know, if someone had said to me, "Yo, you're going to be balls to the wall with a full-on zombie apocalypse, and you're gonna get your hands on a gun," I would have never thought I'd leave it behind. It seems the dumbest of the dumb things to do. But now I'm here, I know I have to leave it behind. Because the one lesson that I learned on that range, like any sad cop in a bad TV movie, is that if you have a gun, you have to be prepared to use it. And I'm kind of frightened I might like using it too much. There will be accidents and recriminations, tears before bedtime. There will be shooting. There will be death.

So I climb down from the roof, and I bury the stupid thing in the corner of the shed beside the green cow pie, which is beginning to crust over again. When I'm done, I shoulder the backpack and emerge from the shed into the foggy half-light.

A moo. Another moo. And some kind of bleat.

Huge black-and-white shapes lumber out of the mist.

Oh, crapola. The cows have come home. And it sounds like they're Undead — and unfed.

I run back into the shed, dig the damn gun back up, load it, and pocket it in my jacket with the safety on. I'm about to leave when something skitters into view around the door of the shed.

The bleating sound. It's a goat. A small, white, bouncing goat with teeny little daggerlike horns and cute gnashing teeth. Blood is dripping from its mouth and butt, as if its body can barely contain the rancid fluids within. One eye is hanging out on a stalk and dangles around on the goat's hairy cheek as the sad thing bleats at me. I feel the bile rise in my stomach.

The goat paws the ground with a leg that buckles the wrong way, and gives a nifty leap into the air.

Oh god, no.

Cows are big and slow and I can outmaneuver them. But this is a horse of a different color.

It bleats again, lowers its head, and charges for me — it's unsteady but quick on its feet. I dodge out of the way like a matador, but it turns on its little pointy cloven hooves and runs again. This time it catches my sleeve in its teeth, its remaining eyelid peeled right back, showing the pink around the good eyeball, ripping part of the cloth away from the jacket. I shove it away.

"Jeez! This jacket is Kevlar, dude!"

The goat laughs in the face of stab jackets. It rushes me again, I step back, slip on the green cow pie, and fall backward onto my butt. The goat clashes against my chest, I lift it up by its scrawny front legs, and as the teeth snap at my face, I hurl it across the floor as far as I can, which is about five feet.

It scrambles. I scramble. The gun is out, safety off.

Aim. Breathe. Squeeze.

The force of the kickback and the shock of the noise fling me back onto the floor again. I dare to look up. The goat is lying on its side, half of its face blown off. And dead. Absolutely, positively dead.

I cry. Allow myself a huge old sob. Get it all out — Grace, nearly drowning, the hopelessness of my task, and the poor little kid on the floor.

As I dry my tears and emerge carefully out of the shed, the cows look at me warily, too fat and stupid to climb the slope to the shed. I spot a gap and go for it, and as I'm moving as quickly as I dare down the mushy hill, I see lights moving in the distance.

A car?

The lights move in a straight line, then they extinguish.

I have to chance it, have to gamble that that's my crew out there, looking for me. I shove the gun back in my pocket and pick up the pace, mud squishing through my pulverized toes, barely able to see a few feet in front of me in the mists, which are thickening again, helpfully.

"Night soon, Bob." Smitty's there. My familiar. My guardian angel. The monkey on my back. *"Ever feel like things are going to get worse before they get better?"*

The sun has long since slipped behind the clouds again, and there's the odd splat of rain on my face. The darkness is descending, and it's going to pour. But above all that, the fog has thickened, and spread. For a while I could see it like a wall in the distance, first ahead of me, then to the sides. Now it is all around, and it won't be long before it consumes me entirely. Where did the car go? Fear of being abandoned alone rises in my chest.

"Yo, mo-fo." Smitty pokes me in the ribs. *"You're not alone. I'm here, aren't I?"*

"No, you're really not," I say out loud. "If you were, then I wouldn't have to frickin' find you, would I? Plus, FYI, they won't just leave me. We never left anyone behind."

"We did," Smitty says. *"Remember back at the castle? Little boy Cam and sister Lily? We left them, Bobby. They were infected, but we might have had time to save them. We'll never know now. Cam was only a kid —"*

"Shut up!" I yell at him. I walk on, tentatively stretching my hands out into the fog in front of me.

"Very zombie, Roberta."

I ignore him. The occasional spit of rain is now quickening into something a lot more annoying. The *splat, splat, splat* on my bare head is like

Chinese water torture. Didn't people go insane with this? Isn't it against the Geneva Convention or something? I would pull the hood of my jacket up, but frankly it feels like the equivalent of stuffing cotton in my ears. My senses are on full alert, they ping with every little noise or shadowy movement. The sharp smell of wet pine burns my nose as I force myself forward. My legs *swish, swish, swish* as the material of the waterproofs rubs together, and suddenly I am hit with the ridiculousness of my situation. I'm heading back into the red zone.

Pine smell. Trees. I must be near the road. I speed up.

A sudden root, or a clump of grass — and I'm falling flat on my face and screeching stupidly loudly, kissing the ground with full force, the wind knocked out of my lungs, a gnarly twist of sopping undergrowth soaking me almost as much as the river did.

Ow. Least the gun didn't go off.

It's comfortable down here. I might give up. I quickly pull myself up to sitting. The thought of surrendering to the earth is scary. Gotta get up.

Turning to see what I tripped on, I'm greeted by a bloody face.

I fall back onto my behind again.

What used to be a man. Empty sockets, eyeballs pecked out by crows. No nose to speak of. A neat hole in his forehead. But his mouth is closed in a firm line, like he's disappointed in me for kicking him in the ribs as I fell.

I scream.

16

I immediately feel stupid. Only amateurs scream, and I'm way past that. This is what it's supposed to do to you, all this mayhem and bodies and gun carrying. You get numbed. Like my feet, exposed to cold and harshness and cruel sharpness of sticks and stones.

Forcing myself to look at him, I take in the camouflage. A soldier, probs? But not Xanthro. He's not in black, and there's no little yellow *X* insignia. Bog-standard British army? And shot, once, in the forehead, sniper style. Maybe he wandered too close to St. Gertrude's, and the Xanthro men took him out? They don't want any interference from the government while they're trying to modify their precious *Walking Dead* weapons.

Could there be more army dudes around? My heart jumps. I could do with finding some of the good guys. This one's been here a while. I know that because he's starting to smell. He's past turning; if he was going to go zom I think he would have done it by now. And it could mean his pals are long gone.

A door slams somewhere in the gloom, and my head jerks up. I can just make out a figure moving toward me. I don't think I have it in me to run away. If it's not a friend, I'm toast.

Russ stops just before he reaches me, and stands there, chest heaving, eyes on the soldier. I allow myself to breathe again, a huge wash of relief tumbling over me.

"Dead?" he pants.

"Very."

"And you're OK?" He searches my face.

I nod. "Good to see you again. I was beginning to think I might not."

"We thought we heard something. Hoped it was you." A huge smile of relief spreads across his sunny face and he does a weird kind of double fist pump. "Nice one!"

He rushes at me and picks me up. I kind of lift up my knees and before I know it we're kind of hugging in a really sappy, barfy kind of way. And I don't dislike it. It's so good to feel a live, warm human; especially a big, strong, cuddly, handsome one. He holds me tight and then runs his warm hand over my bald head, which is totally embarrassing for both of us, because I think he'd forgotten my no-hair thing for a second, and I'm mortified that I feel stubbly and gross in the extreme. We break apart.

"The helicopter," Russ pants. "Back at the bridge. I dropped the rope. And then we had to make a run for it. I'm so, so sorry."

"Hey, don't sweat it," I say, embarrassed.

"We were hoping they hadn't spotted you under the bridge."

"Well, they had," I say. "But I swam away. It was no biggie."

"You were in the river?" Russ shakes his head, rubs his face with shame, makes a whole deal out of it, then hugs me again. "You've still got the backpack, though?" he says as he strokes my back.

"Yeah. Dead soldier guy wanted it, but I told him no." I sort of pat his back, not wanting to seem unfriendly, but not wanting to be totally PDA in front of the others.

"Oh, she's really milking this one," I hear Alice snark from the Jeep.

A door opens, and I can just make out Pete.

"Where have you been all this time? Have you been bitten? What was in the backpack?"

"Nice to see you, too, Petey." I try to walk nonchalantly back to the Jeep, but it's kind of tricky with wobbly legs and no shoes. "I floated downstream a little, hung out with a few Undead animals, and chowed down on a granola bar." I delve into the bag and toss him one. "Enjoy."

Pete catches the bar and frowns at me. "Livestock has been infected?"

"Nothing 'live' about it." I lean on the Jeep to steady myself. I'm so tired I could sleep for another six weeks. "Zombie cows, zombie goats. Somebody call PETA."

"That's worrying in the extreme." Pete shakes his head. "Has Xanthro been experimenting on them, too, or have they been bitten by humans?"

I shrug. "Maybe folks got hungry. All I know is we're not going to be ordering Angus burgers anytime soon." I nod at the bar in his hand. "So eat up your granola."

"Anything more interesting in there?" Russ pats the pack on my back.

"These waterproofs." I pinch the fabric on my leg. "Water-purifying tablets. And there was a postcard from my mum."

"No way!" Russ says. "Show it to me."

I delve and hand it over.

"Wish you were here," he reads, frowning.

And it sounds even lamer said out loud.

"That's all?!" Alice exclaims. "Would it have killed her to say where?"

Pete gives her a doleful, pale green eye. "Maybe it could have. Or killed us."

"Yeah, right," Alice says.

"There is something a bit weird," I say. "The postcard. That lighthouse. Look familiar at all?"

They all examine it.

Pete shakes his head. "Should it?"

I grimace. "Martha's room. The pinboard."

Everyone looks at me blankly.

"There was a postcard of a lighthouse there, too. In fact, I think it was the same one."

"Are you sure?" Russ says.

I nod.

"And this is your mum's handwriting?" Pete taps the card.

"Without doubt," I say. "She's a doctor. It would take some talent to forge that scrawl."

"Oh god!" Alice huffs. "For once, couldn't your mother do something straightforward?"

I'm about to come back with some witty retort — although I'm kind of agreeing with her — but my ideas are snuffed out by an ominous noise from above.

Russ looks up and swears. "They're back. The fog will only keep them away for so long."

"Get in," Pete says.

"I can't see them. Can they see us?" I look up as I climb into the back-seat beside Russ.

"They may have infrared," he says. "Go, Pete!" He opens the window and sticks his head out to listen as Pete takes off as fast as anyone can in thick fog.

"I can't believe you lost my skirt," Alice gripes from the front seat.

"Yeah, because that's what matters, Malice." I delve into the back and retrieve my longed-for boots.

"Shh!" Russ hisses at us. "I think the helicopter's losing us."

Pete grips the steering wheel, and how he's managing to keep to the road, I don't know. It's the weirdest feeling, barreling along in the gray, not able to see where you're going. I hope we don't hit another Undead cow.

After a few seconds Russ comes back in. "It's gone. But we should get as far away from here as quickly as possible."

"But Grace said Smitty was near," I say. "We have to find him." I lean forward to Pete. "Have you got the numbers? We need to work them out. Now."

He flicks a hand at me. "Check out your window. We've been laying low and doing precious little else since you last saw us."

Somebody has written the numbers in the condensation of the window.

55461760328189
5555006005959

"First one is for Smitty, the second for your mum," Russ says. "After we got away from the helicopter, we drove into the woods and hid for an hour or so, and tried to work out what they meant. But we drew a blank."

I stare at the watery digits. I'd love to have a eureka moment, but it's not going to come easy.

"Both numbers start with five five," I mutter. "Both numbers are the same length; that has to mean something."

"Yes. Could be there's a word in common?" Pete twists round. We are so ending up in a ditch.

"But look at all those fives in the last set — what word has four of the same letter in a row?" I touch the second number lightly and the pressure of my finger on the glass pools a dribble of water.

"There are codes where the same number means different letters," Pete says. "But you need special algorithms to work them out. So that means a computer, or a really big brain."

"My mother would never assume I'd have either of those things."

Russ drills his fingers on the back of the seat in front. "Let's think about this logically — because your mother is nothing if not logical, right?" He looks across at me.

"And then some."

"So back to basics." He rubs his forehead, like he's trying to warm up his brain. "She tells you to find Smitty. We can only assume that the number after his name tells us where he is."

"Yes!" Alice slaps the dashboard and makes us all jump. "That's what I was thinking all along."

"Er, great." Russ clearly wasn't expecting quite this level of enthusiasm for his stating of the obvious. "So will these numbers spell out a street name? A building, perhaps?"

"Oh, no." Alice isn't happy at that. "Not a building — a place."

"What?" I curl my brow in irritation at her.

"Not what, where." She leans over the back of her seat and dabs a finger on the window. "The numbers are where!"

"Yes, and?" I shout back. "5546 . . . whatever . . . that's not a word."

"It doesn't have to be," Alice says, like she's talking to a very slow person. "It's those point thingies. The lines on a whatsit. So many north or whatever."

"What on earth are you talking about?" I roll my eyes.

"On earth. Right!" She looks at Russ. "Finally she gets it. Only she still doesn't know she gets it." She shakes her head.

Pete slams on the breaks.

"Coordinates," he groans quietly. "Longitude and latitude. Why didn't I see it before?"

"So obvious, now that I look at it," Russ says.

"Huh?" I say dumbly, mostly because I'm flabbergasted that everyone seems to think that Alice is right about something that requires brainpower.

"The numbers are, like, degree thingies on the globe. We did it at school, Dumbo," Alice explains to me.

Pete turns off the ignition and bounces up and down in his seat. "You know — fifty-five degrees north, say, then so many west or east or whatever. It's how you find stuff when you're in the field. Basic geography."

"*Basic* geography, Bobby," Alice purrs at me.

"The seventh number — six — is text code for *N*, meaning 'north.'" Pete jumps in because heaven forbid that someone else should get a chance to explain it all. "The six numbers preceding it measure longitude." He takes a breath, relishing the chance to tutor me. "There are three pairs of numbers." He reaches over and touches Smitty's number on the window, putting commas in to separate the first six digits: 55, 46, 17. "So fifty-five degrees, forty-six minutes, seventeen seconds north. That's how it's measured, and it points to a specific spot on the map." He screws up his brow, thinking for a moment. "It *is* somewhere near. Fifty-five would make total sense; Edinburgh is fifty-five degrees north."

I look at him. "How do you even know that kind of thing?"

He looks back at me blankly. "How do you not?"

I blink. "OK. So how does *she* know?" I point at Alice.

Pete shakes his head gravely. "These are weird times in which we live, Bobby." He continues, "So the next six numbers are degrees of latitude, and the final number in the sequence will be indicating 'east' or 'west' — it's nine, so that's text code for *W* . . ." He begins to do commas again, and the first set of digits now reads:

55, 46, 17 N, 03, 28, 18 W

"There!" He sighs happily. "That's it. That's where Smitty is. All we need to do is go to those coordinates on the map and we'll find him. I bet my life we'll find him."

And I believe it. For the first time since I woke up this morning, I feel genuinely chipper.

"So how do we do that?" I ask Pete. "How do we follow the coordinates?"

"Easy!" he positively sings. "We have a GPS."

He turns on the ignition again and reaches for the button that turns the satellite navigation system on, and for a kind of embarrassing second, he doesn't realize what we've all remembered.

The GPS screen blinks out at us, smashed, unreadable.

"Oh god." Pete looks like he's going to cry. "I didn't know . . . I didn't think we'd need it . . ."

We sit there in silence and watch the screen blink, the only form of light inside the car. The engine hums quietly. Outside, the fog begins to thin, showing the trees to either side of us. I want to cry, too. So near, and yet so far. There we sit, all worked up and nowhere to go.

"Oh, well," says Alice after a minute, "I suppose we'll have to use the map thingummy, like in the olden days." She shifts her pert behind and pulls out a wad of papers marked with curvy lines and numbers. "I've been sitting on this all the time, *très* uncomfor-taahble." She flutters the paper. "It's what gave me the idea of the numbers in the first place, it's got them scribbled all over it." She takes in our open jaws and incredulous stares. "What?"

Russ grabs the map from Alice and pores over it with the flashlight. "This is it," he breathes. "This is what we need — the longitude and lati- tude, it's all marked here." He points at the map. "This must be the river — and here — the farm buildings, and the bridge." He nods, a smile breaking over his face. "We can do this!"

I lean over him. "You think this is for real? These numbers, that's what my mother was trying to tell me?"

He looks up at me. "Well, she's *your* mother. Do you think it's some- thing she would do?"

I don't even really need to think about it; it's totally something she would do. And now that I do think about it, my cheeks burn as a long-forgotten memory surfaces.

A trip taken just before we went to live in the States. My mother and me in a tent — a camping weekend. It was the kind of thing I usually would have done with Dad — mainly because my mother was always far too busy to spend whole weekends with me — but she managed to surprise me with a last-minute adventure.

We went somewhere by a lake; it was summer, and the sun burnt my skin red as I played in the icy waters on the first day. Then there was a campfire, and insects — midges and wasps and a big beetle with antlers — in my sleeping bag. Mum told me not to be silly, not to be scared by the little things.

And the next day, we went orienteering. There was an important pile of rocks that marked something, called some ridiculous thing like Folly's Cairn or Bluff's Outcrop, and we had a map and a compass and we took bearings. We traversed hillsides, marched determinedly through woods so thick and pine-scented it brought on Mum's asthma.

I didn't really get it; she tried to teach me how to use the compass with the map so we could find our way, but I couldn't make it happen. I was *nine*, people. I was still checking out the shadows of the woods for fairies and Bigfoot.

But life with Mum had taught me, if you don't know what you're doing, blag it. So I blagged it, big-time, pretending like I totally understood where we were going, and getting it right by pure chance more often than I got it wrong. I was pretty amazed at how lucky I was. I blagged it so damn well that toward the end of the walk, just as my stomach was beginning to rumble and I was beginning to look forward to going back to school after this epic journey, we walked out into a clearing, and Mum handed me the map and the compass, and told me I was on my own.

"I know the way from here." She pushed the hair out of my eyes. "But I want you to make it there by yourself. Use the coordinates, and I'll see you at Dead Man's Pileup." (OK, so I clearly can't remember the name of the rocks, but you'll forgive artistic license at a time like this.)

With that, she strode off into the woods.

As I looked along the narrow pathway, the map heavy and floppy in my hand, I knew my mother wasn't coming back. This was one of her tests: If I passed, the weekend would have been a success. If I failed, I obviously wasn't her daughter after all.

Gripping map and compass tightly, I stepped onto the path. Maybe I'd walk for a few minutes, the trees would disappear, and I'd find a field with a big ol' pile of rocks and Mum sitting on top of them like a leprechaun at the end of the rainbow? Easy peasy.

But, of course, it wasn't like that. And this is where my memory gets a little fuzzy. I know that I walked and walked, the woods getting darker, and I remember that sinking feeling that this was going on far too long to be the right way. I remember finding a stream and following it because streams always lead *somewhere*. And then came night. After that I don't remember much, because I think I blanked it out. Just waking in the parking lot, and the police car's flashing lights, and Dad shouting at my mother.

Turns out, I had wandered way off track. I'd actually ended up going in a huge circle and almost retracing our steps back to where we had left the car the day before. I had no clue how to use the tools my mother had given me to find some arbitrary pile of rocks, but I had followed my nose and found my way out of the woods on my own terms. They found me asleep, curled up on the ground outside the locked passenger door of my mother's car. She was embarrassed, Dad was furious, and I had learned never to expect my mother to come for me, but to help myself out, to find my own way home.

We never spoke about that weekend again, ever. But she must have figured that I'd never forget about coordinates. I know that by leaving me this clue, she's kind of giving me another shot at finding my way again. I should have known what the numbers were, but again, I wasn't paying close enough attention.

"Give me that map." I hold out my hand. "And make some room in this Jeep. I'm finding this place, and we're rescuing Smitty."

17

We are standing on a sodden hill overlooking a field lined with a forest. The field is featureless apart from four low stone walls, which make up an empty sheep pen.

"Ooh," Alice murmurs. "Give Bobby a Girl Scout badge."

I worked it out, and we drove here, only a few miles from where they picked me up. This is the point on the map where the coordinates meet. The fog has mostly cleared on the higher ground, it's raining lightly, and the Jeep beside us is threatening to slowly sink into the mud.

"So now what?" Pete looks grim.

"This is the spot," I say, as if that will make Smitty materialize. Why am I feeling so frightened? I should be yelping in excitement. My mind is all Smitty — but he's fled from me. No voice in my head now. I could be too close to the real thing.

"There's got to be something else here." Russ shakes his head. "Let's check out that sheep pen at least."

We begin to slide down the muddy bank. My mind races. What if Smitty's lost it? Who knows what can happen to a person in six weeks if he's on his own and living off the land? Especially one who is full of zombie bite and zombie antidote, fighting it out. Maybe he'll be crazy —

have no memory of me, or be running round the field in his underwear and bits of leather fashioned from the hide of one of the dead cows.

And not only that; how will he greet me? What will we say to each other? It's been forty days and forty nights. In Teen Time that's like a year. Granted, I have been unconscious for nearly all of that, so to me it's a bit like I saw him yesterday. But presuming he's lived every minute of that time, he's had an opportunity to . . . well, get over things. Get over me.

Maybe he won't like me anymore.

I'm so stupid. Like any of that matters. This is about Xanthro and Osiris and zombie epidemics and saving the world. Or it's about Mum and me, and about getting these kids in this car home. It's *not* about my burgeoning love life or lack thereof. It's not about a kiss or a warm hand to hold or the quite mortifying way my body tingles and churns when he's near. It's not about missing him; it's not about feeling — for the first time in ages — that I'd finally got someone who gets me.

Leapin' lizards. It took going into a coma to even admit all that stuff to myself.

Oh god. The coma. The bald head. I look like an *ugly baby.*

No! This will never do! I can't have this huge, full-on reunion as Bald Bobby. I look appalling. I have waterproofs on, for goodness' sake — I go *swish-swish* when I walk. I smell of rotted cow and formaldehyde and river mud and dead soldier juice. And nobody else looks as bad as me in comparison. Alice — I swear it — has glossy, *brushed* hair. There's no hope for me. I might as well knock out a couple of my front teeth and have done with it.

It's hard going down the bank. We pause halfway to catch our breath and dislodge some of the caked mud from our feet.

"If he's here, he's well hidden." Pete shivers beside me.

There's nothing unusual about the pen. It's one of one of those old-fashioned ones they make out of big lumps of stone that all miraculously fit together without any cement. There's no roof. Nowhere to hide.

"We're here. Let's look." Russ tries to sound enthused. We continue to make our way down, mud still thick around our ankles, sliding diagonally in a way that reminds me of my crappy boarding efforts in the snow of a few weeks ago.

There's a gap in the wall right at the other end. We clomp along there and enter.

Once inside, there's quite a lot of shelter; I'm amazed how the wall keeps some of the rain off. The ground is sprinkled with hay (or straw, still unclear on the hay-straw diff), and there are a couple of large metal feeders that presumably dispensed food to hungry sheep. No hungry sheep, though. And definitely no Smitty. Well, what did I expect? To see him crouched in a corner, chewing on a turnip? Maybe I did. I walk around the wall, past the first food trough, toward the second.

"There's nothing here." My voice sounds awful. Croaky, rough, raw. It's tired. I'm tired. I'm almost ready to crash out in the back of the Jeep and let Pete take us wherever he can. I'm almost done with the whole damn thing.

"So we keep going," Russ shouts. "In the same direction. It's got to be close."

The hay or straw looks soft in this corner by the trough. I think I'll just hunker down here. I'm already wet through, and this way I don't have to put up with Alice's in-Jeep entertainment. Yep, that's decided. I'm staying. I halfheartedly rake a boot across the hay-straw, like a dog scraping at the ground, preparing to lie down.

Jackpot.

I clear some more, holding in my yelp before I've made certain. And then I'm on hands and knees, and I am certain, but still I don't share.

There's a small wooden trapdoor. There in the earth.

I take a moment, just for me, to steady myself, because once they know, we're going in and we'll have found him and I'll have to deal. A rush of hope and wonderfulness runs through me. I feel incredible. This is it. *I found him, Mum.* I found him.

I stand slowly on wibbly-wobbly legs, and turn around to let the others know, but they're already there. They must have seen me scrabbling and they've come up behind. Silently I point at the steel ring that acts as a handle.

Russ nods.

I bend to lift the door. It's heavier than I thought it would be, but it moves on well-oiled hinges, and I can manage.

A few steps down. To a squat tunnel that disappears under the wall.

"A shelter?" Pete whispers.

I head down the steps, ducking my head to fit in the tunnel. Russ hands me the flashlight from the Jeep.

I shine the flashlight, but there's not too much ahead of me. Barely a few feet away is an opening into a larger space. I scuttle along, squeeze through, and find I can stand up and pan the flashlight around me.

A small room. Corrugated tin walls, a stone floor. A camp bed on the far wall. Some stuff in the middle of the room — a cardboard box, some kind of lantern. Candy wrappers. To the right is an alcove with a curtain across. I pull at it; behind is a dirty sink with a faucet, and something that looks and smells suspiciously like an adult-sized potty.

The others follow me in, and suddenly the room is crowded. Russ has found the lantern and has turned it on with a flick of a switch. The room is bathed with watery white light.

"He's not here." Alice sounds irritated, like her dad didn't turn up on time to collect her from the mall.

I sit on the camp bed. I'm tempted to lie down, smell the bed, see if I can tell if he slept here. But that would be slightly loony.

"Someone was." Pete holds up a box of empty food cans. "Maybe your mother took him. She could have moved him to a safer place. She might have left a message here for us."

It's true, but I can hardly summon the energy to look. The disappointment is stinging me from the inside, pushing its spikes through my gut and up, out of my chest and my throat, threatening to choke me in tears. I look under the pillow on the bed, under the bed, on the walls and floor. I don't see anything.

"This could be nothing," I hear myself say, getting up slowly. "For all we know, he was never here. Maybe this is the wrong place after all. Who knows? Dammit!" I reach down and toss the bed up, and the metal frame springs up and clatters against the wall.

"OK," Russ says. "So we gather anything that's useful to us, and we go on."

"Where to?" Alice shouts.

"Farther." He sounds sure. "It must be the wrong place."

"No," Pete says. "This is the spot, I'm sure Bobby got it right."

"Who cares," I say. "He's not here, and we're wasting our time."

I'm about to flounce off, sucking in my tears until I'm outside and the rain will cover them anyway, when I notice a shiny red thing down by my feet. It must have been dislodged from somewhere when I kicked the bed, perhaps between the mattress and the frame. I crouch low and pick it up, feeling the smoothness of the material in my hands. It's a small Chinese silk purse. I unzip it. There are four silver coins inside. Quarters. The ones I put there back in the States, in case there was ever an emergency. I gasp.

"What is that?" Russ said.

"This is mine." I grip it in my hand. "Smitty must have gone through my pockets at the crash and stolen it from me." I smile. "That's so him."

"He could be nearby," Pete says, heading for the door. "Maybe he heard us coming in the Jeep and ducked out, thinking we were the enemy."

I cling to the purse and follow him out the door, but as he gets to the end of the short passage to the surface, he stops and turns round.

"Helicopter," he whispers.

I tune in my ears. Yes, it's there. The juddering sound of the air being sliced through, the copter hovering very close by.

"Stay here, or make a run for it?" Pete's green eyes are strained and bloodshot.

"The Jeep." Russ pushes from behind. "Have to get to it."

"Up that bank?" Alice squeaks. "I can't run up it."

I don't think any of us can.

"We're hidden here," says Pete.

"The Jeep isn't. And maybe they saw us heading in this direction," I say. "Presumably they know about this place? If we've disappeared it's pretty much the only place we could have hidden."

Russ nods, pushes past. "Wait here." He disappears through the hatch for a minute, then emerges, red-faced.

"They've found the Jeep. The helicopter is at the top of the hill. We've no choice but to make a run to the woods."

"Are you serious?" I say. "Leave the car?"

"Bobby, they're on foot, heading this way. We go now, or we get caught. When we get the chance, we double back. Come on!"

He pushes us up through the exit, like we're going over the front. The light is blinding after the dim of the shelter; at first I can't see the men, but then I spot them, about a third of the way down the slippery bank behind us. Three men, like before, all in black. I duck down behind the wall and make my way toward the gap in the pen. There, over an expanse of rough clumps of grass, is our only hope. A dense forest, green trees peeling away into the horizon, seemingly endless. A great place to get lost in. But getting lost is our only hope.

Russ is at my side.

"We run. It's the only way." He takes off and, with a quick glance to check that Pete and Alice are with us, I do the same. We only have a few seconds' head start; they'll see us, and then the rifles will be trained on our backs. Even if they're under orders not to shoot to kill, that doesn't stop them from shooting us to bring us down.

"Stop!"

Sure enough, the now-familiar rasping voice rings out.

"Stop, or we'll shoot!"

"Keep running!" I yell at the others.

The trees are achingly close now. But a single shot and I'll be far, far away.

But it doesn't come, and as I reach the forest first, I fling myself into the undergrowth. Alice is next, thundering past where I'm lying.

"Bobby?" she cries. "Where are you?"

Then Russ, almost dragging Pete, who is purple, gasping for air.

"Get up!" Russ shouts at me. "They won't stop!"

I know it. But they want to catch us alive, of that I'm sure. I scramble up and follow where Russ leads, branches pinging back and whacking me in the face, roots tripping me, moss-covered rocks threatening to make me land on my back again.

"Keep together!" Russ gasps. "When they hit the trees they'll spread out, try to corner us."

He seems to know what he's doing, and we follow. He takes us into thicker undergrowth still, and to the foot of a steep bank. We keep on keeping on, leaning into it, pulling ourselves up by saplings and rocks and clumps of grass. Reaching the top first, I collapse and lie for a minute, lungs pumping painfully. The others thump down beside me, Russ wriggling on his stomach for a better view.

"Hostile at twelve o'clock!" he whispers. One of the soldiers is some way below us, but on course for a rendezvous if we stay where we are. "The others will have gone round, either side." He indicates left and right. "Damn! We need to keep going, or they'll have us." He springs to his feet. "Wait here a second." He dashes off, and we lie there panting, barely able to do anything else. I keep a beady eye on the soldier, who is sizing up the bank. If he decides we've come this way, he'll be joining us in a minute or two.

Russ comes back. "This way." He beckons and we rise, keeping low, following him through the trees until he crouches down, hand flattening for us to do the same. "The way is clear — we go down the bank and out of the tree line in the open. Then we can double back and up the hill to the Jeep — it's our only chance."

This bank is steeper than the first — almost a cliff in parts — and it has less cover, and fewer trees to grab. It is slick mud from top to bottom, and to our right is a ravine with a fast-flowing stream tumbling down jagged rocks.

Pete shakes his head. "I'm not sure . . ."

"Slide from trunk to trunk," Russ says, demo-ing on his backside, sliding to the first tree and catching himself on it. "Just follow my lead and you'll be fine."

Alice nods, not wanting to be left behind this time, and crashes into Russ before he can move to the next trunk.

There's a noise behind us, somewhere in the undergrowth. Could be a deer. Could be a soldier. Pete and I shoot each other a look and take off down the bank, not waiting for a free trunk. We're surfing on our asses, feet out straight, arms trying to slow our descent. I have mud in places I don't like to think about. We both overshoot Alice. I lean to my right in an attempt to steer, and catch a trunk, while Pete sails past me and out of sight. I'm impressed he manages not to yell, but it's kind of unsettling that I don't hear him land.

Russ skids down after him, leaving Alice indignant and still cling-ing to her first trunk. She opens her mouth to shout, and I gesticulate madly to her, shushing her before she can make a noise. I glance up the hill, and then down, and when I look again Alice has set off on the diagonal toward me, half on her feet and leaning back, and half rolling uncontrollably. *Shit.* As she nears me I brace myself for the collision, but it never happens. At the last minute she slips down past me and rolls again, off the edge of the ravine and out of sight. I swallow a squeal, but Alice doesn't do as well. She gives a long scream, followed by an "Oh!" and a short yelp. Then silence.

Oh god. Not good not good not good.

With Russ and Pete in god-knows-what shape at the bottom, it's up to me. I look up the bank again — is that movement? — and then I'm crawling on my belly toward the edge, pulling myself forward as far as I dare.

I look down into the abyss.

I don't see her. The gushing stream, the sharp-looking rocks, yes — but no Alice. I pull myself a little farther down to the point she fell off, and lean over again.

She's there. I see legs. She's lying on her back, partly obscured by a bush, on a wide grassy ledge that is maybe fifteen or twenty feet below. I can't see anything above her knees, but she's not moving. I don't think, just lower myself over the edge, grabbing at anything I can, feetfirst, scrabbling for any kind of hold, blinded by dirty, running water from above. It's more of a controlled plummet; I ricochet off things and plunge to the grass below, landing on all fours and rolling over like I meant it. I'm winded, but uninjured. I look up, and that's when I see the man bending over a lifeless Alice. At first I think — I *hope* — it's Russ, but he's slimmer, and all in black. A soldier. He has his back to me, bent over her like he's feeling for a pulse or strangling her, I can't tell which.

He hasn't seen me. I pick up a piece of branch, and creep toward him.

Just aim for the back of the head. As hard as you can. You only get one shot at this.

I raise the branch, all slimy and green in my hand, and grip it tightly.

Wait! Is he kissing her?

I pause, branch aloft. His head is bent over her face, and there's a weird lip-smacking noise.

I gasp.

Before I can whack him, he spins around on his knees and looks up at me.

The branch falls from my hand.

It's Smitty.

18

I blink. This time, I'm definitely not dreaming.

I shoulda recognized the leather jacket.

"Hey, Roberta. 'Bout time you showed up." Smitty sits back on his heels beside Alice's body, wet ink-black hair over his face, a broad smile playing on his chops like I just brought them breakfast in bed. "How the bollocks are you?"

He stands up and looks like he's going to do the whole hugging and kissing thing. I won't allow it. I back off. I've thought about what I'll do if — when — I find him. I've tried to mentally prepare myself, but now every instinct deserts me.

"Yeah, I'm OK. We looked for you."

He nods, smile fading. "I waited. Your mum said she'd leave clues."

A hand clutches my heart. "You've seen her?"

He shakes his head. "Not for weeks."

I swallow, move round him to Alice, and squat down to her. I see her chest rise and fall, and as I move her hair to look for an injury, she moves her head and coughs.

"Were you kissing Alice?"

It's the dumbest thing to say, but it slips out.

"Kiss of life." Smitty frowns at me. "Good ol' Malice practically fell on top of me. I was worried she'd stopped breathing, I was giving her a little mouth-to-mouth."

He manages to make it sound *disgusting*.

"We should go." Smitty hauls Alice up. She moans slightly, and he puts her over his shoulder, fireman-stylee. "You've got some men in black after you."

"I noticed." I inject as much venom into those two words as is humanly possible.

I can't help but be impressed that he's still got his strength, but I hate that I'm impressed.

"This way." He takes off along the grassy ledge. "Watch your step."

What is wrong with me? I should be thrilled and filled to the brim with joy that he's here, but I think I preferred Dream Smitty.

The ledge winds down to the bottom of the hill, and suddenly there's the tree line with the field beyond.

"Psst!"

I spin round. It's Russ and Pete, their eyes as big as saucers, taking in Alice and the apparition who's carrying her. Pete flings back his head and starts to laugh silently. Russ casts a look to him and then to me, and I can see that instantly he knows who the tall dark stranger is. He runs toward us lightly, Pete cantering behind. He slows down a couple of paces away and looks Smitty up and down. I clear my throat.

"Russ, this is —"

"Smitty!" Pete rushes at him and hugs him, which causes Smitty to lose his balance a little and almost drop Alice on her head. "I knew you'd be here. I knew it."

"Good to see you, too, Petey-Poos," Smitty laughs. "Love the hairdo."

He turns to Russ. "New recruit? Can't recommend hanging out with these freaks, they'll get you into trouble."

Russ grins tightly and thrusts out a hand. "Russ. I was on the bus when it crashed."

"Hey, Russ from the Bus," Smitty says. "You'll forgive me if I don't shake, I've got my hands full of blonde at the moment. She's still heavier than she looks."

"Is she OK?" Pete asks.

"Breathing, but out cold," Smitty says. "Which, I think we can all agree, is our favorite kind of Alice." He smacks her behind. "She'll be fine. She's got a thick skull."

A noise from behind makes us duck down.

"We need to get to the Jeep now." Russ takes the lead, turning to his left. "This way —"

"Nice idea," says Smitty. "But wrong direction." He points to the right. "Jeep's this way."

"No." Russ frowns. "We left it on the hill."

"You did." Smitty begins moving through the trees. "And that's where I nicked it from."

We follow him, aghast.

"I let off the brakes and freewheeled down the side of the hill. Quite a ride."

As we reach the tree line, we see it — parked conveniently by the last tree. Smitty opens the back door and dumps Alice inside. He tosses the keys to Pete. "All yours again." He jumps into the back, where I join him. Russ and Pete climb into the front, and Pete fires up the ignition, while Smitty shouts directions from the back. As we pull away, I spot two of the soldiers emerge from the trees a way off from us.

"Faster, Pete!" I shout. "They're behind us!"

He puts his foot down and a splatter of mud hits the windows as the wheels spin. But then they catch, and we bounce away across the clods, away from the trees and across the field, Pete cleverly keeping us on the right side of a small hill so that our pursuers can't train their guns on our tires.

"They'll make for the helicopter. We have to find cover before they get airborne." Russ grits his teeth.

"Keep driving, Petey," Smitty says. "The road's just over that hill. They're not going to be flying anywhere for a while."

"How do you know that?" Russ stares at him.

"Because I tied a nice fat chain around the tail rotor." Smitty grins.

"Whaat?" Pete cries, turning round. "That's genius!"

"Knew you'd be proud, Petey," Smitty says. "Oh" — he smiles to himself — "and I pissed in the cockpit. All over the controls. That's got to do some damage."

"Classy," I murmur, but I can't say I'm not pleased. "So you saw us coming?"

"Nope." Smitty shakes his head. "I was in the woods when I heard the helicopter. Figured they were after me. Then I saw you lovely people running for your lives. Did the business with the chain, got the Jeep, and motored back to save your sorry selves."

Pete lets out a peal of laughter. "We were looking for you, and you found us first."

This puts the sulks on me, for no good reason. And Russ is glum, too. He grunts and turns around in his seat. Smitty puckers his lips behind Russ's back and blows him a kiss.

I ignore him and lean over the back to check on Alice, making sure she's comfortable. There isn't a mark on her. I pull the tarp up around her a little so she'll be warm. She still has her bag around her neck, and I carefully remove it, laying it beside her.

"There's the road," Pete says. "Where are we heading?"

"Martha, our babysitter at the hospital," I explain to Smitty, "said we weren't far from Edinburgh. We keep driving until we see a road sign; we're bound to hit a gas station or somewhere that has maps."

"Hmm," Smitty says beside me. "Because gas stations treated us so well last time. So where's your ma hanging out, exactly?"

I avoid his eyes. "I was kind of hoping you'd tell us. But she left us these numbers — coordinates — that's how we found you. And the second set of numbers has to be where she's hiding, but we need a map covering a bigger area."

"And there's the postcard," Russ says.

"Yeah." I fish it out of my backpack and thrust it at him. "Random lighthouse. Don't know if it's full-on cryptic, or if that's where she's hanging out. Mean anything to you?"

"Nope," he says. "So where are these coordinates, then?"

"They're here." I twist round to the window to show him. But there's nothing on the glass.

"What's wrong?" Pete hears the pause.

"They've gone," I say. "We wrote them in the condensation," I tell Smitty, "but they've melted or something."

He gives me a look, then leans over me and breathes on the glass. His leather jacket creaks, his body warm and heavy against mine. He breathes again, and the glass steams. But to no avail. No numbers come up. The glass has been wiped clean, on purpose. I feel the panic rise in my chest.

"Pete! You wrote them down on some paper," I shout at him.

"Take the wheel," Pete says to Russ, slowing the Jeep, then wiggles his hands into his pockets, checking and checking again, looking down the side of the seat and on the floor. He slams on the brake, does a face-palm.

"You lost the paper?" I yell at him.

"Fifty-five, fifty-five, double zero north," he rasps. "Write this down."

"You don't lose stuff, Pete," I cry. And he doesn't. He's Mr. Organized. If I could rely on anyone in our gang to actually not lose something, it would be Petey-Poos. What's up with him?

"Fifty-five, fifty-five, double zero north — write it down, Bobby!" He shouts at me.

I search for the old map on the floor, find it — and Russ gives me a pen. I scribble the new numbers next to where I'd written the old set of coordinates.

55, 55, 00 N

Pete screws up his eyes.

"Double zero . . . fifty something? I think the last four numbers repeated . . . fifty-four, fifty-four west?" He slaps his forehead. "Or was it thirty-something?" He shakes his head like he's got a flea in his ear. "I can't remember."

I add to the sequence:

55, 55, 00 N, 00, ??, ?? W

I put the pen down. "You did good, Pete. None of the rest of us could do any better."

Russ shakes his head. "I should have memorized them. I can't believe I could be so sloppy."

"Hey, don't beat yourself up, Russ from the Bus," Smitty drawls. "Petey here was always the brains of the crew, and it's clear nothing has changed since then."

Russ turns on him, eyes blazing. I shoot out a hand.

"Stop! Don't turn this into a pissing contest." I nod to Pete. "Get driving. We have something to go on, and that's a lot more than we could have."

It is dark. We can't risk headlights, so we crawl as fast as we dare, which is not very fast. The road is long, straight, and lonely. Hard to tell what the countryside is doing out there beyond the dark and the clammy, opaque air, but we don't see any buildings yet. Pete keeps slow and steady. As I begin to relax slightly, the tiredness moves in. It is undeniable and inevitable and I hardly have the strength to fight it, like drowning in a vat of thick, suffocating mud. I rub my face and try to focus.

"Sleep," Smitty says to me, unexpectedly softly. "I'll wake you when we get attacked by something."

Of course, after that I want to stay awake. But my eyes are so heavy. I let them rest for a moment, and then before I know it I'm coming to and I hear the boys discussing something. Russ is outside with the flashlight; I see a flash of green, a road sign.

EDINBURGH 8

Sleep is heavy on me like a leaden quilt, pressing me into my seat. I allow my eyes to close again for a second, and I'm fast asleep.

There's a bump, and I'm jolted awake. I blink my eyes, but for some reason I can't quite get them to open properly. But even through half-closed eyelids I can see the dazzling sunlight coming through the back window. The rays are like liquid, piercing the mud-splattered glass and bathing me in warmth. How long have I been sleeping?

I sit bolt upright. Red-orange light everywhere. The windows are steamed up and I can't see out. For a moment I wonder if we've been beamed up on the Xanthro mother ship. I'm alone in the Jeep. Everyone's gone. They've abandoned me.

A little snort behind me makes me jump. Alice is still fast asleep, with Smitty's leather jacket over her. I feel a small stab of jealousy, and then feel ridiculous. At least I'm not completely alone.

I gather my backpack, ease open the door, and step outside. It has stopped raining. My boot finds gravelly ground, and I push myself out of the Jeep and close the door quietly. The light dazzles me, like I've never seen light for months, like I'm a troglodyte surfacing for the first time.

The Jeep is on a hill, on a rough track leading upward. And beyond is . . . I blink against the light. The glitter of water, the dark rising of buildings, black spires and towers and glowering hills far into the distance.

Farther up, where the track narrows to a path, I hear voices. I lope as fast as I can to the top and am greeted with a full panorama. The sun is like a burning red ball, hovering over the horizon to my right. Smitty is perched, shivering and jacketless, on some kind of carved stone in the middle of the summit, his hand up at his eyes, shading from the sunrise. Russ and Pete are a ways off, looking over the city.

"Edinburgh?"

Smitty looks over to me.

"Pretty, isn't it?"

"Pete had the idea to come up here," calls Russ. "Scope things out before we get in above our heads. Bright of him."

"This hill is Arthur's Seat." Pete comes over, ever the tour guide. "You can see the Firth of Forth in the background. And see that little raised bit of land in the center? That's the Royal Mile, with Edinburgh Castle on top."

"Awesome view." I mean it. It's probably the most beautiful thing I've ever seen. To the east, the sun is rising so quickly I can actually see it move. It draws me to look at it until I'm forced to blink, black spots dancing on my eyelids. As it rises it casts orange on the east-facing sides of all the buildings, illuminating roads shining like yellow rivers, dotted with cars that have long ago ended their journeys. No smoke floats out of chimneys, no boats float on the water.

And yet there is movement. At first I think it's my sun-dazzled eyes, but then I realize the others are seeing it, too. The streets are moving, dots are converging, swarming, moving together and then apart. People, or what used to be people.

"There are hundreds of them," Pete says.

"Thousands," Russ corrects him.

"Did you see any on our way here?" I ask them.

"A handful," Smitty says. "But nothing like that. I think they like company; strength in numbers and all that."

"Xanthro has been tinkering with them," Pete tells Smitty. "They were developing them to use as weapons; it's incredibly clever, really. These new zoms can work together as a team. They understand some language. They can think ahead — plan, even."

"Great." Smitty gives a low laugh. "Reckon that was just the ones at the hospital, or do you think they've been crop-dusting the general populace with Osiris Version Two-point-Oh? Because if these zoms are intelligent, we shouldn't go anywhere near the city."

"Some streets look clear." Russ squints. "They seem to all be grouping in specific areas. Maybe they're contained?"

"Nice eyesight, Superman," Smitty snarks.

"No matter." Pete waves a hand in front of him. "I've been thinking about it, and we need to go south, anyway. The new coordinates are south of Smitty's hiding place. Before I, er, *killed* the GPS, we could see that Edinburgh looked north of us. So this isn't the right direction. We need to head away from the city, not into it."

"I'm fine with that," I say. "But we still need a map."

Pete nods. "Most places we passed that might have had maps were burnt-out, or it was too risky to stop. But now that we know the score here we should head south and try every garage and corner shop until we strike lucky."

"Agreed," Russ says. "Back to the Jeep."

I nod. "We need to check on Alice, too. She's been out an awfully long time . . ."

Russ smiles. "Always thinking of others. That's what I love about you, Bobby." He squeezes my arm, and hurries away down the path, with Pete following.

Smitty chuckles mockingly. "That's what I *lurve* about you, too, Bobby."

I turn on him. "Shut up!" I say. "So what if he's actually nice to me. It makes a great change to have someone around who actually gives a damn."

Smitty shakes his head. "So why did you even come and look for me, then, Roberta? If you were so happy with the Terminator there, why give a crap about me?"

"Because my mother told me to," I hiss at him. "She didn't lose a wink of sleep about dumping me in that frickin' Xanthro nuthouse, but she was oh-so-desperate that they didn't get their hands on you!"

"You're wrong," Smitty says. "She was worried about you." He jumps down off his perch, winces as he starts to straighten his leg, tries to cover it up, then walks to the edge of the hilltop.

"How's the leg, anyway?" I ask him.

He shrugs. "Beats your head scar any day."

I touch my head. I forget the scar is even there sometimes, forget my bald head and the things they stuck in me at the hospital, forget that piece of paper in Martha's office that said they were testing Alice and me. But I shouldn't. Because all these things are confirmation that I'm different. And maybe that's why they're after me. After me, and now after Smitty.

"I don't remember much about the first couple of weeks at the shelter, I was out of it a lot." His face is glowing in the morning sun. "Your mum took care of me, then she was gone. Then she came back and told me to wait for you, she had to go on ahead and sort things out."

"What things?" I say.

"Make a plan so we could escape Scotland, I suppose. She told me not to leave, not even to poke my head outside, whatever happened, until you or she came for me. So I hung out as long as I could." He shakes his head. "Do you know how mind-numbingly dull it is in an underground shelter on your own for days on end? What was I going to do?" He gives me a halfhearted wink. "There is a limit to how much self-abuse I can handle."

"How long did you last?" I gulp, and flush red. "In the shelter, I mean."

He raises an eyebrow. "Course you do. There were a few days where I really didn't know if it was night or day. But when the fever died down, I started counting the days. Two weeks of eating out of tins. Then the food started running low and I was having whole conversations with myself. After that, I reckoned I'd rather be out there with the hordes. I started going out, trying to see where I was. Spotted the men in black and a few zoms a couple of times, but always managed to stay hidden."

I watch a seagull fly into the light, imagining Smitty breaking out from his shelter. We both escaped our underground hell, and we found each other. That is the main thing.

"Did you see any of those Undead cows?"

He gives me a look. "You been hallucinating again, Roberta?"

"For real," I say. "And a goat." I shudder. "The goat was the worst, I had to —" I nearly say "shoot it," but then I remember the gun is my big secret. Smitty gives me a weird look, but as he does I'm distracted by the seagull again, as it swoops low — too low — and makes a swipe for Smitty's head with its huge claws. It's no seagull. It's big, dark, and evil-looking.

I run at him and push him out of the way at the last moment, and we both fall to the ground and he yelps, thinking I'm giving him a bit of rough-and-tumble for that last remark. For a brief moment we hold each other in our arms, and then the flying monster appears again, a blood-curdling scream in its throat while it tries to rip out ours.

"What the hell?" Smitty kicks up at it with a boot, sending it to the ground a few feet away from us. I spring to my feet and pull him up just in time for the thing to recover and make a run at us, wings flapping.

"What's going on?" Pete arrives at the top of the path with Russ, who doesn't ask but just acts, kicking the huge creature so that it tumbles away from us again. "Good lord, that's an Egyptian vulture."

"I don't care if it's Big Bird, we're out of here." Smitty grabs me and we all run down the path; Russ has found some rocks and is flinging them at the vulture with all of his might.

"Where did it come from?" I pant.

"Must be Edinburgh Zoo," Pete says as we reach the Jeep. "Vultures eat carrion. Dead things. Probably feasted on a zombie. I wouldn't be surprised if many of the animals have escaped and eaten infected flesh."

"Like what?" I say.

Pete shrugs. "Lions, tigers, and bears, oh my!"

"Wonderful." Smitty slams his door, and Russ flings himself into the front seat as the vulture makes a swoop at the roof of the Jeep. "Not only do we have humans live and dead to contend with, we're on safari with Zombie Simba, Timon, and Pumbaa? That's the Circle of Life all right."

Pete revs the engine, reverses down the track at speed until he finds a place to turn, and then we zoom downhill, the vulture circling now, waiting for the next victims.

19

"Pete, mate," says Smitty, a jovial tone in his voice, "remind me exactly why we're heading *into* the city. Anyone would think you're leading us to our certain death."

There are Undead rats running down the streets, hideous and screeching and fighting one another. The bigger ones chomp on the smaller ones, who scream, their guts spilling out onto the road before being greedily gobbled by their friends. Makes you want to keep your hands and feet inside the moving vehicle at all times.

"We're really *not* going into the city," Pete says, his hands gripping the wheel. "It's just the fastest route out of town is the start of the A1 — I remember it from the numerous times we've driven here with my family — and I'm following the signs, OK?" He turns round, and I see the veins standing up at his temples, the muscle in his neck. "Look, the alternative is I fanny around trying to make my own way there, and to be frank, I don't know where I'm going."

"Calm down, Pikachu." Smitty puts a reassuring paw on his shoulder.

"He's doing a great job," Russ says. "So far, no crazies. And we trust him. Just let's not dawdle, Pete, eh?"

Pete looks like he's going to cry, but nods and takes a deep breath.

We head up the wide, dark street. Every flicker of a streetlamp, every shadow cast across a storefront makes us jump. It's so damn eerie. But at least the zombie rats have gone. Maybe the zombie cats ate 'em.

The road is littered with debris; some we can push out of the way with the Jeep, some we have to drive around. A couple of times we even have to run out onto the road to pull a bunch of tire-bursting trash out of the way so that we can continue. Every car is burnt-out, useless. It's a mess.

A lot can happen in six weeks; it doesn't take long for people to turn criminal. As we get farther into the city center, all the stores have smashed windows and look like they've been looted. Food shops and restaurants — yeah, I can see why — but also electrical stores and jewelers. Makes no sense to me. And this being Edinburgh — cashmere shops have been raided, places that sell tartan, and a fudge kitchen. OK, I get the last one. It's calories. But, really, you're telling me that the apocalypse strikes, and you take the opportunity to get that wide-screen you've been jonesing after or a pashmina or a kilt? People are friggin' weird.

"Whoa!" Russ puts a hand up. "Slow down."

In front of us is a pile of cars in the middle of the road. Not just left there or crashed or whatever, but deliberately placed. We crawl closer. There is a park bench on the pile, too. Some wheelie trash cans. A supermarket cart.

Smitty whistles. "It's a barricade."

Instinctively we all glance behind us. I look out of my window to the side — on the street there's a church to my left, and a mixture of houses and shops and offices along the rest of the street.

"History repeating," Pete murmurs to himself.

"Whazzat?" I know he wants to share.

"In plague times, hundreds of years ago, the stories go that they closed this area off. They bricked up the streets and wouldn't let anyone in or out. Left the infected run mad and die within the city walls."

"Nice," Smitty says. "And effective. Let them go unfed, unless they want to take a bite out of one another. Leave them to hunger and die."

The Jeep is dawdling. I do not like this scene.

"Pete, make a *U*. Now," I urge.

Pete stops and cranks the gear stick.

"Hang on," Russ says. "Do you reckon there are survivors here? If this was an army barricade it wouldn't be a bunch of crap on the road, it would be a proper barrier."

"Yeah, but why would survivors build a barricade?" I say to him. "Think about it. They're either keeping zoms away, or they're stopping other survivors — and not to shake their hands and give 'em a cup of tea. This could be a trap."

Pete nods, and he's about to make the turn when I see a figure step out into the road. My hand shoots out to stop Pete. The four of us sit there in silence as the figure walks slowly toward us. It's a young woman, I think. It's too shadowy to see her face, and she's wearing jeans and a jacket and some kind of headgear. She's skinny, but she's female-shaped.

"Zom?" Russ whispers.

"Doesn't look that way," Smitty says. "Pete. Get ready to move, bro."

As she gets closer, there's another movement by the barricade. This one is unmistakable. Pure zom. Short and stocky. Bent almost double, stumbling, clothes ripped. And it's seen her or seen us, because it's heading this way.

"Oh, dear," says Pete. "You see it?"

"Course I do," I say. And then there's another movement. Another figure — another male — this time a tall teen with straggly hair, dragging a leg, stumbling.

"One more!" Russ cries.

"We're going," Smitty says. "Pete!"

Pete flicks on the headlights.

The girl, blinded, holds up a hand to shade her eyes. She's not much older than us. Dark hair spilling out of a woolly beret.

Pete lowers the window. "Hurry!" he shouts. "They're behind you."

"Pete!" I lean over and try to get the window up. "Turn around. We don't know who she is."

He smacks my hand away. "You're going to leave her? To be eaten?"

Damn. He has such a great way of putting things.

"There are more . . ." Russ points to the barricade, where a couple of zombinos have appeared.

Whoever this girl is, she's got quite a following. And suddenly she realizes it. She turns, sees them, and starts running toward us. Waving her hands desperately.

"Keep the doors locked," I say.

"Bobby, no!" Pete starts, but he closes the window anyway, because anything running toward you has a tendency to make you do that. The girl reaches us and slams into the car, rounding the hood and slapping on the windshield, screaming.

"Help me! Let me in!"

Pete stays where he is. The girl starts to cry, tugging at Pete's door handle. Meanwhile, the Undead posse are fast covering the ground between them and all of us.

"Don't let her in, Pete." My Spidey Sense is firing off on all cylinders. This just ain't right. And when something smells off in this world, it's generally well dead and stinking to the heavens.

"She's going to die," he says, but I think we've convinced him. He's about to make the turn when someone runs out of the barricade. A smaller figure and moving fast. It's a boy, maybe nine years old. A live one. He dodges a couple of zoms, heading toward us, doing really well.

"Zac!" screams the girl. "You can make it."

And then, just as he's almost clear of the posse, he slips, and he's down.

"Zac!" the girl screams again, rushing to him.

"Oh, shit it." Smitty flings open his door and runs after her.

"Damn!" Russ opens his door, too. "Bobby" — he turns round to me — "stay here." And then he's gone.

Smitty and the girl seem to be struggling to help free the boy from something he's caught a leg in, while Russ circles them, waiting for the zoms to descend. Then the girl does something weird. She leaves the boy, runs up to our car, and beckons for Pete to get out. Some of the zoms decide to follow her. Flummoxed, Pete opens his door.

"Get out," she shouts at him. "We need your help."

Pete bends low to pick up a piece of wood, preparing himself to hit the nearest zom. The girl grabs him.

"Don't try, they're strong ones," she says. "Just save my brother."

Pete nods and takes off, and the girl slips into the driver's seat.

I look at her. "What are you doing?"

She looks me up and down, and speaks with a quiet but firm voice. "Get out."

"Excuse me?"

She raises an eyebrow. "You heard me. Get out."

"But . . ." I gesticulate toward the monsters. And then they do an even weirder thing. They stop moaning. They straighten up. They start to laugh, and they leg it toward us.

And suddenly, the boy who was so very trapped a moment ago is sprinting back to the Jeep.

I knew it. I frickin' knew it. And still I got duped.

"That's your cue to leave," the girl says to me calmly. I look at her and realize she's holding something in her hand. A shiny, pointy thing. Looks like something she'd use to break up ice. Or my face. "Get out now, or my friends will hurt you." She winks at me. "And so will I."

At that moment, the nearest "zom" flings open the door and pulls me out. I think about fighting them — they're only teens — but there're four of them, plus the girl and the little boy, and I can't take them all. Smitty, Russ, and Pete are running back to me, but they're going to be too late. The girl has already started the Jeep, and the kids are piling in.

Doors slam, and I jump out of the way of the Jeep as it turns with a screech.

"We're survivors like you," yells Pete at them. "We're all in the same boat."

The girl lowers her window and shakes her head. "Ner, we're not in the same boat. We're in the car, and you are walking." With that, the boy leans over and blows us a raspberry, and the Jeep powers off down the road.

"Bloody kids," splutters Smitty.

"We would have done the same," Russ says.

I turn to him, eyes blazing. "We would not!"

"You wanted me to drive off and leave the girl," Pete says to me accusingly.

"I was only trying to protect us," I shout at him. "I knew something was off!"

I *could* have protected us. I have my gun. As soon as I'd seen that barricade I'd remembered it, had even put my hand on it. But what was I going to do, shoot a bunch of kids like us in cold blood?

"Shit," says Pete. "Shit and shit and shit!" He throws himself down on the cold, wet street and has a little gurning fit. Russ kicks a trash can. Only Smitty and I stand silent, looking into the distance where the Jeep has gone.

"Jesus," Smitty mutters. "Oh, sweet Jesus Christ."

"I know," I answer. "I cannot believe they took our ride."

"Forget about the car," he says. "They took Alice."

He runs, flat out and furious, after the Jeep.

I wait for a minute to pick my jaw off the floor, and then I run, too, just as the Jeep turns down a steep side alley. We follow, not caring about the slippery ground or the prospect of Undead joining the chase. Russ and Pete have realized what's going on and they run after us. As the Jeep reaches the bottom of the alley and is forced to make a sharp turn, we gain on it, and I can see the kids in the back flipping us the bird and sticking their tongues out. They think they've got us beat, but I'm counting on all the detritus littering the road to slow them down some.

The hill gets steeper, and now with added cobbles.

"We can cut through — climb over," Russ shouts, pointing to a barricade to our right. "They're heading down the other side of the hill."

We race to the barricade. I can see what he means. We can cut them off if we take the shortcut; it's a quicker route on foot.

"What if this is keeping the zoms out?" Pete shouts as we start to climb.

"I think that's the point," I shout back.

Pete shakes his head. "No! We haven't seen any for streets and streets. Maybe they're all on the other side."

As we reach the top, we see a giant zombie playpen below, filled with lumbering bodies. *Gah.*

They see us and flood toward the barricade, roaring. Some are able to climb the first few feet up, using each other for support, looking for the best route, working it out. They reach up to us, anger on their faces, screaming, spitting, popping sinew, and wrenching muscle to try and get to us.

Smitty shakes his head, shouting above the cacophony. "What happened to them?"

"Told you," I say. "They're clever now. And wicked hungry."

But there are thick rolls of barbed wire halfway up the barricade, and this proves their downfall. Not that the barbs deter them, but they simply get caught in the wire and stick there, unable to climb any farther, thrashing in frustration, moldy old fish caught in a net.

Russ is already down and shouting for us to follow him. We go the long way, pedaling feet down the narrow road, not daring to think about how much distance the Jeep will have gained on us by now. But as we round the corner, the road widens and we see it.

Weirdly, it is coming toward us.

We skid to a halt; the surprise on our faces is matched by the look on the faces of the kids in the Jeep. They look shocked out of their lives and terrified. Now I can hear a familiar thundering noise, and I watch as a black shadow swings round a tall building.

The helicopter is back.

20

The helicopter swoops down to a few feet away from the car.

Russ pulls me back into a shop doorway, and Smitty and Pete duck into their own alcove a few doors down.

No mystery why the kids look so spooked. The helicopter is firing at them. And it doesn't take long for the gunman to find his mark. A tire explodes, and the Jeep slides, colliding with a lamppost. The helicopter lands, throwing dust and litter into the air, and two men in black jump down and make toward the Jeep and its dazed passengers.

"Come on," I urge Russ. "We've got to get Alice."

Russ holds me tight from behind, squashing the pack on my back, his arms flattening mine to my sides.

"What are you doing?" I twist my head round, trying to look him in the face.

"Stay still," he rasps at me. "We wait here until they've all gone."

"Like hell we do!" My voice rises, and he slips a hand across my mouth.

"Bobby," he says, all too calmly, "you need to do what I say, or you'll regret it. Don't you know that by now?" His voice sends chills through me, even though he's just being macho. "Don't you know how precious you are?" OK, now he really is being weird.

I try to look down the street for Smitty, willing him to know something's wrong. But I can't see him. I dig my heels in and push backward on Russ, throwing him off balance for a split second. He takes a step back, and we clatter through the door of the shop and hit the floor.

Instantly I can smell them.

I leap to my feet, untangled from Russ, who looks as if he's hurt himself in the fall.

Around us are maybe a dozen zoms. We've fallen into a bookshop, depressingly untouched in the rioting. The Undead stand there staring. They're all adults — preserved, almost pristine compared to their outside cousins. Sure, hair is mussed, blood oozing, and flesh sliding, but these guys have been sheltered from the months of relentless wet.

A woman holds her hands out to me and tries an unpracticed moan; she has a barely marked tweed coat. I freeze, hardly daring to breathe, the air is so thick with the odor of rotting flesh. Behind her, a man stumbles forward, sporting a shirt and tie with minimal spatter. They look surprised to see us, and as if they've forgotten what to do. But it's not going to take long for them to remember. Somebody locked these guys in here weeks ago, they've read everything they're ever going to need, and they want out. More appear around the stacks, and begin to stagger toward us, hungry.

For a second I think I'm going to leave Russ lying there, but in spite of that weird little death cuddle we just had in the alcove, I can't do it. As the tweed-coated lady lurches toward us, I pull him to his feet and we sprint out of the store and into the street.

The men in black are in the process of pulling kids out of the Jeep; they all start as they see us. For a moment I catch sight of Alice's stricken eyes peering out over Smitty's leather jacket from the back. At least she's awake. I think that's a good thing.

Then our bookworms follow us out into the open.

Instinct tells me to run toward the Jeep, and the zoms follow. Instantly the men leap into action, firing on the Undead. Kids spill in every direction, and in the chaos I fling open the back door and offer a hand to Alice.

"Who are all these people?" she spits at me, like I've invited everyone round for a barbeque. "And where the hell are we?"

OK, so last time she had her eyes open she was falling off a hill in a forest, but I haven't got time to fill her in. "Can you walk?" I say.

"What?" She rolls her eyes, and swings her legs to the ground. "Of course I can — oof!" She tries to stand, crumples, and is caught by Smitty, who has appeared beside me as if in a puff of magician's smoke. "You!" Alice looks up at him. "About time you turned up!"

"Thanks!" He takes a second to free his leather jacket from Alice's clutches, and then loads her up piggyback-style and runs for the alleyway.

The men still fire on the zombies, and another has rounded up two of the kids and is taking them back to the helicopter.

"No, not them, you morons!" shouts the man in the shiny balaclava to the soldiers. "The others!" *Uh-oh.* Time to scarper.

We duck down the alleyway, which opens up onto a wide road leading over a bridge.

"Where are we going?" I shout at Smitty.

"Out of town," he replies. As we pelt across the bridge, I look down. *Oh god.* This bridge is not over water, there are simply streets below us, and a train track. And there they all are. All the zoms we could see moving from Arthur's Seat. Hundreds of them, shoulder to shoulder, groaning and shuffling and waiting for their breakfast. Their clothes every shade of gray through brown, rotting into their fetid flesh, all wet from weeks of constant rain. This is where they've been all this time, all the Edinburgers.

And then I hear a pulsing beat from the brightening skies. The helicopter is airborne again, already sweeping over the city, looking for us.

I tear my eyes away and keep running. Ahead of us is a huge barricade. It's the biggest yet, it dwarfs the one we just climbed. It looks like a professional job — wire fencing — but one that failed and has been reinforced with all the usual barricade stuff: cars, furniture, bits of tree. It must be fifteen or twenty feet high, and pretty wide from the looks of things. I'm not sure that we're getting over it easily.

Smitty doesn't think so, either, apparently, because just before we get there, he unloads Alice, leans her against the wall, and swings a leg over the side of the bridge in an act of crazy. Is he going to jump off? Into that sea of monsters?

"We have to climb down," he shouts at me.

I smack into the wall beside Alice and peer over it, my head spinning. There's a drop to a vast frosted glass roof below — nothing that will kill, but enough to break an ankle or two. Thankfully there are ledges in the stone, somewhere to put my reluctant feet.

"We can make it onto that roof," Smitty cries.

Yeah. As long as we don't slip. Because street level is one hell of a drop.

I swing a leg over, and Smitty grabs the back of my jacket like a mother cat snagging her kitten. The stone is slippery and freezing cold. I cling to the top of the wall with cold fingers and feel for the ledge below with the first foot. I have it. I ease both feet down, and then Smitty lets go and I'm my own.

From above, I hear the others helping Alice. I feel my way down the side of the bridge, and drop carefully onto the roof.

Alice is half thrown down past me, and with a scramble and a tumble of arms and legs, Smitty, Russ, and Pete follow. The rotting faces below us smack their chops in delight; above the helicopter lands on the bridge.

"Which way now?" I shout to Smitty.

He takes off over the roof at speed, which is hard to do, because as well as being slippy, it's zigzaggy; lots of little peaks and troughs, just high enough to be difficult to scale on one side, then slide down the next. We push, pull, and cheerlead each other along, following Smitty. There are sections where the glass is clear, and I look down below. We're on the railway station roof; I can clearly see the tracks and platforms. And also the zombie commuters, wearing ragged suits and clutching long-dead phones, waiting for trains that will never come. I really hope that Smitty has a plan he wants to hurry up and share, and I really, really hope this glass doesn't break in the meantime.

There's a *thump* somewhere not far behind; two soldiers hit the roof. They set off toward us, but they're not as nimble, and they don't help each other like we do. There's a lesson for you: Teamwork wins.

I hear a yell.

My head whips round to see, and I gasp; one of the soldiers is hanging, his torso on the edge of the roof, his legs dangling in the air. The zoms are below, waiting. Everyone stops to watch, we can't not. If anyone has the upper body strength to save the situation, it's this guy. But he's fighting a lost cause, and we all know it — even he knows it. He tries to use his hands like suckers to pull himself up on the slick glass, but there's nothing to hang on to. Every effort makes him slip another few inches. His mouth stretches across his face in a gnarl of desperation and sheer bloody effort.

"Grab my hands!" the second soldier cries, and he's sliding headfirst down the sloping roof, reaching for his fallen comrade. But just as the dangling soldier looks up at his would-be rescuer, his friend slap-bangs into him, and the two of them fall off the roof and land with a dull *thud* somewhere below. The noise of the groans rises, and then there's the screaming. So many bodies down there. I can't see, and I'm glad I can't, because there will be ripping flesh, teeth scraping bone, and guzzling. Eaten alive. "Here!" Smitty has moved. He's beckoning frantically, and we wake up from our nightmare and get moving again. Above us, the copter moves off. Are they going to land somewhere, catch us on foot? No time to worry. Smitty's by a window within the glass, a hatch that somehow he's managed to open. I look through the opening and into the train station, with its arrivals board and coffee shops and platforms. By me, at the ceiling, I spot a network of metal beams leading to the walkway. *Oh, nuts.* Just as I think things can't get any worse. He's expecting us to go all Cirque du Soleil across the ceiling.

He points to a walkway, down and to our right. "Just walk along that beam and jump down to it, it'll be easy."

I try not to let my nerves show as I ease myself onto the beam.

"Meet there." He points to the bridge over the tracks directly beneath us. "You'll be safe. Wait for me."

"Why?" Russ says. "Where are you going?"

Smitty doesn't reply, but winks and disappears off across the glass roof again.

"Great." I cling to the hatch, half in, half out.

"I wish I'd stayed unconscious," Alice bleats beside me.

"All the same, I'd seriously like to get off this roof," Pete spits at her. "So move your behind, Alice."

"Fine," she says, and braves the hatch first, shimmying across the metal beam toward the walkway. Smitty was right, this is easier than you'd think, provided you have a concussion and can't grasp the mortal danger of the situation.

Pete's close behind, and then Russ beckons for me to go next. I frown at him; I haven't forgotten how he acted in the doorway. That was just wrong. And kind of weird. But I go ahead anyway, thinking if we make it out of this one, I'll question him later.

Alice leads the way to the walkway, and then we run, skibbling down steps, then up a different set of steps onto the bridge. The zoms on the platform check our movement, of course, and start to groan with excitement.

"Where's Smitty?" yells Alice.

"He better get here soon." Russ is looking down the other end of the bridge. A dribble of monsters is heading our way. They must have spent the last few weeks honing their step-climbing skills.

"Typical." Alice sighs. "Bloody typical."

I follow her gaze. There's a small train moving very slowly along the tracks toward us. It's one of those little local commuter rail–type ones, in cheery fried-egg yellow.

And there in the front cab, waving at us from the window, is a very happy Smitty.

"Good grief," Pete mutters. "He's driving the train."

Smitty is gesticulating. Making walking fingers at us. Then the walking fingers jump off something.

"He's expecting us to jump onto the roof of the train," Russ says.

"Totally," I reply.

"Jesus Take the Wheel," Alice says. "I am not leaping onto a speeding train."

"It's not exactly speeding," Pete says.

"Go on, then!" Alice shouts at him. "Fling your skinny malinky-dink self down there, see how you enjoy it!"

The train is approaching. As are our Undead friends. I climb over the railing.

"You're not really doing this?" Alice looks at me disapprovingly.

"No choice," Pete answers for me, and joins me over the railing. "Come on." He holds out a hand to her, and she looks this way and that, taking in the zoms, the train, everything. She takes his hand, but then changes her mind and snatches it away again violently.

"It's crazy!" she yells.

With the ferocity of her movement, Pete slips. I shoot out a hand, but it's too late.

He falls backward off the bridge.

His timing is excellent; he lands with a smack on the slow-rolling train, which has just arrived below us.

But then he doesn't move.

We fling ourselves to the other side of the bridge and look down at the train below — a surreal moment when we all take a time-out to watch him, carried by the trundling train, splayed on the roof below. Even the zoms pause to watch.

And then he's up, springing to his feet as if surprised to find himself still alive. He's winded, can't speak, his eyes bulging out of his face with the strain of trying to breathe again. He staggers to keep on his feet, because even though the train is moving slowly, it's still moving. As he drops to his knees to find his breath and his balance, it suddenly occurs to me that he's the lucky one. The Undead are moving again, moving toward us — from either side they come, and they're not letting up.

"Gumpf!" Pete cries, his eyes panicked, an arm outstretched to us on the bridge. At first I think he's crying in desperation because he's being carried away, but just as he regains his wind and gives the shout-out another try, I realize what he's suggesting. "Jump!"

"Not on your nelly," spits Alice.

"Yes." Russ clambers over the rail. "He did it, we all can."

"He didn't jump, he fell," Alice yells at him, but she's already sizing up the jump. We all are.

"It's nothing, Alice," Russ calls. "Pete didn't even hurt himself!"

Pete, currently bent over except for his pale and wretched face, might take issue with that. But he sure wants us to join him.

"Hurry! It's speeding up."

Oh, great. Smitty put his foot down and Thomas the Tank Engine is about to become the Flying Scotsman. Truth is, regardless of that, we don't have time to think this over. Zombies are making their entrance onto the bridge, stage right and stage left. Russ and Alice clamber over and join me on the other side of the railing, and we're all going to make the leap.

Russ goes first, an athletic bound into the air, landing in an acrobatic squat. He runs lightly down the moving train, then walks on the spot directly under us, like this is just another workout.

"I'll catch you."

I turn to Alice. "Come on, we'll go together." I hold out a hand, nodding.

"Get your filthy paw away from me!" she screams. "Don't trust you an inch."

I glance up at the bridge; they're nearly on us.

"Do you trust them more?" I shout back. "Because if you do, then totally, hang out here and have a party for all I care!"

The first zombie roars at us from above, the fish smell hitting me like the worst kind of putrid sock. Sod Alice, this train is leaving and I'm going to be on it. Who is she kidding? She's going to either jump or fall off after me, and I want to be out of the way so she doesn't break my skull when she does. I ready myself for the leap.

"Bobby!" Russ is pointing frantically at the end of the train. The end of the train, which is fast approaching the bridge. "You have to jump now."

I lower myself slightly, take a breath, and —

"Help me," Alice whimpers. "Please."

"You got it." I nod, and take her hand. "After three. One, two —"

"Aargh!" Alice falls before I finish, and takes me with her. As our feet hit the train's roof, her hand is wrenched from mine and we both fall over backward, not able to stick the landing. I make the perfect backward roll and end up on my hands and knees. Alice is somewhere behind me. I turn to look — and she's gone.

The end of the final carriage is all I see as we leave the bridge behind, the zombies waving us off from above.

21

"Aliiiiice!"

I scrabble toward the edge, hoping to see her pale pink fingernails clinging on. But they aren't there. I hardly dare look down. But I make myself.

There she is, below, lying on her side on the little kind of mesh iron balcony that sticks out of the back of the train. She's lying there, and she's groaning, arms wrapped around herself in a hug, rocking as the train judders along, picking up speed.

The cold rush of air makes my head hurt. I have to move — it's going to get drafty up here soon. "Hang in there, Alice!" I scream. I look for some way to get down to her, and I spot the ladder.

In a second I'm down there and she's swearing at me for stepping on her; there's not exactly much room to move. "You're doing OK, then," I growl as I pull her into a sitting position.

"Did I ever mention how much I hate school trips?" she splutters out at me. "I never thought I'd miss the nice, cozy bus." She looks down behind us. "Ew, gross. Smitty is running them over."

The train tracks run red. Every now and then we judder as we hit bodies. They must be pretty mushy, they're not putting up much resistance.

There are bits of zom on the track; some still moving, some decapitated. He's just mown them over. Pretty good, really. You can do that if you're driving a train. I look around. We'll be clearing the station in a minute. I remember the horde outside. We'd better get inside this train before it gets seriously busy around here.

"Bobby!" It's Russ from above. "You both all right?"

I nod as Pete appears on the roof, too. "We'll live. But let's not do that again, huh?"

Russ is suddenly down the ladder with us, squashed together. He puts an arm around me and gives me a sudden squeeze, on the charm offensive. "I thought it was awesome." His face is beaming. *Wow.* He really did love it. "How often do you get to jump onto a moving train?"

"Luckily not very often." Alice uses me to lever herself upright. Once she's up, she transfers her arms around Russ, effectively cutting him off from me. Which is totally fine by me. The train speeds up a gear, jostling us against one another. "Door." She points behind us. "Now can we go inside, please?"

Russ and Alice go in. I wait for Pete to come down off the roof.

"You OK?" I look at him. His goggles are around his neck and he's breathing kind of heavy. He nods at me.

"Guess we solved our transport problem."

I pull a face. "Guess we did." I gesture for him to lead the way into the train. "Smitty's got skills."

"And passengers." Pete's brow is crinkled. At first I think he means us, but then I look where he's looking. There, through the glass door at the end of the compartment we've just entered, are the passengers in question.

Oh, fudmukker. Zoms on a Train.

I walk slowly down the corridor to them, not getting too close, because we all know what happens if you get too close. The nearest zom is squashed against the glass door, one bloodied hand slapping, a hat on askew, a little machine slung casually around his shoulder.

"It's the conductor," calls Alice, behind me. "I hope we all remembered our tickets."

Behind him, there are more — five or six? Hard to say how many, but enough to be a problem. I sigh inwardly.

Alice doesn't do inward sighs. "God!" she harrumphs. "Didn't he think to check the stupid train before he went full steam ahead? That is so typically Smitty."

"OK, so this is fine," Pete gabbles. "We simply walk on the roof past that carriage, then climb down and uncouple the final two carriages. The Undead will be left behind on the tracks, and we are safe."

"And you're down with 'uncoupling,' Pete?" I shoot him a look. "Do it all the time?"

He shrugs. "How hard can it be? Smitty has apparently learned to operate a train."

We go out into the fresh air again, amid Alice's protests. She's all leaden legs and green around the gills, and I feel her pain. We're leaving the station behind, and this is quite a way to see Edinburgh and its occupants. Suddenly there are so many of them — every street I look down, they're there, and on the tracks, and looking out of doorways. It's like Zombie Town proper. I'm über-grateful we're on the train; we never would have made it out on foot.

"It's getting slippery up here." Russ is first to hit the roof, and yes, it's raining again. Not a full-on torrent, but the kind of soaking, fine drizzle that the UK specializes in. Makes everything kind of slimy. I grab the ladder and carefully pull myself up after Alice, who, despite her protests, has clearly decided she doesn't want to get left behind.

The train isn't exactly going flat out, but it jiggles from side to side as it goes, which means the safest way to traverse the roof is kind of like a zombie stagger: feet spaced wide, arms held up in front, hands outstretched and ready to grab. Except if we're grabbing anything, it's going to be a piece of roof as we fall. Or each other. Russ reaches the end of the first carriage, and then drops to his knees.

"It's no good, the carriages aren't separate," he shouts back at us. "We can't undo them."

As I get closer I see what he means; the train is segmented so that it can go around bends in the track, and there are individual carriages separated by internal doors. There probably is some way of adding or subtracting carriages, but not one that four teenagers on a rainy roof can figure out or execute.

"What now?" Pete shouts.

"We have to go back inside, we can't stay here," Alice whines.

"We need to warn Smitty." I start zombie-ing up the train again.

"And how do we do that?" Alice yells after me.

I have no idea, but we can't all ride this train together. Smitty clearly doesn't know about his stowaways, and they could be sneaking up on him. Then we'll be missing a driver. That would be unthinkable — and I'm not just being sentimental. The only thing worse than being on a train with zombies is being on a runaway train with zombies.

By the time I get to the front of the train, I'm crawling. Smitty's clearly loving the need for speed. We're coming out of the city, and the view would be pretty damn impressive if I wasn't so frightened of falling to my death. Vivid green hills, and I can see the sea, the fog lingering over the water. It's on my left; as we all know, my geography pretty much stinks, but I think that means we're going south, so at least that's something. I flatten myself against the roof of the train and edge forward.

"What are you going to do?" Russ has caught up.

I answer him by reaching down and slapping the windshield below with my hands. Russ joins me. Then Alice is at my other side, and we're all slapping away, trying to alert Smitty to let him know we're here.

The train speeds up. A bit. Then a lot.

"He thinks we're the friggin' monsters!" Alice screams.

Damn, she's right. He's speeding up to try and shake us off. I wiggle forward on my belly.

"Keep tight hold of my legs!" I shout at the others, trying to banish thoughts of the soldiers slipping off that glass roof to the horror below.

"Oh my god, don't do it!" Alice flops down on my right leg anyway. *Ow.*

Russ grabs my left leg, and I feel the pressure of my ankles being held. I pull myself forward until I'm hanging upside down over the front of the train, looking through the windshield. It's surprisingly secure, the force of the train moving forward pinning me there like a bug. And there's Smitty, leaning forward and peering up at me, his hand resting on a lever, his expression barely concealed panic.

"It's us! Slow down!" I slap the window some more, perhaps a little too much, because he jolts upright and the train suddenly lurches forward faster. "Stop the train!" I shout. "We can't get in."

He gets control over his face and the train, and we slow right down. But he clearly can't hear exactly what I'm saying, because we're not stopping.

"Stop the train!" I scream. "Stop it!" I slice a hand across my neck. He gets the message, I hear the brakes screech below us, and I'm pulled up roughly from behind.

"What are you doing?" Alice says as I clamber back onto the roof. "We can't stop here. Look at them!"

I hadn't exactly been scoping out our surroundings as I was doing my Spider-Man routine. But now I see where we're at. Out of the city, yes, and surrounded by fields. But in those fields — well, I can only describe it as the Nightmare Highland Games. Zombies in kilts stumbling around a soggy field. And now I know what that screeching noise was — not the brakes on the train, but bagpipes. These zombies are playing for us, wheezing and squeezing what has to be the weirdest instrument in the world at the best of times. It sounds like someone is torturing donkeys.

"That's quite impressive." Pete squints into the distance. "And I do believe one of them is tossing a caber."

"And I do believe the rest of them are coming this way," Russ yells. "No time to lose!" As the train draws to a halt, he slithers down off the train, and lands on the gravel below with a *crunch* and a bit of a yelp, then holds his hands up to help us. There are rungs down one side, and we use 'em. The driver's door opens, Smitty offers a hand up, and one by one we are safe in the cab.

"Why didn't you go in the door at the back?" Smitty fiddles with the lever and tries to start us up again.

"We did," I say, "but we had company. Didn't you think to check you didn't have any zoms on board before you picked this train?" I ease the door to the carriage open a crack. "Looks like this carriage is clear, and the next, but it's hard to tell."

Russ pats me on the shoulder. "Leave it up to me, I'll check." Alice smiles at him as he strides off into the carriage.

"He's handy to have around, isn't he?" Smitty snarks. "So I had some easy riders? Oops." He presses some buttons on the dashboard. "It's not like I had hundreds of trains to choose from."

"Yeah. How come you can drive a train, you loser?" Alice snarls at him.

"Oh how I've missed you, Malice, let me count the ways . . ." He goes to tally on his fingers, then makes an *O* with finger and thumb. "That'll be none." He busies himself with the train controls again; we're not moving yet. "I turned a key, pushed a lever, pressed a pedal. Ran a few of them over while I was working it out, but that's no bad thing."

"Well, can you get a move on now?" Alice points out the window, and we see the line of kilts staggering out onto the track.

"Hopefully," Smitty says. "Might have been a fluke, me starting this thing last time." He cranks something, and the engine starts up, and the train moves forward slowly. We all breathe a sigh of relief. "Sorted." He leans back and puts his feet up on the dashboard as we slowly squish a hairy man with a huge sporran.

Russ bursts through the door, making us all jump.

"They're only in the one carriage, the second to last one, where we saw them. We've got two clear carriages between them and us here, and I'm pretty sure we can secure the door if someone gives me a hand. I can detach one of the seats and wedge it in front."

"I'm in," Pete says.

Alice watches them go, then looks at us, rolls her eyes, and schleps out of the door with a groan.

Smitty looks at me. I look back. His eyes are different: older, sadder, but they still have the twinkle. His face breaks into a weary smile and he winks at me.

"Alone again, Roberta." He affects my accent. "Wanna make out?"

22

I roll my eyes. I know it's a lame, Alice kinda thing to do, but I have no witty comeback, so it'll have to do until I dredge one up.

Smitty sighs, leans back in his chair, and sticks his feet up on the dashboard again, where I'm perching.

"So Alice is after Russ, then?"

"Huh?"

"You know." He makes some gross pelvic-thrusting movement.

"No!" I shout, unnecessarily loudly. "God." I shake my head. "Well, she might be. But I don't think he's that interested. He didn't seem to be too bothered when she went for a ride with the teens from hell."

Smitty laughs, overly casual. "So he wants to get into *your* pants, then?"

"Smitty!" I practically choke. "No! What is wrong with you?"

"What is wrong with *you*?" Smitty chuckles at me. "He seems all right for a meathead. You should go get you some, Bob."

"Shut up." I don't know what else to say. I can't believe tears are pricking at my eyes. *What's up with that?* I turn away and look out the window so that Smitty can't see my face reddening. This is so not how I'd pictured the big reunion. He obviously doesn't care who I lust over, and he certainly doesn't think it will be him. Which means he couldn't give a damn about me like that. "Truth is, I don't even know if . . . I trust Russ."

"No?" Smitty looks up. "Why not?"

Focus, focus. It is so not about my love life. I stare out at the sodden countryside, feeling utterly miserable.

"He stopped me from running out into the street and saving Alice." I bite my lip. It sounds like nothing now that I say it out loud. "Held on to me."

Smitty whistles and laughs. "Bet he did, Roberta. He's the protective type, you should like that." He twiddles a bit of hair girlishly. "Did he cop a feel?"

"God! *God!*" Still that witty comeback is elusive. And I've nowhere left to go on the indignation scale. I turn away from him and concentrate on the outside instead.

We're trundling along at a good pace now, leaving behind the McZoms in the field. The rhythm of the train is vaguely comforting, and my face cools. In the distance, the fog hangs ominously over the sea. It will come back; it does that. We don't have too much time, and I need some questions answered. I clear my throat.

"You've never told us exactly what happened. After the crash."

Smitty raises his eyebrows. "You remember anything?"

"I remember you trying to help me." I look at him steadily. "And then I blacked out. When I came round, you had gone. There were just these men in black."

"Xanthro."

"Presumably. So you hid?"

"No!" His turn to get angry. "I went looking for something to get you out of the wreckage, get that crap off your legs and pull you free. We were in the dark, in the trees, there were bodies everywhere . . . some of those kids on the bus had already turned. I wandered into the woods, looked some more. And then suddenly I was out of it."

"You fainted?"

"No!" Angrier still. "Your mum coshed me. On the back of the head with a branch."

"She did?" I suppress a laugh. Although I can believe she did it. She's all for extreme measures. And let's face it, I've been tempted to knock him out a few times, too.

"When I woke up, we were in a hut in the woods." He plays with some lever on the dashboard. "I don't know how long I'd been out. It was still dark outside. Your mum left me there — for a day, I think. I was a mess: I had a fever, my legs were all screwed from the bites. She came back; she must have given me something for the pain. And she'd brought" — his face wrinkles at the memory — "a needle and thread." He pulls up one leg of his jeans. "She sewed me up."

I look. His leg is a real horror show. I have no idea how he's been able to move at all, let alone run. It looks like he's had a fight with a great white shark and been patched up by Dr. Frankenstein. Two huge, curved, jagged lines run around both sides of his white calf. There are purplish-red raw places where I guess the skin wouldn't quite stretch over. It looks wet to the touch. And there's a smell — a smell I've been aware of for a while, but only now can I see the source. Yellow stuff oozes from the stitch marks. It is not a good scene.

"Sexy, eh?" He smiles. "I think it must have stung a little when she stuck the needle in. Good thing now is that I seem to have lost most of my nerve endings. Reckon I'm going Zombie Hybrid?"

I don't know what to say.

"I'm still waiting for my superpowers to kick in." He brightens. "She sewed me up, then we shipped out. We went to the shelter. I was unconscious most of the time; she was there, then she was gone. I do remember her saying your name, saying you'd be coming."

I give a low laugh. "That was optimistic of her."

Smitty looks at me. "She wouldn't have just left you, Bob."

"Yep. Well, she did." I shake my head. "And guess who she sent to help us?" I don't wait for him to answer. "Grace."

"What?" Smitty shouts. "Blondie, from the castle?" His face clouds as he thinks. "Shiznuts. That makes total sense. When we went to the bunker, we went on a Ski-Doo with a sled. Remember the ones at the castle? She must have met Grace there." He shakes his head. "Why on earth would she trust her to get you out? And why would she think you'd trust her?"

"Apparently it was her only option."

"And what happened to our Gracie?"

"Xanthro shot her," I said. "When we were escaping. They took her down." My voice cracks a little. "Right in front of us."

Smitty sucks air through his teeth and looks off down the track. "That sucks for her."

"Xanthro is divided. We heard the soldiers in the hospital say as much. Grace told us it only makes them more dangerous. So far, I've got to agree. Smitty . . ." I can't hold back any longer. "Why didn't my mum come for me herself? Why did she leave me there? In the middle of Xanthro territory? Why didn't she come and save me?" I can't prevent the sob. God, I hate it, but I can't help one teeny, tiny, pathetic sob from escaping. "All this time I've been wondering the same thing, and it's been tearing me up inside. She left me. She saved you — she hid you, because you are valuable to her — and she left me to fend for myself."

Smitty looks at me, shocked, and the sorrow on his face makes my stomach churn.

"She told me you were a survivor," he says simply.

Suddenly the rain starts to pour, and the sound of it hitting the windshield makes us jump. Smitty flicks a couple of the switches until a wiper starts to sweep across the glass. We both watch it for a minute or two, and then he finally speaks.

"You know what, Bob? She told me she couldn't go back there. She said that if she tried to rescue you they'd know, and they'd kill you both."

"She did?"

"She did." He thinks about it. "She said you were far safer there than out here with her, and that she'd help you get out OK when the time was right."

"Really?" I try to smother the glint of hope in my heart. "But I wasn't safe." I pull out the piece of paper that I found in Martha's office, the one with my name and Alice's on it, and show it to Smitty. "Xanthro was testing Alice and me for something. I don't think they found anything with Alice, but on my medical chart they said I was some kind of carrier. I think that's why they've been after me all of this time. I think Mum knew it, too. So why risk me?" My head hurts thinking about it.

Smitty reads, shakes his head. "Better stick with me, kid. Mutants together."

I swing the conversation to a safer subject.

"Did you learn anything about the outside when you were with Mum?"

He shrugs. "Pieces. The infection spread really fast. A lot of people fled south, but then they shut off the border to England. The army was rounding survivors up for a while, but when it got too bad, they stopped the rescues." He shifts on the chair. "But that news is weeks old. Once your mum disappeared, so did my info. I figured I'd hang out for you for as long as I could, then see if I could find her." He glances at me. "See if I could remember where she told me she was going."

I almost choke. "You know where she is?"

"I didn't say that." He puts his hands up. "Here's the thing. She told me, but I kind of forgot."

I stare at him. "What?"

"She mentioned it. But I had a fever." He rolls his eyes when he sees the look on my face. "Don't freak on me! I was mainlining Osiris, rolling stoned down the rabbit hole. When the fog cleared, I couldn't remember what was real and what wasn't."

"You just told me a bunch of stuff you remembered. How come you didn't remember this?"

"Maybe she didn't even tell me, maybe I overheard her, I don't know." He kicks the dashboard. "I had the idea she'd been planning a way to get us out of Scotland." He pauses. "And I remember something about a . . . pixie."

"Huh!" I snort. "So she's at the end of the rainbow with the magic leprechaun?"

"It all feels like dreams." He sighs. "Look, I have this random vision of pixies . . . They were coming out of your mother's mouth."

I stare at him. "This is one of your perverted fantasies, isn't it?"

"I know it sounds ridiculous, but I'm serious." He reaches out a hand to my arm. "I'm sorry."

In my head, the light switch flips. I stand up from my spot on the dashboard, moving away. The tears begin to rise, and I fix my eyes on the track ahead, willing myself not to cry.

"She didn't say all that stuff about me being a survivor, did she?" I can't look at him. "She never said I was safer at the hospital. You just made that up to make me feel better."

He's silent.

"Thanks," I mumble, "for trying to help. I appreciate it."

We let the train rumble over the tracks for a few beats, the rain making me wish that this was all washed away, all this bad stuff, all the fog in our heads, all the dirt that has lodged in our brains. Smitty finally rises up out of his chair and turns to me.

"I looked for you, Bobby." Our eyes lock. "After I left the shelter, I went looking for the hospital. I couldn't find it, and I began to wonder if I'd made it up, if she'd even said you were in a hospital, or if it was anywhere nearby." He chances a hint of a smile. "I was hoping that I'd spot a town full of little people and that would be my screwed-up vision of mouth-pixies."

My stomach bounces up into my throat, and I feel the blood drain slowly from my face. Smitty's expression changes, the half smile replaced by an alarmed stare.

"What's wrong? What did I say?"

I quickly reach round into my backpack and pull out the postcard. There it is on the back of the picture, the words printed in tiny black letters.

I shove the postcard at Smitty. "Smitty, I take it all back," I say, my voice trembling. "Check out the name of the lighthouse."

He turns it over, reads the print.

"Elvenmouth Light. What — ?" Then he gets it. He shakes his head in disbelief. "This is my pixie fixation, isn't it?" He looks up at me. "She told me the name, and my medicine head turned it into that rubbish."

"So now all we need to do is find Elvenmouth," I say. "With a map . . . that we don't yet have."

"Still, this is huge, Bob." He's smiling again. "This is way better than a bunch of numbers we can only half remember." He twinkles at me. "And you can relax about me having some weird fantasy about your mum."

"What?" I blurt. "Why would I care about that?"

"Oh, I dunno, Bob." His eyes twinkle in that annoying way they have. "Perhaps 'cause you were jellybags?"

"Huh?" I almost shout. "As if —"

He reaches over suddenly and touches my collar. Then he slowly pulls me toward him, his eyes never leaving mine. I let him. Our faces are apart by an inch.

"Miss me?" He's smiling, but his eyes are deadly serious.

I can feel the heat coming off his body. I open my mouth to make some wise-guy retort, but I'm all out of clever. I want to kiss him. I hate that I want to. I hope he makes me do it anyway.

Pete bashes into the cab. "You've got to come and see this."

We spring apart guiltily.

"The zoms are still contained?" I shout unnecessarily loudly.

"Yes, yes," he says, waving his hand at us. "But come and see. I've worked out where your mum is."

He hustles us out of the driver's cab, then down to the bottom of the first carriage, jumping up and down like he's obviously dying to show us something. That always makes my heart sink. We pass Alice, who is gently snoring. As we approach, I can see Russ in the next carriage down. It looks like he's secured the door to the zom-carriage, and he's kind of pacing and checking on it. I knock on the glass and beckon him to join us.

He throws me a smile as he punches the button to open the connecting door.

"There are six of them in there," he reports. "The conductor, one youngish girl, but the rest are oldies. They definitely smell bad, but I don't think they'll be giving us any real trouble, so long as we keep the barricade up."

"So." Pete is practically hyperventilating from waiting on us. "A map of Britain." He taps the wall with a pencil. There, in a thin metal frame, is a grubby cardboard map with all the major cities and rail routes marked.

"Nailed it, Petey," drawls Smitty. "And are you going to write 'Here be Monsters' on it?"

Pete gives an impatient titter. "Glad to see you're just as witty as ever, Smitty." He draws an arrow to a point just west of Edinburgh. "I memorized the digits of Smitty's hiding place, and here're the numbers we remember from the second set of coordinates." He writes:

SMITTY = 55, 46, 17 NORTH, 03, 28, 18 WEST
BOBBY'S MUM = 55, 55, 00 NORTH, 00, ??, ?? WEST

He clears his throat. "So we can tell that the two locations aren't too far apart. But the difference is that the second location will be south a little, and then three degrees farther east," Pete says patiently.

"Yeah?" I say.

"Look." He draws a vertical line that goes through Edinburgh. "We know this is close to three degrees west. Then we move east a little . . ." He draws a vertical line that goes through London. "We know London is at zero degrees."

"We do?" Smitty says.

"Yes, because zero degrees is Greenwich, that's where it all starts." Pete flutters his white eyelashes at us. "Like the clock. Greenwich Mean Time, from when England was the center of the world."

"OK, I'll take your word for it." It rings a bell with me, but I'm not going to admit it.

"So in summary" — Pete knows he's talking to morons — "we know the location for the second coordinates is marginally south and significantly east of the shelter, at zero degrees." He traces a finger on the map. "And if you go a little bit south and across to zero degrees, where will you end up?"

I look at the map. Britain hunches over like a witch riding an invisible broomstick. Or possibly a prawn. But I can see what Pete means.

"Zero degrees would be in the sea," I say blankly.

"Yes!" He slaps the map. "Far out to sea. It's impossible to go to zero degrees and be on land, unless you cross into England. And then you'd be way too far south to still be at fifty-five degrees north."

"Then we've got it wrong, the code?" Russ says. "The second number means something else."

"No." Suddenly it's clear to me. "She's in the sea." I look around at the staring faces. "Think about it. The border's closed. She's hardly going to be smuggling us into England by land. And I think chartering a jet plane might be a tad difficult at short notice, even for my mother. So what's she going to do? She's going to get a boat." I show them the lighthouse postcard. "The whole nautical theme. This is her idea of a total hoot."

"All righty," Smitty says. "We swim out to meet her, or . . . ?"

"Zero is *far* out to sea," Pete interjects. "Many miles."

"She did that so there'd be no doubt we'd guess she's in a boat." I nod my head. "We go to the lighthouse. Flash the damn light at her — something — she'll have a plan."

"I can estimate where that spot might be, but without a GPS it's going to be one hell of a big guess," Pete says.

"Doesn't matter, we just watch for the lighthouse," I say. "We're following the coastline. When we see it, we stop."

"What's happening now?" Alice has chosen this moment to wake up, and is looking at me with a full face of filth. "Is there going to be a storm?"

"No doubt, Alice. The storm is definitely coming, and the lighthouse is our way home." Outside I can see the beach, dipping in and out of the fog. "I just hope we haven't missed it."

23

Smitty's back in the driver's cab. He enjoyed filling Alice in on all the details, right up to the point where she flung a water bottle at him. Now she's locked herself in one of the train's bathrooms and will no doubt reenter looking pristine, as is her trick.

Russ is in the carriage next to the zoms, on lighthouse duty, and Pete is glued to the window in here, intermittently drawing lines on his map. I'm hovering by the seats next to the driver's cab, willing Elvenmouth to suddenly spring into view. I want to go and talk to Smitty, but on the other hand, I don't want to make it too obvious that I want to go and talk to Smitty. Least of all to Smitty.

Alice comes back. *Wowza.* She doesn't look pristine at all, she looks green.

"You OK?" I expect the usual defensive slap in the face from her, but she just rakes her hand through her hair.

"No, I'm not." She wipes the corner of her mouth with a delicate pinky. "I just spewed again. I never spew, and these days I'm all about the spew. It's utterly gross."

"Pregnant." Pete doesn't look away from the window. Again I expect Alice to spiral into a tantrum, but instead she just rolls her eyes half-heartedly. I chance putting a hand on her shoulder, and she lets me.

"You fell into a ravine. You got kidnapped. You jumped onto a speeding train. It's a lot for one day."

She almost smiles.

"Rest." I self-consciously remove the hand. "We'll wake you up when it's time to move. I promise."

She raises a blond eyebrow at me. "You'd better."

"Hey." I spot some drinks in a box under a table. "Thirsty, anyone?" I pull out a can. It's bright red and orange and reads NECTA! in a whirly retro font. "Is this stuff for real? Not another Veggie Juice they just made up?"

Alice takes one and cracks it open. "No. They did ban this stuff in a few schools because it woke the students up. *Beaucoup de* caffeine and sugar. For all we know it could be the cure." She drains the can and lies down on a seat.

"Hit me." Pete holds out a hand, and I toss him a soda.

"I'll give this one to Russ," I say. Pete nods as I head to the other carriage. *Goody.* Now I've got an excuse to take one to Smitty next. *Gah! Like I need an excuse.* How ridiculous.

So I'm kind of in my own head as I push the button for the door to open, and as I walk through and it closes behind me, I don't immediately see Russ. I'm keeping one eye on the sea for that lighthouse, and the other on the far door, looking through to the zoms beyond the seat barricade he's made. They're still there, of course, just swaying with the train and not much else. They've probably given up trying to get to us. For now.

". . . mfluffle . . . effer contact .˙. . blumm fer update."

A tinny voice stops me in my tracks. Where's Russ? That wasn't him. The noise was coming from the far end of the carriage. I tiptoe toward it. I can still hear the voice, but it's very muffled by the sound of the train, the rain.

". . . thesser situation . . . ollow, over?"

Last row of seats, on the left. Can't see anything from here, but I'm still walking slowly toward the sound, a cold knot solidifying in my gut. That's a walkie-talkie. Sounds just like the ones in the morgue. The memory makes my blood freeze. *Where's Russ?* Jeez, did he go in the carriage with the zoms? The voice has stopped.

I reach the end of the carriage. Russ is crouched low, with something in his hand. He turns round and yells in shock.

"God! You scared the life out of me." He clasps his free hand to his chest; the other hand, with the thing in it, sneaks behind his back.

"What's that?" I point.

I watch for the twitch; some tiny little microfrown in that split second when he's working out how to answer me. But he's not guilty of anything, or he's really, really good . . . his brow smoothes over and his mouth gives a relieved smile.

"So glad it's you. I found this." He holds out the walkie. "In Pete's stuff." *I didn't know Pete had any stuff to speak of.*

"I heard the voice." I search his face. "What were they saying?"

"I don't know!" He does exasperated. "Couldn't make any of it out."

Well, that's a lie, because I was several feet away and I clearly heard some words. "Is it the one from the morgue?" I ask him.

He shrugs. "Could be. Maybe he thought he'd keep it and it might come in useful?"

"But don't people have to be quite near to talk to you on one of those?" I take a small step backward. It's instinctual, I can't help myself. But Russ notices, and he knows that I notice him noticing.

"Maybe he's been contacting someone." He steps toward me.

"Maybe he has," I say. "Maybe he has been contacting someone all along, and that's how they've known where we are at every turn. The helicopter . . ."

"That would make total sense." He looks at me, face frowning. "I mean — crazy, but I have been noticing a few things that worry me about his behavior. Haven't you?"

"What like?" I think I can guess, but I'm not going to volunteer anything.

Russ grimaces, as if this is causing him actual pain. "He smashed the GPS. He lost the paper with the numbers on, and then he was the one who had the chance to wipe the numbers in the Jeep."

I think about it. Yes, I clocked those things, too. "He remembered the numbers, though."

"*Some* of them," Russ says. "Enough to divert suspicion, but not enough to be seriously helpful. And even before that, the phone went missing when he was the last one to have it — and now this walkie turns up in his things." Russ shakes his head. "He's always been fascinated with Xanthro, hasn't he? Maybe they got to him in the hospital. Persuaded him to come on board."

I gasp. But, yeah, I've had the same thought.

Russ holds a hand up. "We're probably just being paranoid. I feel awful about doubting him." He shrugs. "Let's keep this between us. I'll hang on to the walkie for now."

I don't say anything. I just stand there, because I really don't know which way is up, and I can't help thinking that Russ has just swung this whole conversation round to make himself look better, and Pete look worse. But then again, that might be That There Paranoia at work.

"Get in here!" Pete shouts down the carriage, making me jump out of my skin.

We're both glad of an excuse to move, and I watch Russ pocket the walkie. He puts a protective hand over the bulge. I also have a full pocket, let's not forget. Just because I haven't pulled it yet doesn't mean I won't. Only I have to have a good enough reason.

Pete is holding the map from the wall and is up by the door of the driver's cab, with Alice. I run as fast as I can up the wobbly train to get to them.

"Slow down, Smitty!" Pete is shouting, flinging the door open. I get to them just in time to see Smitty's shocked expression. "Slow right down." Pete is firm. "We're in the zone."

"What are you talking about?" Smitty replies.

"Here." Pete puts the map on the dashboard and stabs at it. "I've calculated the spot as best as I can on the map, and I've located the area indicated by Bobby's mother, give or take a few miles. Judging by our speed of travel and cross-referencing the minor conurbations we've been through — not to mention the fact that we're in the section of track that hugs the coast and runs parallel to the motorway — I estimate we're within shouting distance of our destination."

"Eh?" Alice says.

"We're nearly there," I translate. "So how big's this zone, Pete? How much could you be off by?"

He shakes his head. "Bobby, this map is hardly detailed. It may not even be to scale. And I'm working without those remaining numbers. It could be as much as five, ten miles out."

"So do we stop? Where do we look?" Alice cries. "Do we just get out and walk along the beach and hope we see something?"

"Maybe that's exactly what we do." I lean forward against the windshield, eyes darting. "No obvious Undead out there."

"The fog's getting worse," Smitty says. "Just saying."

It's moving off the sea, coming inland, like a slow-moving tidal wave. As the train descends a slight hill, we get a view of a bay up ahead. It's different from the gently undulating coast we've seen so far, startlingly so. It's a perfect little crescent of pale sand against the slate-gray water and the white wall of fog. The shape of the bay is so uniform it looks almost man-made.

"Wish 'U' were here," I murmur. "It looks like a *U*."

Oh god, Mother. Would you like some extra cheese with that? I feel a chuckle in my throat as I take in the candy-colored houses that line the harbor. I know this place, I remember it.

"The lighthouse!" Smitty cries.

There it is, at the harbor, the top poking out of the encroaching mist. I remember there's a red house on a hill that looks like a face with windows for eyes . . . I remember sunburn, ice cream from a van, being bitten by a horrible hairy fly that wouldn't get off my arm even when my mother swatted at it . . .

"This is Elvenmouth," I say. "We came here for a vacation. More than once, I think, when I was very little." I murmur. "I didn't even know it was Scotland. But I remember it well. She would know I'd remember it."

"Thank god," says Alice. "So what now?"

"We go to the lighthouse, turn it on, wait for the boat." Smitty flings out a finger. "We should get as close as we can, stop the train, make for the harbor."

I nod, and as I do, Alice screams, "Stop!"

"Be cool!" Smitty says. "Just let me get —" But then he's facing front again, and he doesn't need to finish his sentence.

There in the middle of the tracks, hovering, is the helicopter.

We all scream, and Smitty hits the brakes, slamming us against the wall. But the train won't exactly stop on a dime.

"Can you reverse?" Pete yells.

"You tell me!" Smitty yells back, fiddling with the controls. The train's brakes screech, but we're still moving forward.

"We should make a run for it," I say.

"I am not going out there now." Alice starts to cry.

"Stay calm, everyone," Russ says.

The train slows to a reluctant halt, the helicopter still hovering up ahead of us, ten feet or so off the ground. We fall silent, and we don't move. We can see them looking at us, and for some reason, it makes us want to stand like statues.

"What do we do?" Alice whispers.

"Hit the gas. Maybe just crash into them?" I half joke. "They're not going to think we'll have the nerve. They'll get out of the way in time, you'll see."

"I don't think they can land on the tracks," Pete says.

"We just sit tight," Russ says.

"Or go backward," Alice says.

"I don't know how to do backward." Smitty grits his teeth.

"They can't hover there forever," Pete says. "They'll have to go off somewhere and land, and then we hit full speed ahead."

"Better believe I'll be ready." Smitty wipes a bead of sweat off his brow. We wait.

But then the doors on the helicopter open, and three men in black lower themselves onto the legs of the helicopter and jump onto the ground.

"That's that idea busted," Pete says.

"Drive, drive, drive!" Alice cries. "Make them move!"

Before Smitty has the chance to crank the engine, there's a *ping* and a *crack*, and we all hit the deck.

"They're firing!"

"Is this thing bulletproof?"

"What are we going to do?"

"Stand up slowly!" A voice rings out through a megaphone. "All of you! Now!"

We don't move.

"Don't make us come in and get you," the voice continues. "Stand up slowly, and you won't get hurt."

Smitty gives me a hug. "I'm going to give myself up. It's me they want, after all. I'll stand up really slow, and you guys make a run for it through the back."

"Don't be so frickin' self-centered. You don't know they're after you. They were plenty interested in the rest of us before we even found you." I grab him. "I hate it when you pull this crap."

He shakes his head. "I'm going to stand up nice and slow, like they want. And you good folks are going to get the hell out. I'll distract them long enough. So make the most of it."

"He's right, we should go." Russ pats my shoulder, and crawls past me.

Smitty raises an eyebrow. "My, that was easy."

"He's going, I'm going." Alice scrabbles across the floor and opens the door.

"How's it going to work?" Pete hisses. "This distraction thing? They'll shoot you."

"Go, Pete," I urge him. "I'm staying to help Smitty. We are not done yet. Trust me."

Pete gives me a questioning look, but then he nods and crawls out.

They've all gone. It's just me and Smitty. Stubborn, wonderful Smitty.

"Are you ready for this?" I ask him.

"Got a white flag?" He grins back.

"I'm all out."

"On three?" He gives me a wink.

"Just like the good old days."

"Not quite like the good old days . . ." he says.

I frown at him.

He leans in, puts a warm hand on my cheek. Then he kisses me. "*Now* it's just like the good old days," he says, then kisses me again. I close my eyes, and wish everyone would just vamoose.

"This is your final chance." The megaphone booms. "Stand up where we can see you!"

"Pervs. They want to see us." Smitty chuckles. "You ready?"

I nod.

We raise our hands above our heads and get up slowly.

A gun pointing at us. The gun is attached to a man standing by the side of the tracks. The mystery man with raspy voice and shiny balaclava is in the middle of the tracks, arms folded.

"Wanna see what happens if I try and run 'em over?" Smitty murmurs to me.

"I wouldn't do that if I was you." A voice comes from behind. We whip around; a third man in black, a second gun. "Move yourselves." He waves the gun, and we gingerly move past, stepping into the first carriage. "Any more of you I should know about?" he says.

"No, we're it," I say. I hope we gave the others enough time to get away.

Through the doorway, I spot the two men who were on the tracks appear on the grassy verge below. *Damn!* Alice and Pete are also standing out there, and they're looking up at us with really weird expressions on their faces.

Are they trying to tell us something?

Then it registers: Russ is nowhere to be seen. My heart sinks with the confirmation. He's probably cozying up to the bad guys after all. He called them on the walkie, and now he's delivered us straight to them.

The mystery man takes a step forward and opens the door. His eyes flash, but other than that I can't see his face because of the stupid balaclava. But I kind of think he's smiling. He waves up at me.

"Hello, Bobby. It's good to finally catch up with you properly."

24

Smitty looks at me.

"Friend of yours?"

The man glances at him. "Hello, Smitty."

"Er, hello." Smitty frowns at him. "Do forgive me; I can't quite place your husky voice."

For a moment I think I recognize that voice. Close-up, it's muffled and rough-sounding, like he's got some über-case of tonsillitis. But is there something familiar? No, it's just 'cause he knows our names. They want Smitty, they want me. We're two hybrids or half-breeds or something. We're doomed to a life of being experimented on in some secret hospital far underground.

"How are you feeling, guys?" With some difficulty, the man climbs the steps up into the train. There's not much room for us all in this little area beside the exit, so I kind of back into the carriage. The guy with the gun raises it at me. *OK, mister. Not going anywhere.* I slowly perch my behind on the edge of a table.

"You've done a good job running from us," the man continues. "And you survived. That's not to be underestimated." His voice is really raw-sounding. Maybe that's just the evil, like a job requirement. "I told them you'd be resourceful. They didn't believe me — said you were just kids — but you see, I was right, wasn't I? I generally am. They're beginning to appreciate that."

OK, so this is getting weirder. His eyes — something about them, something familiar, I know it . . .

"Can't tell you how glad I am we've finally all got this chance to talk." He gives a kind of gurgling chuckle.

Smitty shoots me a look of pure flummox.

"We ended things on a rather ugly note back then when we were hanging out." He gets really close, and I can see his eyes. Brown. And the skin around them, just red, bright red skin. "And I'd love it if there could be no hard feelings." He raises a hand and touches my bald head, then carefully, almost with affection, runs a hand down my cheek.

Smitty springs forward to leap onto him, and instantly I'm transported back to the kitchen at the castle. A hand caressing my face. A dog fight between Smitty and one of the students. That déjà just won't stop vu-ing. I know who this is, and it makes me sick to my stomach.

Smitty tussles with the man on the floor, and the guy with the gun jumps on top of them both. It's not an even fight this time. Smitty's outnumbered and outplayed. The guy with the gun pulls him to his feet, and the man on the floor starts laughing.

"You know who I am, don't you, big man?" He turns from Smitty to me and raises his hand to his balaclava, ready to peel it off for the big reveal. "But you still look a little puzzled, Bobby."

"Not so much, Michael."

I burst his bubble before he can get to the payoff. His hand pauses, and he lets the balaclava stay in place.

"Sorry to steal your special moment." I take a bold step forward. "You always were a little bit slower than us."

His eyes narrowing, he whips the balaclava off.

"And this is what I've got to show for it."

My stomach lurches, and a gasp escapes before I can stop it. Michael's face is distorted beyond all recognition. One side has slipped, like the skin and muscles have been pushed down and stayed there. Red and black, his eyebrows burnt off, only tiny wisps of hair cover his scabbing scalp. His lips are wrinkled and his skin slick where the outer layer has disappeared. But it's his nose that's the most shocking: It's gone. There is just the rise of nostrils, no tip left; it's like it has melted clean away.

A victim of his own hand. In an attempt to scare the hordes away with a can of gasoline and a lit torch, he only succeeded in setting himself alight. The last time we saw him, he was a human inferno, and this is the result.

He looks worse than a zom, and that must really, really suck. And by the look in his eye, I know that he blames us for it.

"How did you . . . ?" I have to ask, I can't help myself. "I thought you must have died."

"Oh, I was lucky," he swaggers. "I knew where there was a really, really good hospital."

"They took you in?" Smitty shouts from underneath two gunmen. "Last time we heard, Xanthro wanted you dead!"

"Hmm, well, it's amazing how these things turn out, isn't it, Smitty?" Michael turns on him. "I was the last living connection to Osiris that they had. Grace missing-slash-presumed zombie, Shaq a crazy Undead, and her mother" — he jabs a finger at me — "in the wind. They knew the stimulant and the antidote were gone from the lab, and then they found the stimulant at the site of the bus crash." He turns to me again. "Thanks for just leaving it lying there, darling."

I use every last ounce of strength trying not to react, and he sees it, and turns away, laughing. Something catches my eye down the train.

Russ, in the next carriage. The top of his head shows through the glass, like he's ducked down. His eyes are wide, he's clearly stressed to the max. And then I see why: Behind him, shadows loom. The lurching shapes of the Undead, and they're at the far end of his carriage. He's let them out, moved that barricade, and now he's baiting them up toward us. *Bloody hell.*

Michael's none the wiser. "So they get to wondering where the antidote has gone to. And then they put a bunch of security-camera images together, and some mobile-phone calls that they hacked, and what do you know? It turns out that Dr. Bobby's Mummy is in the mix, and not only has she come back to save the day, she's come to save her daughter." He smiles at me.

"Yeah?" I try to look down the train again without him noticing. Russ is still there, and the figures are getting closer. He's mouthing something at me. I raise an eyebrow at Michael. "Took you long enough to work it all out."

"Would have taken them longer. They didn't know who you were at first. But as I was there at the hospital, I was able to help them out." He leans in. "Given your daddy's special talents, they were really interested in you. They did a whole bunch of things to you while you were out cold. Have any exciting dreams?" His face close-up is raw and oozing. "You couldn't do anything to stop it. Did you just lie back and enjoy the ride?"

Smitty yells, and I swing a hand back to punch Michael in his pus-ridden face. But for once he's quick, and he knocks my hand aside. The force pushes me over, and I hit the carriage floor. Smitty goes ballistic, and for a moment they're all on him — even the man who was guarding Pete and Alice — and nobody is looking at me. It's my chance. I leg it as fast as I can down the carriageway and punch the door open. Russ looks at me, and without words we fall together toward the carriage's exit door, wrenching it open, tumbling out onto the grassy verge outside. I reach up and shut the door just as the first zom appears — the conductor. Unable to reach us, he spots some other folks in the train who don't have tickets, and starts to stumble toward them.

"Smitty!" I cry. Russ and I begin to run up the outside of the train. Just as we reach where Alice is standing, bewildered, on the grass, Smitty appears, falling out of the door. Russ reaches up to slap the button, and the door hisses back automatically.

Gun shots ring out. At first I think they're firing at us, but then I realize they're shooting our travel companions, who are now making their way through the first carriage.

"Run!" I scream, pulling Smitty to his feet. It's not exactly going to take long for them to press the button and open the door.

"Where's Pete?" Russ yells.

A white Mohawk appears out of the door of the driver's cab. Pete jumps down, grinning.

"Hoped my timing was right. Locked them in."

"How?" I'm already running.

"The main carriage doors all have electrical locks," Pete pants. "Pulled all the wires out and hoped for the best."

He might have done something right, because for now, there are no bullets flying by my ear, and no men in black chasing me down. But I'm not going to hope those doors hold them for long, or that they'll waste much time getting out through the driver's cab. And there's the little matter of the helicopter, which, having left the track, is now circling ominously above us.

"Head to the harbor!" shouts Russ, up ahead. We run through a field of long grass, the wet stalks whipping my thighs as I plow through. There's a five-barred gate, and a lane that curls around into a village green opening up onto a beach.

There in front of us is the fog. Rising off the sea and creeping toward us through the village — patches of clear air here and there on the beach and the harbor wall, but for the most part, thick and impenetrable.

We stop in our tracks.

"Can you hear the dead?" Alice breathes.

We don't need to answer her — we can all hear them. The moans rising like the fog. Somewhere in that soupy gray of the harbor, there are bodies, many of them, jostling, stumbling, waiting for us.

The top of the lighthouse is just visible above the fog. Can't go around, can't go above or below. Have to go through.

"They can't see us," whispers Smitty. "Wanna play Freeze Tag, anyone?"

I look behind us. The train zoms and locked carriage doors will only trouble the men for a minute or two; they'll be hot on our heels.

"Be quiet, be quick," I hiss at everyone. "Lighthouse or bust." I've got to lead by example; I take a deep breath. "This way!" I make the decision and peel off to the left into the mist.

I feel the fog envelop me like cold dread sliding down my skin. I'm blind, tiptoeing as fast as I dare through the fog. In all my adventures underground, I never felt as claustro as now. Hands out, no way of telling who's ahead of me, to the side, who's ready to loom out of that clammy blanket of white that threatens to suffocate. Unlike in the forest, I *know* they're out there — sometimes mere feet away — I hear them, I smell them, and I catch glimpses of stumbling outlines, almost feeling their breath on my neck. My heart thumps in my ears, hot blood running to my head and prickling my outstretched fingers. I must focus on moving forward or I'll freeze, my hands clawed as if I'm clutching at the last shreds of bravery that is fast leaching out into the mist.

Behind me I can sense that Smitty and Russ are near, and every now and then I hear a half-concealed squeal above the moans and groans. Alice is following. If she is coming, then I know Pete is there somewhere. We can only move forward, we can only keep going. Underfoot there are discarded fishing nets, curled ropes, and lobster pots; we must be almost at the harbor wall.

Please, Mother, be waiting for us. Please be in a boat, a fast one, preferably one that turns into a submarine and gets us out of here, out of the monsters' way, far from the men with guns.

I stub my toe against a low wall. I've reached the harbor — I can smell the sea lapping somewhere below. And then I see boats looming out of the mist.

Row, row, row your boat, gently down the stream,

If you see a zombie, don't forget to scream . . .

I use the wall to guide me along the harbor until I see steps leading up. We're here, we've found Elvenmouth Light.

I run up the steps in the fog. There's a door, bright blue and thick with years of paint. *God, I hope it's not locked.* I try the handle, and it turns easily. Score!

The others arrive at the top of the steps, ashen-faced. Without a word I slowly open the door, every nerve firing, thoroughly expecting to be faced with a monster.

But there are none. Just an empty lobby, with an iron-and-brass stair-case winding upward beyond a modern metal gate, with a barrier above made of a lattice of bars. Russ rushes to the gate and turns the handle, pulling the door toward him. It doesn't open. He rattles it, tries pushing, then turns to me.

"Key?"

I hold my hands out. "What key? I don't have one."

Russ turns to Smitty. "Did Bobby's mum leave it with you?"

"No," Smitty says. "Dontcha think I would have mentioned that by now?"

"Oh god." I pace up and down. "Something we missed. Something at the shelter." I take off the backpack and feel into the lining. Mum must have left us a key. She would never make such a mistake.

"Maybe it's here," says Alice, hunting round the featureless lobby, run-ning her hands over the stone walls. "Or no. Under a rock outside. People always leave keys under rocks outside."

"I'll look," Russ says, and ducks out of the door.

Meanwhile Smitty has climbed the gate and is pulling on the barrier above. Between gate and barrier is a gap of a couple of hands' widths; he tries to squeeze through, but he's too big.

I wouldn't be, though.

"That's how I'm supposed to get through," I say, almost to myself. Before I can climb, Russ bursts through the door.

"The soldiers are out there," he whispers. "Coming through the fog. They're headed this way."

"Can we keep them out?" I say. "Use something to keep this door shut?" But I know the answer. There's nothing here. And besides, to what end? Once they know we're in here, it's not like we've got anywhere to escape to.

I move to the door, my hand in my pocket. "One of you get through that gap and light the damn lighthouse. Pete!" I fling out a finger at him. "You're skinny enough and clever enough. Get on it!"

The time has come. I was hoping it wouldn't, but now it has. Nowhere to run, nowhere to hide, and only one solution.

I reach into my pocket for the gun.

25

I pull the gun out. It's still in plastic. God, why didn't I unwrap it again? Doesn't exactly make for a quick draw. But it is loaded, that much I know. I fiddle with the tape with my freezing hands, trying not to drop it.

"What's that?" Russ demands. "You're not going out there."

"Back off!" I hiss at him. Russ shuffles backward a little. "Pete, get up those stairs *quickly*. Smitty and Alice, you'd better help him." I pull the gun free of the plastic at last, shielding it from them with my body as I check the safety.

"What are you going to do?" Alice whines back. "Stop bossing us around, you baldy freak."

"Get on with it!" I turn round and point the gun at her. It's a really crappy thing to do, I know it. Seriously, do *not* try this at home. But it gives me a couple of seconds' worth of the best laugh ever. Because she sees the gun, and she craps herself and slithers to the stone-cold ground. If I'm going to die in a minute or two — and I kind of think that's pretty likely — at least I finally owned Alice.

Smitty gulps. "What the fu —"

"You, too," I cut him off. "I'll hold them off, you light the way for Mum."

He gives me such a look — of confusion, admiration, shock, and little side helpings of lust and terror thrown in there for good measure — that I nearly crack. But he complies. Because when there's a gun, you do.

"I can't believe she's got a bloody gun. All this time, a bloody gun!"

I can hear Alice going into overdrive somewhere behind me as I open the door, creep out into the fog, and slither to my stomach. This is it. I click off the safety. I breathe, the cold, wet stone beneath me making me shiver. But I'm sweating under my collar. I hold the gun up, look down the barrel. Three figures, in and out of swathes of damp fog, on the beach. But soon they'll be at the harbor, and that will be when I shoot. I'm no sniper with a rifle. This is a handgun. If I'm going to shoot them, I'm going to have to do it when they're closer, but not so close they disappear into the fog.

Michael's pointing down the harbor wall. He's seen us, or maybe he heard Alice having her moment. They're heading this way — just a few seconds more. I find a few lobster pots to hide behind.

Now to do this, now to kill somebody.

Who? Who goes first? I'd like to take out Michael in a heartbeat, but even as much as I hate him, it's more difficult than I thought. I should have just bitten him when I had the chance. If I'm right and I am infected, maybe he would have turned by now. That would have been easier than shooting him in cold blood.

OK, so not him. At least I don't know either of the others. Plus they have guns. Once I shoot, they'll shoot back. Makes more sense to take one of them down first.

Eeny, meeny, miney, mo . . .

In the end, I choose the closest one, the easiest shot. *Sorry, mister.*

I aim, squeeze gently. Nothing. The gun is heavy, makes my hand ache. Squeeze more. Always a little more than you'd think . . .

There's a *bang*, and I nearly scoot backward into the sea, even though I was expecting it. The men weren't expecting it, however, and they jump into the air. They all come down again, all in one piece. I missed. And I realize I meant to. I can't do it. I can shoot at them, but I can't kill. How screwed up is that? They would kill me and not think twice, but I can't shoot them.

Well, maybe in the leg . . .

I go to line up my shot, but they've got wise to the situation and taken cover. I fire one off anyway, so they know the first wasn't a fluke. And now comes the gun battle. The one I know I can't help but lose, because they are trained killers with rifles, and I am a schoolgirl with a good eye but only three remaining bullets and a lobster pot for protection.

But this was never about winning, just about buying time . . . and it works. A minute later and there's a very loud *clunk-clink*, and a *buzz*, and the lighthouse fires up its bulb. Pete did the business; I've never loved him more.

I fire off a couple of shots, then crawl back to the door, flinging it open. Smitty and Alice meet me there.

"Keep low and run — now. Run to the end of the wall!" I wave them on with the gun, and they're off, tumbling down the steps and toward the water. I hunker down, half in, half out of the doorway, the big blue wooden door shielding me.

I think I hear the sound of a boat's engine out there somewhere, but maybe that's just wishful hearing.

Only one bullet left now. Use it wisely . . .

"Pete, Russ," I rasp, not able to tear my eyes off the soldiers' hiding places and look into the lighthouse. "Get moving!"

The soldiers are falling back. Incredible. Do they know what we've done? Know they're too late? That they're defeated? Or are they merely waiting for reinforcements? Only Michael remains, walking out from behind the wall where he's been crouching, looking up at me. I could take him out. Maybe he even wants me to.

There's a noise and a crash from inside the lighthouse, and I twist around.

Pete and Russ are lying on the floor beside the gate. Behind the metal bars is a raving, bearded zombie. He hollers at them, throwing an angry arm through the gate, reaching for flesh. But they're just out of reach.

I scramble toward them.

"Hiding . . . upstairs," Pete wheezes. "He attacked me, made me fall down the stairs."

"But you did it, Pete." I squeeze his arm. "The light. And you made it back in one piece."

Pete looks pained. "I don't know . . ." He puts a hand to his side, and it comes away red.

"Bitten?" Russ says.

"I'm not sure," Pete says. "I hurt myself on the way down." He looks at Russ. "And when you pulled me through the gap."

"Mate, he was on top of you." Russ shakes his head.

"Yes, but . . ." Pete's eyes tear up. "I thought I'd got away . . ."

Russ stands up. "We have to leave him."

I shake my head. "Think again. The soldiers have fallen back. We go, now."

"Not with Pete," Russ says. "He'll turn."

I grip the gun tightly. "Didn't you hear, Russ? I don't leave my bitten friends to die."

"No antidote this time, Bobby," Russ says. Pete looks stricken.

"We have Smitty. And we have my mother. She'll figure something out." I raise the gun at Russ. "I hate to do this. But move your butt. Because I'm done with wasting time."

Russ flings open the door, and I help Pete out, making sure my gun is aimed at Russ the whole time.

As soon as we get outside there's an unmistakable hum, a motor noise coming from the direction of the sea. Then, through the fog, I catch a glimpse. A small boat with an outboard, heading our way. The fog conceals all but the outline of the boat, but I know.

"She's here," I say. "She's come for us."

Smitty and Alice are crouched on the stone steps leading into the water. We lower ourselves down on the ground beside them and wait. I will the boat to get here quickly, my eyes glued to the sea. A little way off, I can just see a round shape floating in the water. At first I think it's a buoy, but it's way too big, and as I look closer, I realize it has a tiny red flashing light on it.

"What —?" I start.

"Mine," Pete stutters. "Tethered, no doubt, but deadly. Explodes on contact. I had been wondering about what they'd do to secure the borders out to sea. Otherwise how do you keep people in?"

Alice stares up at him. "Are you saying it's a bomb?"

Pete nods, sweat running down his pale face. "They'll have them peppered all around the coastline. And a few farther out to sea, no doubt. Mainly as a deterrent."

The boat gets closer — close enough for me to make out a figure on board — and I want to call out to Mum to warn her. But just as she's almost on it, she skillfully avoids it. I breathe a sigh of relief.

But I relax too soon.

There's a shout, a scream — and as I look up the steps behind me, all I see is Pete, arms outstretched, face pulled into a screech, falling toward me.

He's turned? Already?

He clatters against me, my wrist bending the gun against my own body. Then a hand grabs me and pulls me backward, and I tumble down the step. The gun flies out of my grasp, smashes on stone, and discharges with a *bang*. I brace myself to hit the cold water below, and the world goes dark and swallows me whole.

26

I'm floating on my back in the churning, gray water.

The waves are tossing me here and there — actually throwing me up into the air and then catching me again, like my dad used to do when I was a kid. And now, as then, it's kind of fun. I think I should feel scared and cold, and the salt should be stinging my eyes and the back of my throat. But actually, I'm good. Quite happy to be here and helpless and just letting this happen. Because after all this time of having to try and be in control of this crazy, I'm just gonna let stuff happen. Isn't that great? Stop fighting. Smile, even. Let the surf toss me up in the air. Let the sea dash me against the rocks or drown me in the murky depths. It's fine, honestly. Because I'm numb, and I don't even care anymore, and it feels great.

But then I turn my head, and I see Smitty. He's floating, too, but he's not moving. Facedown, arms spread wide, torso bobbing. For a horrible moment I think his legs have been bitten clean through by a shark, but then I see them beneath the water, just hanging there, motionless. I jolt upright in the water, grab his leather jacket, and try to haul him the right way up so that he can breathe, so that we can ride the waves together, so that we can continue the fight until it is done.

He's very heavy. Weighed down and waterlogged. My muscles scream, the cold rushes in, and I realize I can barely keep myself from sinking in this water, let alone support the two of us.

There's a huge boat, just a little way off. Every time the waves carry us up, I catch a brief glimpse. Hope spikes me in the chest. It's going to be so hard, but we can reach it. I just need him to help himself.

"Smitty!" I try to shake him awake, screaming at the back of his dark head. "Smitty!"

Just when I think all is lost, the wave helps me and he turns over, his head lolling, dark hair stuck down over his face. I grab the lapels of his jacket and hoist him toward me. I wipe a hand across his face, brushing his hair back.

Eyes open. A smile.

It's not him. It's me.

My mouth drops open. I gulp a lungful of water and sink five fathoms deep below the churning gray waves.

It's just a dream.

I wake up gasping, like I've been held underwater.

I'm on my own, lying in a bed. The only sounds are my gasps and my heart beating loudly in my ears. Hands gripping the cold metal sides of the bed, I stare up at the bright white ceiling, steadying myself while the room stops going up and down, hanging on, waiting for the calm.

It never comes.

Where the hell am I?

"Hello?"

Bright lights. A room. White walls.

Again? I'm back in the hospital? *Again?*

Bile rises in my throat and I try to sit up. I kick out with a foot and swear as I stub my toes on the end of the bed. I notice a small control panel hanging off the side of the bed. There's a button on it that says CALL.

"Okeydokey, let's call."

A couple of minutes pass. Or maybe less, I'm not sure. And then the door opens and a head looks round.

It's my mother.

Damn, damn, damn, I'm still dreaming. Seriously, wake the hell up already! I look for bits of myself to pinch.

And then she's there, by my bed, like she didn't really need to walk across the room, like she just kind of levitated there like an angel, which is totally fine because this is a dream, and any old crap is possible in a dream.

She looks at me. She takes my face in her hands, her eyes crinkle, and big wet tears drip down her cheeks and plop onto mine. Oh, lordy. This is quite the scene. Now I know I definitely have to wake up. Oh god, she's kissed me, and she's sobbing.

"Bobby! Oh, I've been so worried about you. I'm so sorry, my little girl." More tears fall.

Jeez. The mother in this dream is so wet. Positively soggy. Both metaphorically and literally.

Then the door opens again, and Smitty comes in. And then Pete and Russ. And some muscly guy in black I don't know, and finally a woman in scrubs who fiddles with my wrist. Good god. It's *The Wizard of Oz*, I'm Dorothy, and all these random farmhands who are inexplicably allowed into my bedroom are actually the friends from my dream.

Am I still dreaming?

"Ow!"

The nurse has just stuck me with a needle. "Sorry," she breezes and smiles at me.

"Just a blood test, Bobby," Mum says. "No need for alarm. How are you feeling?"

"You gave us a shock," Russ says. "Cracked your head on the boat. Blood everywhere."

"Not cool, Bobby." Smitty gives me a smile.

"After all your efforts in the gun battle, it seemed rather unfair you should miss out on the rest of it." Pete nods enthusiastically.

"Wait." I use the rails on the side of the bed to pull myself up. "Where are we?" I step onto the cold floor and try to stand up. "You!" I point at Pete. "You were bitten. You turned, you tried to grab me." The floor undulates. I wobble, nausea creeping up into my throat. Everyone shouts, "Whoa!" and Mum and the nurse help me back into bed.

"Pete is fine; he was wounded, but not infected," Mum says.

"They patched me up, Bobby." Pete tentatively lifts up his T-shirt. "I'm absolutely fine. Sorry about what happened on the steps." He shrugs. "It all happened so fast, it's rather a blur — but I can only assume I slipped and fell on you."

"And we're safe?" I twist around to look at my mother.

"This is a hospital ship," Mum says. "We're in the North Sea. We're safe."

I look around the room. There's a frickin' porthole. That should have been a major clue. Though at the last hospital we had tropical butterflies and look how that ended up.

"We were right about the coordinates, then." The room is still going up and down, but at least now I know it's not me. I glance up at Mum. "This is where you've been waiting?"

"We were watching the bay. As soon as we saw that train coming in, I had a feeling it would be you. You tend to find a way." She whistles and shakes her head like she's surprised. "I knew it was the only place we'd all be safe. I pulled some strings. We'll stay here until the worst is over."

"The soldiers?"

Mum pauses. "We discouraged them from following us."

"OK . . ." I look around. "Where's Alice?"

My mum gives a half smile. "She was a little . . . seasick. She's having a lie-down until she feels a bit brighter."

I know how she feels. I'm kind of hoping I find my sea legs sooner rather than later.

"You should get some rest," Mum says.

I squint at her. "Is this the kind of rest where you put me to sleep and then I wake up and everyone's vanished apart from those of you who have gone all monstery on my sleeping ass?"

Mum makes a face at the language. "No, Roberta. It is not. When you've had a sleep, come and find us on the main deck upstairs, and we'll have a bite to eat."

I give her a look.

She puts up a hand. "Not like that. I mean a sandwich."

"Wait!" Something was niggling at me, now I know what it is. "When you said 'Alice is feeling a bit seasick,' did you actually mean 'Alice has been infected and is going to turn into a zombie and eat all of our brains, starting with Bobby's because she hates her the most'?"

Mum shakes her head. "Rest easy. She's been tested — you've all been tested. We did that first thing when you boarded, it was one of the conditions of them allowing you to stay." She licks her lips. "Well, they know about Smitty's special circumstances, but apart from that, you're all in the clear. Now sleep." She and the nurse usher Russ and Pete out, but Smitty lingers by my bedside.

"I totally had the same thought about Malice. Kind of glad she's not on the turn." He grins. "Undead Alice would be such a pain."

Mum, the nurse, and the unknown guy walk to the doorway, discussing something on my medical chart. I whisper to Smitty.

"Weird about Pete. Russ was certain he'd been bitten. He wanted to leave Pete behind."

Smitty shakes his head. "He doesn't trust Pete."

I think about it. "Do you? Russ told me he found a walkie-talkie in Pete's things. One of the ones the Xanthro soldiers were using. And did he slip on the steps? Or was he trying to take me out?"

Smitty raises his eyebrows. "Albino's been in this mess with us right from the start. He's a nerd and a pain, but I trust him with my life. What Russ says? That's just meathead-thinking; guys with muscle don't like guys with brains."

I squint at him. "And which one are you?"

"You know me, Bob." He winks at me. "I don't have either. Just charm and good looks."

I pull a face. "And zombie juice running through your veins."

"Ah, well," he says. "They'll sort me out here — it's a hospital, isn't it? I'll be kushti, Bob. They've got *Fallout 5* on Xbox; we can totally hang here for a week or two." He leans in. "See that bloke? That's my bodyguard. Apparently I am the most important person currently walking the earth, and he has to follow me everywhere. Kind of might make things between us a little difficult." He gives me a knowing look. "Unless you like being watched." He winks, and I go to smack him in the face, and he dodges. Like he always does.

Gah. In front of my mother and everything.

He chuckles and blows me a kiss as he leaves, the red on my face heating up the entire room. I wonder if my bald head blushes, too? You gotta bet it does.

The nurse gives me a juice to drink and leaves. Mum nods at the muscly guy who's been standing in the corner, watching her — and he leaves, too.

"You have a bodyguard now?" I look at her. "Or is he for me?" I down my juice in one gulp, and she takes my hand.

"I'm proud of you, you'll never know how much," she says. "It went against every bone in my body to leave you in that hospital. But I knew you'd be safe there as long as they didn't know you were my daughter."

"They found out." I look her in the eyes. "Michael was there."

She nods. "So the others told me. I had no idea, obviously. I thought the hospital would be the best place for you while you were injured. And if you hadn't broken out of there with the help I sent, I would have been back. With considerable force, you have to believe that."

"Grace got shot," I tell her. Again she nods.

"Regrettable. I should never have sent her after you; it was pure recklessness on her part to release the infected."

"You could say that." I pull a face. "Anyway, you did the right thing to get Smitty away." I swallow. "They would have done anything to get their hands on him."

"Oh, no," Mum says. "They didn't know he was carrying both the stimulant and the antidote in his system. How could they? They didn't witness it. The only person who knew about him was me." She shakes her head. "No, he was never really in danger."

Here it comes. "Then why were we being chased?" I squeeze her hand. "They tested me at the hospital, Mum. I know about it. About how I'm different. That's why they came after us, isn't it?"

"So much for you to deal with. Get some rest. I owe you some more answers, I know I do." She stands and squeezes my hand back before releasing it. "But a little at a time. See you up on the deck in a few hours; I'll explain everything."

She leaves.

Really? OK, so I'm probably as tired as I've ever been in my life, and I'm sure that nurse just slipped me a Mickey Finn in that juice, but as if I'm going to zonk out for "a few hours" after all that's happened! I'll give it twenty minutes, and then I'm totally going up there . . .

I sleep. But no dreams. Not this time. When I wake up, the lights are dim and I have a dry mouth. But I know this is real life. My bones ache.

I get out of bed. Someone has thoughtfully placed some clean scrubs and a robe for me to put on. A fluffy white robe, with bunny scuff slippers. My own clothes are absent, except for my boots and my coat. I think about it and reject slippers for damp and smelly boots. If the last few weeks of my life have taught me anything, it's that you should always be able to run.

So she said they'd all be upstairs on the main deck. I envisage my mother standing at this enormous wheel, wearing a captain's hat, while everyone holds on for dear life. I open the door and step out into the corridor. Not much lighting here, either. And it's deadly silent. Not quite the bustling hospital, then. My nurse sits at a desk bathed in orange light at the end of the corridor. She looks up at me and smiles.

"Feeling OK?"

"Um, yes. Thanks." I walk toward her, trying not to hold on to the walls in case she thinks I'm not up to it.

"Bit rough out there tonight." She smiles. "Still, better conditions than being on land at the moment."

She makes it sound like we're having a bad rainstorm or something.

"They're all up there." She points to a sign that reads MAIN DECK, with an arrow. I give her a nod of thanks and follow the arrow. There's a metal staircase, and I clank up it, holding on to the cold rail. Another corridor, another arrow, and then a sign on a dark wooden door. I open it.

No Mum playing captain, no ship's wheel. The room is a large lounge area, with velvet armchairs and a headache-inducing patterned carpet. There are big windows looking out to the bow and port and starboard, and glass doors to the deck outside; it looks pretty bleak and stormy out there. Smitty and Pete are sitting at a homey-looking gas fireplace; Alice is reclined in a chair, covered with a blanket but deep in flirtation with Russ nonetheless. Seems a bit of seasickness isn't putting her off her stride. My mother and Smitty's bodyguard, plus two of his buddies, are talking at the far end of the room.

Mum spots me as I come in; something makes me think she already knew I was on my way.

"Bobby," she calls. "Are you feeling better?" She strides up to me and squeezes my arm. "Come and sit down. We can begin; we're all here now."

Oh, heck. It's like she's going to announce which one of us is the murderer. I slip into a spot by Smitty on a mustard-colored couch.

"Thanks for your patience, everyone." She stands in the middle of the lounge, like Scout Leader at the Friendship Circle. "This won't take too long, and then we'll feed you, I promise. All that running away must have made everyone very hungry."

The joke falls flat. I die of embarrassment. Alice groans, and Smitty gives me a sympathetic smirk.

My mother continues, oblivious. "Please know you are safe here, and we are not at home to visitors." She smiles. "Whether private or governmental. You may all stay here until such a time as we decide the safest course of action. Scotland is still cut off, but the rest of the UK remains unaffected. Parts of Northumbria have been deemed no-man's-land, but England is ostensibly protected from the outbreak." She pauses. "Your families are all safe. We took the liberty of checking on them as soon as we had your full identities."

Alice starts to cry. Pete is laughing. I look at Smitty. He's staring at the floor, nodding silently. I never stopped to think of their families before now, I was so caught up in my own familial drama.

"You will be able to contact them yourselves shortly." My mother is pleased at how well that news has gone down. "We would hope that this situation would end soon, and we'll expedite your return home safely as a priority, on confirmation of your long-term health."

Smitty looks up. "Meaning you get to say when we go home, not us?"

My mother blinks. "Exactly. But that is as much for your own safety as anything." She strides to the door leading down belowdecks. "Anyway, not to dwell on that — I think it's time I introduced you, or rather rein-troduced you, to someone who can tell you a lot more than I."

With that, she gives a short rap on the wooden door.

It opens, and Martha glides into the room.

27

I spring to my feet, not knowing whether to fight or fly. Martha seems to have that effect on me every time she enters a room.

Pete is jumping up and down beside me.

"What is going on?" he splutters. "At the hospital . . . we saw your ring in the blood on the floor."

Martha sighs and smiles benevolently upon him. "I'm sorry if I gave you all a shock."

How many more so-called dead people are going to turn up? At this rate my mother is going pull back a curtain and reveal my father, jammin' with Elvis and Michael Jackson.

"Smitty," my mother says, "this is Dr. Martha Wagner. No doubt the others told you that she was looking after them at the hospital?"

Smitty nods. "They did mention her, yeah."

My mother gives him her warmest smile. "This is her facility. She is kindly hosting us here for . . . the duration."

It's Martha's turn to beam at us. "I'm glad to have you all. Anna was my student back in her Cambridge days, and we have worked together for many years at Xanthro. She's probably wished a few times since that

I hadn't recruited her." They both have a titter at this, like we're at a jolly cocktail party.

"Wait . . . wait . . ." I'm still standing, and the words come out like a yelp. "You were at the hospital. You work for Xanthro. You told me my mother was dead. You abandoned us when the zoms got out, and let us nearly get eaten, shot, drowned, pecked to death by an Undead bird, and run into the ground by a Xanthro helicopter." I look around me at all the others. "Am I the crazy one here?" I look at Martha again. "Doesn't that make you the enemy?"

She holds her delicate hands up. "I owe you all a hundred apologies." She turns to my mother. "And you, too, Anna." She walks toward me with that hypnotic glide and holds out her hands to take mine. When I don't respond, she sighs. "I told you your mother was dead to minimize the risk of them realizing you were her daughter. And I promise I didn't abandon you. Initially I thought the situation was salvageable. When it became clear it wasn't, I knew you'd all be safe in your rooms for a time. I worked on quickly destroying my links to your mother and securing the things I knew we needed to take with us to establish a fully workable division of Xanthro on this boat. Then I came to get you all, but by that time the corridors were awash with the infected, and soldiers, and you were nowhere to be seen —"

"Back up." Smitty gets to his feet. "This boat is Xanthro? Did I just hear you right?"

"Of course." She looks surprised. "This is one of our main facilities now. This ship houses the majority of our research on Osiris. Everything that was salvaged from the castle and from the hospital."

"Are you serious?"

"This is utter bullshit!"

"I want to get off!"

We're all on our feet now, each working our own little version of meltdown.

My mother steps up. "*Good* Xanthro, Bobby, the real Xanthro. The company that Martha and I both signed up to work for, not the people who launched the virus into the general population and traded lives for profit." She takes me by the shoulders. "We work toward *the cure*. We don't want anyone using what we created to do harm. We have to right the damage and make sure this never happens again."

"Er, excuse me." Pete raises a hand. "You are doing research on this boat, yes?"

Martha and my mother nod.

"Uh-huh," Pete says. "This would involve live experiments?" He gives a wry smile. "Or should I say, Undead ones?"

"What?" I feel the panic rise again. "You have zoms on the boat?"

"A small group," Martha says. "Around thirty individuals. Securely and humanely kept. They pose no danger whatsoever . . ."

"Right!" Alice walks to the glass door. "I want to get off this boat, and now, please."

"There is absolutely no need for concern," Martha says.

"That's what you said last time!" Alice screams at her. One of the bodyguards walks up to her. "Don't even think about laying a hand on me, you big bully!" she squeals.

"You all owe your lives to Martha," my mother says quietly. "She coordinated the rescue from the bus, concealed Bobby's true identity, and ensured as many of you weren't infected as possible. After lines of communication went down completely, the knowledge that she was with you was the biggest reassurance to me that you were all right." She looks at me. "I knew she'd protect you while we were setting things up and facilitate your escape when the time was right."

I stare at her. "But why bother with the coded messages? Why didn't she just bust us out of there?"

My mother shakes her head. "It was safer for all of us if you left separately. Safer if no suspicion fell on Martha, and safer that she didn't know where Smitty was."

I sit, thoroughly shaken.

"Wow," I say. "So, Martha. Out of that whole busload, you only managed to save four. Oh, pardon me — six including Mum and Smitty. You must be so proud."

"Bobby!" my mum snaps at me.

"I wish I could have done more," Martha says. "Saving five was not a good outcome."

"Five?" Pete says.

"No." I count round the room. "I'm including Mum and Smitty. She originally told us four survivors, but actually there were six."

Russ shakes his head. "I was never on the bus."

"What?" I say.

"Of course you were," Alice says. "You're just having a memory fart."

I look at Mum. "What's going on?"

Russ wrings his hands. "Can I tell them, Anna?"

Anna?! Suddenly I feel even seasicker.

She smiles wryly at him. "I think you just have, Russ."

"Oh, this is *good*," Smitty drawls.

Russ looks sheepish. "I am, essentially, a plant."

"Eh?" Alice says. "Like a tree?"

"I asked him to go in after you all, to aid Martha. He was your safe passage out of there," Mum says. "He's army trained, part of a small team that has been working with me sporadically since everything started to go wrong with Xanthro. Remember how I contacted you in the castle? That was through this team; they have been my backup."

"Whoa, whoa, whoa — rewind," I say, turning to my mum. "You sent Russ in to protect us?"

She nods. "To help you escape. I managed to contact him after the crash, and within a few hours he was at the crash site, wandering about like he was one of the kids they missed the first time round. Martha made sure he was picked up."

"How old are you?" Alice sounds appalled.

"Twenty-one." Russ grins. "But my friends say I've got a baby face."

"Oh. My. God." Alice practically spits out her front teeth. I don't know if she's disgusted or thrilled.

"Bobby, I had taken your phone from you at the crash site, and had a few hours to get the coordinates and enter them on the phone's memory," Mum continues. "Russ managed to pass the phone to Martha, and she secreted it into your personal belongings at the hospital."

I look at Russ. "You knew about the messages all along? What they meant?"

He makes a face. "No. Anna didn't tell me that. Obviously I knew the phone was important, but I assumed she wanted you to have it so she could call you on it when we were clear."

"And you knew Martha?" Pete says. "And that we were underground?" He shakes his head. "What a performance."

"I knew a little," says Russ. "But less than you might think. My role was to protect Bobby at all costs, and help her get out of there without breaking my cover. But I had no contact with Anna. Once I was in place, I had no way of knowing what was going on outside."

"And when did Grace come into all of this?" I can't imagine the answer.

"She . . . was a risk." Mum rubs her hands on her legs. "After the team helped me with transport for Smitty, I went to the castle. Grace was there, she was a mess. She'd hidden from Xanthro, and she had nowhere to go. I lost contact with Martha. I offered Grace an option: to go to the hospital and help you all get out. She still had security access codes from when we worked there. It was a huge risk for her, but I told her if she was successful in your safe return I'd shelter her from the bad factions within Xanthro. She knew they would have hunted her down and killed her otherwise."

"Turns out they didn't have to hunt far," Pete says.

"Michael killed her," Smitty tells my mother. "Bet you didn't plan on him turning up."

It's Martha who answers him. "They picked him up at the castle. He was in intensive care for weeks. When he was able to speak, it became apparent he would be a threat to us."

At that moment, an intercom on the far wall buzzes. One of the bodyguards picks up a receiver, listens for a moment, and then puts it down.

"Dr. Wagner," he says, "there's a minor disturbance belowdecks. A very small fire, apparently. Nothing to be alarmed about, but we should assist them."

"Great!" Pete says. "Somebody breaking out of their cage, perhaps?"

"Impossible." Martha shakes her head. She turns to the bodyguards. "Go ahead. We can manage here."

"So." I have to get to the crux of the matter, and soon. "Why was Michael following us in the helicopter? Just to get to you, Mother?" I look at the others. "Xanthro didn't know Smitty was carrying the virus and the cure in his body, nobody told them." I turn back to Mum. "They were coming after me, weren't they? I read my notes at the hospital, they said the Osiris tests could not be completed because of 'other factors present.' I'm like Dad, aren't I? I'm a carrier, but I'm immune?"

That makes them all sit up.

Russ looks sharply at me. "You've got the virus?"

"Bobby —" My mother stands up.

"Oh my god, you're infected?" Alice screams at me.

"Maybe I am." I look from face to face. "Remember little Cam in the castle, turning into a zombie? Ever stop to wonder how he got infected back at the Cheery Chomper? We all assumed he'd been bitten. But I had a nosebleed. I bled on his face, it went in his mouth, a day later he turned. I have the virus in my system, but I have a natural defense against it. I can be bitten, and I'll never turn."

"That's not —" Mum begins.

"No, Mum, it's all right," I say. "God knows, it's all out in the open now."

"Incredible." Russ stands, clenches his fists, and paces up and down in front of the fire. "Xanthro knew this for certain?"

I shrug. "I think they knew something was up with me, and they thought I'd be valuable to them."

Russ nods, and then does a kind of weird little laugh, and shakes his head. "And I didn't have a clue."

Mum raises a hand. "Let me put a stop to this right now." She walks over to me, places her hands on my shoulders. "Bobby, you are wrong. You are not a carrier."

I stare at her. "But those tests! I read that —"

"You have mononucleosis."

"Oh my god, what's that?" Alice says, shifting away from me in her seat.

"Glandular fever," Mum says. "A relatively harmless virus. Very common among teens; in fact, they sometimes call it 'the kissing disease' because of how it's often spread."

I flush red and make a point of not looking at Smitty. Beside me, I can sense him doing the same.

Mum continues. "It makes you feel tired and run-down for a while, sometimes extremely tired, but the symptoms go away after a few weeks. It is no Osiris, believe me."

"So why were they chasing us?" I mumble.

"Well" — she looks around the room — "yes, they did want to capture you in order to lure me out of hiding. But there was another reason. I was going to do this slightly differently, but . . ."

"What?" I snap at her.

"You're not the carrier," she says, walking across the room to Alice and Russ. "Alice is."

Knock me down with a feather and call me Mavis.

"Whaat?" I say.

Smitty swears, and Pete tops it.

"Me? What?" Alice looks up at Mum like she hasn't been following this at all.

"It's OK. In fact, it's great news." Mum smiles at her. "You're the carrier. We have the facilities here to ensure you don't get sick, and to harvest your natural antibodies. You're the key to the cure, Alice. Between you and Smitty, we'll nail this yet."

Alice stands up and backs away. "I'm a zom? You're going to *harvest* me? You want to make me *do stuff* with Smitty?" She starts to cry. "No! I want to go home! All I've ever wanted to do is go home."

Mum takes a step toward her, and she starts to scream.

"Stay away from me!"

"It's all right, Alice," Mum tries to soothe her. "You're not one of them. You won't turn. And you're safe in my hands."

"But, but . . ." Alice sobs. "Bobby's dad . . . he was a carrier, and he died. Am I going to die?"

Mum shakes her head. "We've learned so much, even in the last few days, you have nothing to worry about."

Russ pulls Alice toward him. "Come out with me, get some fresh air and clear your head."

"What?" Alice looks at him as if he's crazy, and I'm kinda wondering myself — it's blowing a gale out there. "No, I don't want to —"

He marches her to the door anyway. "Come on, Alice, it's for the best."

"What are you doing?" Alice says to him.

"This way." He slides the glass door open.

"No!"

"Hey!" Smitty stands up and moves toward Russ. "She doesn't want to."

"Yeah. Too bad." Russ fumbles behind him, and a second before he does it, I guess what he's going to do. He pulls out a gun. I recognize it. The one I thought I'd lost in the sea. "And guess what, Smitty? You're coming, too. Outside, now." He waves the gun at Smitty and Alice. "Both of you."

"What. The. Hell." Alice freezes to the spot.

"Do not move, anyone!" Russ shouts. "Don't even think about it."

"Gosh," Pete says, "the classic double cross." He frowns at him. "You bit me, didn't you? In the lighthouse, during the scuffle with the zom. You wanted them to think I was infected. And then when that didn't work, you pushed me down the steps onto Bobby's gun."

Russ chuckles. "Couldn't resist, Petey-Poos. Thought you had me figured out. Turns out I was the paranoid one." He looks at Mum. "Sorry, Anna. Bad Xanthro pays way better than you do, even with your hot daughter thrown in. Alice comes with me. Thanks for just confirming what we thought. Truth is, those tests back at the hospital weren't quite as reliable as you might think. We knew one of them might be a carrier, but not which one. So thanks for saving me the trouble of taking them both. Now I've got a space for Smitty. Bonus. The bosses won't believe their luck." He gives us his best boy-next-door smile, the one with the dimple.

And then the sirens start.

28

"Please tell me that's the fire alarm," says Smitty.

Russ guffaws and shakes his head. "No, mate, Pete was right. He generally is; you should trust what he says." He winks at me. "I put a little incendiary device on the door of the containment room. Any minute now those thirty or so crazies are going to be heading upstairs to say hello."

"Russ, no!" Mum's face crumples.

"Good god!" Martha gasps.

"Sorry, ladies. Time to boogie." With that, he shoves Alice outside. Smitty faces up to him, but Russ sticks the gun in his face and Smitty backs down. They step outside, and Russ slams the glass door shut.

Mum dashes to the intercom on the wall and presses a button.

Russ smiles at her through the door. Alice's face is twisted, she's screaming full out.

Mum shouts into a phone while I race to the glass. Russ looks at me blankly; he holds the gun up to Alice's head. I freeze.

"Where does he think he's going?" Pete says.

"A powerboat. One on each side of the ship," Martha says. "He'll get them in there, lower it down."

We watch them move past the windows, bent double against the driving wind and rain. We're helpless.

"Someone'll see them, won't they?" I say to Mum.

"Won't work," she says. "They think Russ is on our side."

"Yeah. The whole having-a-gun-set-to-two-kids'-heads might change their minds, nope?" I mutter.

Something pings off the sides of my brain, not unlike a bullet, an idea, a memory . . .

"Only six." I have it. "There were only six bullets."

Before anyone can question me, I fling the door open, and then I'm skidding on the slick deck, chasing them as they stagger toward the boat suspended off the side. I know I let off six shots. One on the poor goat. Four at the soldiers. One misfire when I fell in the sea. And I know there were only six bullets. So Russ is carrying an empty gun.

Unless there was already one in the chamber.

The new idea nags at me, but I won't let it. I loaded that gun. I should know. But truthfully, it's all foggy. And there's always the frightening possibility that Russ had his own cache of ammo — but then again, why would he, I think as I skid around a funnel, because if he had ammo, wouldn't he have his own gun? I'm betting my life — and Smitty's and Alice's — that Russ is currently toting a big fat nothing.

They've reached the railing where one of the powerboats is lashed to some kind of pulley system. Russ smacks a button, and the boat begins to lower into the water. The ship pitches as we are hit by big waves, and I cling to the icy-cold railing, pulling myself toward them before I can change my mind. Russ waves the gun at Alice, forcing her down a ladder off the side of the ship to the boat below. I'm only a few yards away when he swings round and points the gun at me.

"You're out of bullets!" I shout at him. Behind me I sense the others running up toward us.

He laughs and shakes his head. "Don't you think I would have checked that, Bobby? I'd be pretty amateur if I left something like that to chance."

"Maybe you did check," I shout back, edging closer toward them. "But you're counting on the fact that I wouldn't remember how many I'd fired. And guess what? I do remember."

He points the gun at Smitty's temple. "Want to risk it, Bobby? Risk losing the only remaining source of the cure? Want to risk your *boyfriend*?"

I wish people would stop calling him that.

"Russ, how can you do this?" Alice screams at him, clinging to the ladder. "You looked after us. You came after me when those kids drove me away."

"I went after the Jeep, you stupid cow." Russ's lip curls. "The Jeep was my best chance to get out of town. *Anna* is so paranoid, she didn't even tell me where she was waiting for us, so I had to follow the pathetic clues along with the rest of you."

My mother gives a hollow laugh. "Turns out I was right to be paranoid."

"Yes, well." Russ looks around, and I follow his gaze. In the distance I spot three black dots moving through the sky. The helicopter went away and came back with friends. Russ smiles. "Lovely as this chatting is, we've got another little school trip to go on, people." He flicks the gun at Alice on the ladder, and she jumps down to the boat with a yell. "You next," he says to Smitty.

And then I see the shape behind him. Out of a doorway comes a figure, arms outstretched, mouth torn back in hunger, teeth gnashing.

My eyes widen; I take a step back.

Russ laughs. "Nice one, Bobby. But I'm not falling for the oldest trick in the book."

It's Smitty who does it. He looks behind him and gives a convincing yell, dodging out of the way as the monster lurches toward Russ. Russ is only human; he turns his head.

A moment's distraction is all it takes. I barrel into him, knocking him against the rails, the gun flying out of his hand. He's shocked, but he's way stronger than me, and it only takes him a second to recover. But that's all that's needed for the zom to pile in after me. He goes in low, lifting Russ up, ready to plant a kiss in Russ's stomach. A lucky wave lifts the boat, and somehow the two things happen just right to make Russ and zombie clear the rail, headfirst. A hand shoots up. One body falls and splashes, the other dangles. Russ has grabbed a lifeline from the gray, frigid water below. He hangs there, looking up at me.

"Bobby . . ." He gulps. "Please help me . . ."

Fingers grab at my heart. I can't let him fall. I hold out a hand.

But at that moment the ship rises again, and his grip fails. He falls, looking up at me all the while, irritation and surprise on his face. There's barely a splash, it's like the sea just eats him whole.

"Where did he go?" Alice yells from the boat below.

I don't know. I keep waiting for him to come up, like when you see a bird dive for fish. You always watch the same spot, and then they totally surprise you by coming up in a completely different place. So I scan the undulating waves, feeling sick to my stomach. But he doesn't surface.

Another body appears in the doorway, and then another.

It's enough to make up my mind.

"Into the boat!" I shout at Pete. I grab Smitty and start down the ladder to Alice.

"What are you doing?" Mum calls to me.

"Zombies. Helicopters." I yell back, still climbing down. "That's our cue to leave. It's kept us alive so far."

"No!" Pete is still at the rail. "We should stay, they can help us here. *Good* Xanthro, good Xanthro, Bobby."

"Come back!" Mum cries.

Martha has arrived with some armed men. They shoot at the infected while Pete and Mum cower against the deck railing.

I press a button, and the boat falls the final few feet into the water below with a huge splash.

"Drive this thing!" I shout at Smitty. "You managed a Jeep and a train, this should be a breeze!"

"We're leaving Pete?" he shouts back. "Your mum?"

"They made their choice!" I shout. Besides, my mother will follow us, I'm sure of it. Because she's left me to fend on my own too many times to not follow me now. But let her follow, and let "Good" Xanthro clean up shop before we board the *Titanic* again. I'll give them a run for their money.

Smitty has us going, and going fast. I steady myself on the side of the boat, carefully moving up to where Alice sits at the bow in silence. What a life change. She's just gone from Most Popular in the Class to, well, Most Popular in the World. She and Smitty are the Osiris Homecoming Queen and King. I wonder if they'll make them have lots of little immuno-babies together. The idea makes me want to hurl.

"Come sit back here with us," I tell her. She nods, we make it to Smitty, and we sit in a row, all three of us.

"It's not over, is it?" He looks out to sea. "It's never going to be."

"We head to England," I say confidently. "They have to take us in, we're only kids."

"Or we could go to Norway," Smitty says. "They only have trolls there. Trolls would be a doddle after this." He looks at me, a rare flicker of fear on his face. "But for me. And Alice. It's never going to be over, is it?"

The fog has lifted, but the light is fading. Off toward the land I see the dark shapes moving through the air. They look like crows searching for carrion. Is it my imagination, or is there a little black speck bobbing in the sea over there? Could it be Russ? Have they come to pick him up?

"I'd like to go home," Alice says. "While there still is one."

I throw an arm around her and give her a hug. "We're not home yet," I tell her. "But we'll get there. I promise you."

She growls at me. "Get off me, you freak." But she puts her head on my shoulder, and slips an arm around my waist.

The helicopters get louder, and there's a roar of the ship's engines going into full power.

"They're chasing us," Smitty says. "Your mum won't leave us."

I twist around to see.

What chance do we have of outrunning Xanthro? We've done it up to now, though the odds seem stacked against us in our tiny little boat. But they have other things to contend with; helicopters have reached the ship, and one is attempting to land.

A huge explosion rips through the air and the water beneath us; instinctively we all hit the floor of the boat, Smitty losing the rudder, bringing us round in a slow circle to face the ship.

"Jesus," Smitty chokes. "They must have hit a mine."

He stops the boat just as a huge wave hits us. Lucky we were facing it; the small craft rides it without capsizing, bobbing over the aftershocks. Some distance away, the ship is on fire, black smoke filling the air. One of the helicopters is on its side on the top deck, propeller still trying to turn and flying off in different directions.

"Mum," I mutter.

"There!" Alice points. A small powerboat is coming toward us, two people aboard. One controlling the rudder, the other standing at the bow, his Mohawk flopping over against the wind.

"They're OK." I breathe again. Smitty throws his arms around me and kisses me.

"Oh, gross." Alice makes a retching noise. "Get a cabin."

He breaks off, and we look back at the approaching boat. My mum looks so pissed with me. I'm definitely grounded now.

"Shall we wait for them?" Smitty says.

"We should get going," I reply. "Fast as you like. Just watch out for mines."

Let Mum chase me for a while. I feel like it will be good for both of us.

We can't stop yet. That's the rule around here now. I should know. Keep moving, and you live to struggle through another day. Sit still, and you're Undead.